SIDE
SHOW

SIDE SHOW

by Loma A. Phegley

Writers Advantage

New York   Lincoln   Shanghai

Side Show

Writers Advantage
an imprint of iUniverse, Inc.

For information address:
iUniverse
2021 Pine Lake Road, Suite 100
Lincoln, NE 68512
www.iuniverse.com

ISBN: 0-595-24854-3

Printed in the United States of America

Life Is Like A River, It Will Surround You.

But You Gotta' Keep Swimming.

For my family. Especially my Grandson, John, who has dedicated his life to me and has given me two of the most magical great-grandsons any old woman could dream for.

And for his wife Cary for staying in school, and to my husband of 58 years who made it possible for me to not have to starve in a garret in Paris to be able to write this. Of course to my dearest friend Peri LeBeck who knew I could do it. And to the dogs in my life who gave me joy and satisfaction. Pepsi, the Boston Terrier, Midnight, the stray cow dog, and to Lux and Schooner, the two prize Newfoundlands who slobbered and ate their way through every day as we laughed at and loved them.

Credits

Thanks to Suzan Vaughn for her help in editing the first draft. Grateful to Dianne Somerville for her expert advice and to Eric Rush, who trashed my work and expected me to thank him. I don't think so!

Also, with gratitude, I thank Amber Valdez for her expert editing skills and for swooping in at the last moment to save the day. *Viva la cavalry.*

Contents

The Good, The Bad And The Ugly

William S. Bailey___Founder and owner of a small traveling circus in the mid 1930s. Father of a murdered child. Also known as Mr. B and to Star as "Beelee"

Maude Damon Foster Bailey___Wife of William S. Bailey and mother of the dead child.

Ivan The Terrible___Billed as a Russian strong man who was neither Russian nor Terrible.

Teodoro De La Porto___AKA Tico Tico, or just Tico for short. A cruel twist of fate made him a dwarf. A fine substance of character made him a man among men.

Charlie "One Shoe" Wonshu___Ringmaster, musician, and friend.

Hiram___A talented clown with the stage name of "Uncle Toby Toontuck." An even more talented drunk, wife-abuser and liar. Not only bad, but ugly, as well.

Mary Lou Franks___From abused child to abused wife of Hiram to a life in the circus as "Tilly The Fat Lady," she was one of the "Good Ones."

Angel___Known to Tico as *Angelica*. Born deaf and mute and abandoned by her family in an insane asylum to be raised by whoever wanted to use and abuse her, she was one of the "Good Ones" too.

Star___Starshine Moonstone, Hungarian Gypsy, a fortune-teller who "saw all, knew all" but kept much of it to herself.

Phillipe___Self-styled lover of beautiful women, debonair, handsome ex-flying ace and husband of Apalonia Caesar. Prone to getting into trouble with his father-in-law.

Julius Caesar___Patriarch of the family of Sicilian trapeze artists, chef, vintner and protector of his family.

Doctor John Brady___A "Defrocked" Physician, who found a home with the circus.

Jack and Sylvia Flannigan___Keepers of the Cats.

Pete "Skookum" Mathers___Made the best hot dog on the circuit.

Mirriam "Madame Zia"___Crazy, but in control, most of the time. She killed men just for recreation. But to her, it was all perfectly justified.

Barbarrosa and Sinbad___Two man-eating tigers.

Arnold___The Baby Elephant and "common sewer" of fine fruits.

Hey y'all, let's don't fergit Ol' Cooter and Gator, two Cultured Southern Gentlemen.

Chapter One:

The Beast

Who Knows What Evil Lurks in the Hearts of Men?

She lay there mute, her sky-blue eyes wide with terror and bewilderment. Her young mind was simply unable to grasp the what and the why of what had just happened.

Her eyes followed his movements. She watched as he stuffed his now limp penis back into his pants, buttoned them up, and smoothed his hair back.

He lifted his huge foot and stomped it into her tender six-year-old belly. She felt nothing when his fingers encircled her tiny throat, and squeezed until she stopped breathing.

He scooped up the child's corpse, lifted the edge of the tent and carried her little body to the rain-swollen Feather River, throwing it out as far as he could into the raging current. He didn't even watch as the wild water carried her away and she sank from sight into the cold, clear watery grave. "The Beast" was satisfied, at least for now, so he went to his own warm bed and slept until way past dawn.

Even though he was normally an early riser, these events tired him out emotionally and he always slept in after having encountered that black, hideous side of himself that had to obey "The Beast" at any cost. His mind seemed to be programmed to forget these deeds as soon as they were accomplished except for this lingering mental tiredness. It would stay for a day or two and then the memory of the happening would fade away into a part of his mind that would lay dormant until the evil urgency would again visit him and "The Beast" had to be answered. There had never been a question of his ability to control it. It was like a freight train with no brakes. It could not be controlled nor stopped by any force of which he knew. It was just something that happened, like an involuntary bodily function. It just was.

First came the restless urgency, then the futile attempt at resisting that urgency, next came the excruciating pain of "The Beast's" claws digging into his back and his guts and then into his very soul. Finally, the surrender to what he knew was inevitable, and then the unnatural euphoria—the rapture that surrounded him like a cocoon and isolated him from the rest of humanity. That way he could do his deed in a private ecstasy and total detachment to reality while he accomplished what was preordained that he do. "Fait accompli." After it happened, he had this uncanny ability to just forget it ever happened or ever would again. Sick twisted, evil. The world was a playground of little blonde angels and he never failed to find one when "The Beast" overtook him.

Chapter Two:

Getting The Act Together

William S. Bailey owned the circus he called "The Biggest Little Circus In The World," and when he told someone his name he was always quick to add that no, he wasn't any relation to the Bailey of the Barnum and Bailey outfit. It took him four years to put together the little band of performers that made up the crew, and it wouldn't have happened at all unless his Uncle Janus had died and left all of his worldlies to his nephew.

Uncle Janus had not left much, but it was a tattered circus in the making…a huge barn filled with circus equipment including tents, knock together bleachers, a couple of old trucks, a calliope, some musical instruments, concession stands, some tools, and a dozen trunks filled with colorful costumes. There were animals too. At first, Billy wondered what in the hell he was going to do with three elephants, eight camels, six white horses, two boxing kangaroos, three aging lions, a dancing, bike-riding, skating Russian Sun Bear named "Peter The Great" and a trick seal named "Sweetie"—complete with her own habitat, which was a fifty gallon galvanized stock tank that acted as a dandy pool, as well as a bathtub for Mary Lou, the circus fat lady. Since Maude refused to sell or give up Laurabelle and Libertybelle, her treasured milk cows, she added them to the menagerie. An unlikely group they were at first. The two milk cows had no place among the performing animals, however, they did provide thick, rich cream for everyone's coffee and milk for any orphaned animal along the way.

But Maude had some good ideas about how to turn the whole group into a profitable venture. Maude's folks in her home in Georgia had been businessmen. Well, if you can call running moonshine in the dead of night a business. She had learned how to manage cash flow, assess clients' motives and was overall a pretty shrewd entrepreneur. Billy listened to her and began to see the 10-foot pile of canvas and the giant ball of ropes more as an asset than a liability. Why hell, Maude had been able to make money with a couple of chickens and the two wonderful Guernsey cows they had received from her father as a wedding present. Laurabelle and Libertybelle were great milkers so Maude sold their milk and butter to all the neighbors and anyone who came to buy it. Along with her ability as a waitress, that kept them alive during part of The Depression already. Now, with a few resources, Billy figured he ought to start listening to her, not to mention it would make him a boss of sorts, an idea that had some appeal to him.

Uncle Janus had never really been in the circus business. He had loaned the circus owner a considerable sum of money, but since the owner had skipped town, he had left the collateral in his creditor's barn and pasture. The animals had been enjoying a life of leisure for some months now, and feeding them was expensive. He hoped he wasn't leaving his nephew an albatross, but it and his small farm were all he had, and he had no one else to leave it to. Most of the old man's cash had gone to buy Irish whiskey and to feed the animals. He had been alarmed at how much hay an elephant could eat.

Billy and Maude literally rolled up their sleeves and began to work it all out. Billy sold the little farm for a fair price and formulated a business plan. With those funds, along with the three thousand dollars of saved up moonshine money Maude's grandmother had left her, they seemed to be looking at a bright future.

The Baileys got the wheels rolling by putting a "Help Wanted" ad in the Sarasota Tribune. It wasn't long before the Baileys started to hear from performers all over the country. Many circus performers had that paper sent to them wherever they were. Sarasota was winter quarters for almost all of the circuses in the U.S. They could always count on good warm weather so they need not remain idle and get out of shape by not practicing their routines because of inclement weather

First he got a telegram from some clown named Hiram Lockstep. It was signed off "Tobey Toontuck at yer' service." When he did arrive, Bailey took an instant dislike to him, but this was generally the reaction of most people when they met Hiram. He was dumb, but shrewd, he was crude and ugly and a drunken, loud-mouthed braggart, but he was a helluva' clown. Bailey figured he didn't hire the bastard for his personality, but his talent, so he resolved to try to get along with him as best he could.

However, the best thing about Hiram was his wife, Mary Lou. She had some real talent and wanted to be the new Fat Lady. He soon discovered that she could design and sew costumes, cook gourmet meals and most of all she could sing like an angel. What a voice! Not only that, but she had a musical repertoire that would put Kate Smith to shame and a spectacular voice that was every bit as lovely. Her husband, Hiram, insisted on making her change her name to "Tilly." He claimed it sounded more like a name a fat gal might have.

Next he heard from a guy who claimed to have the best hot dog concession on the planet. That was "Skookum" Pete Mathers. And his claim to fame turned out to be true. Not only were his hot dogs the best of any circus, Skookum was a performer, as well. He loved being a clown and helped out the act when he wasn't too busy. He did not like Hiram and tried to upstage him at every opportunity. Skookum was sometimes known as "Slippery Skookum Pete." It was a name he had earned in the old days as a bootlegger in Miami. Smuggling Cuban rum from the island to Miami and to New York was his specialty. Skookum Pete knew Lucky Luciano, Alphonse Capone and Dutch Schultz. He had worked for them at one time or another. He had done some time up at Sing Sing, but was now going straight.

He also had received a letter in old country script from the Caesar Family, Sicilian trapeze artists of the highest renown. Bailey knew of them and shot back a letter that they were hired. Come at once.

Bill called a long time friend of his, ol' Charlie "One Shoe" Wonshu, to come and help out. They had once worked on a bridge building project for the W.P.A. together. Bill had the perfect spot for Charlie. Actually several spots, as Charlie was destined to become the man who could do it all, and often was called upon to do so. Charlie was destined to become "The Ring Master." It was perfect for him. He was big and impressive and had a voice that was well suited to the job.

Charlie recruited a friend of his to serve as the doctor of the circus. He had met "Doc" Brady when he had done a three-day stint in jail for driving while under the influence of the old demon rum. "Doc" had been doing time for manslaughter. He had operated on a young girl for an inflamed appendix. The girl had died because Doctor Brady had been not only drunk, but high on cocaine at the time of the operation. Doc Brady's license to practice medicine had been taken from him for life, but he was still a skilled physician since he had sworn off all alcohol and drugs. The circus did not require any kind of license to bind up the wounds and cure colds and hangovers. Doc Brady was about fifty when he came to the circus, and he was grateful for the job. He was a fine looking man, neatly and expensively dressed, generally in a custom tailored three-piece suit of very-conservative-but-classy cuts. He stood tall, distinguished, well put together with graying hair, combed with a part on one side, and cut short in the fashion of the day. He wore gold-rimmed pince nez glasses and spent most of his spare time reading medical journals, scientific papers and any newspaper from any part of the country he could lay his hands on. He was a true intellectual, but never flaunted his education among these people. Doc was well liked by the crews and by the Baileys, as well. He seemed to fit in quite well with these people, in spite of the fact that he was so well educated, and they were mostly not. Doc Brady and Tico became regular debating opponents and enjoyed many hours of conversation and chess playing.

A big time cat trainer with an outstanding reputation, Jack Flanagan, who had just returned from a Safari in Black, Africa and was already in Sarasota, came by to make a deal with Bailey. The man accepted and soon Jack Flanagan arrived at the circus quarters with his wife, Sylvia, a beautician. Jack came with his own stable of well trained cats and set to work straight away to get his act together for the Big Top soon to open.

It did not take long before Bailey had enough performers to begin putting a credible show together.

Bailey's prayers were answered when "Skookum" Pete showed up with the big Turk and the dwarf, Tico Tico, in tow. There was his Strong Man, huge at six-foot-seven and a handsome fellow as well. His name was Abdoul, but Bailey had other plans for his name. He changed it to another and also changed Abdoul into a Russian, naming him "Ivan The Terrible." He was neither Ivan nor was he terrible, but the name somehow fit his appearance. His head was shaved slick and he had a big black moustache that drooped down on either side of his wide mouth. He looked fierce and he looked just like an Ivan the Terrible should look. He was actually quite handsome and Bailey knew he was a show-stopper just from the look of him. But Abdoul, who was to become Ivan, had many skills that suited the operation of the circus. He seemed to be able to make sense and order from the pile of ropes and canvas. He could erect the bleachers, set up the big top and manage a crew of men. He was an expert at overseeing the needs of the animals. After all, he had tended camels, donkeys and even goats in his long career as a caravan trader.

Abdoul was born in the poorest section of Constantinople, and he was a long way from being Russian. Being the 12th child of 16, his family was the most wretched of the poor in Istanbul, Turkey. Allah had surely blessed this family with so many children, but that is where the blessings stopped. The Good and Great Allah had failed to provide enough food or blankets, much less luxuries like shoes or medicine, and schooling was out of the question.

Abdoul's father sold hashish and mended pots. His mother, who was blind, begged on the streets for food for her children. There was always a snotty-nosed urchin with his or her hand out, hanging onto the ragged hem of his mother's garments. The children were also expected to bring in a few coins as well. His mother sold hashish too, and opium when she could get it, and both his parents were known for supplying good quality stuff. They had a steady flow of customers, but the drug was cheap, and with so many mouths to feed, they barely got by.

The whole family lived in a squalid little hovel that passed for a dwelling. It was wedged between the pot maker's shop and a filthy coffeehouse. It was made of old pieces of tin, cardboard and even rags stuffed into the holes, but in the winter the cold was still numbing. It was mostly the body heat of all those children that made it possible to sleep in wintertime, but the instability of this poor hovel did nothing to keep out the flies, cockroaches, scorpions and fleas. Life was rough, at best, for this family, filled with minor childhood diseases that became major illnesses with no medicine and such unsanitary conditions. Death was a frequent visitor to this neighborhood, where the children especially were already weak from malnutrition, exposure to the cold and rat infestation. Abdoul spent the nights huddled around a trash can fire in a makeshift shelter of sorts, along with some of the other young boys from the neighborhood. No one noticed when he was gone. Throughout his childhood, Abdoul did not know any other life existed. At the age of 6 years, Abdoul began to work for the brass pot maker next door.

Abdoul was grateful for the work and the warmth of the shop in winter. And there was plenty of food at dinnertime, which was part of his pay. Day by day, he grew stronger and taller. The food was plain but plentiful, and the pot maker treated him kindly and instilled a strong work ethic into the boy. He was rewarded for hard work by an extra coin now and then, which he stashed and didn't tell his mother. The pay was poor, but he seldom saw his wages anyway. The meager compensation was handed over to his mother, before he even saw it. Except for the few coins he stashed when his employer had a big job to do and the project made him a decent wage.

Abdoul was as honest as he could be under the circumstances. He did not steal nor did he use the readily available hashish, except rarely. He worked hard and long hours, making more muscle than money.

At first it was all the boy could do to lift the heavy hammers, so he was put to work sweeping and polishing the finished pots. But the pot maker saw that a portion of Abdoul's days were spent lifting the hammers so he could develop the strength it required to become useful at the craft one day. The boy learned well and as a part of his salary, Abdoul was allowed to eat at the pot maker's table. The food was plain, but plentiful, and the pot maker treated him kindly. Abdoul and his family were grateful for the work and Abdoul was praised by his family, which gave him a great sense of pride for his contribution to feeding this family who Allah had abandoned.

At the age of twelve, Abdoul had grown to be much larger and much stronger than his brothers or any of the other boys in the neighborhood. He became the protector of the weaker children and earned the reputation of being a person who one did not wish to provoke. It was rare, indeed, when any of the other boys decided to tempt fate if a beating from Abdoul could be the result.

One lovely spring day, the pot maker sent Abdoul on an errand into the open-air marketplace in downtown Constantinople. The youngster was fascinated. He saw things he'd never seen before, in fact, did not even know existed. Bare-breasted women, their eyes stained with kohl, who danced, it seemed just for him, moving their hips in ways that made this young boy feel as he had never felt before.

He saw women selling fruit and foods he had never seen and never tasted, exquisite cloth, jugglers and sweet meats like baklava, dates and nuts with honey. Bread such as ekmel and sisi. He was awe struck at the sight of so much meat cooking and longed for just a taste of the heavenly smelling kabobs roasting on the coals. There were magic tricks, snakes in baskets, monkeys and birds and, Allah be praised, the smells! Spices like cinnamon, cardamom, anise and saffron. Coffee roasting, tobacco burning in the hookahs, and the perfume of the ladies that seemed to want to get closer to him. The perfume, mixed with the musky smell when one of the belly dancers thrust her self close to him, sent a tingle down his spine and signals to every other part of him that he was unsure of but it was intoxicating. He loved it! All of this new excitement took hold of his soul and would not release it. He was drunk with the knowledge that here was the Heaven he had heard so much about. He had found it and was not about to leave it.

Now Abdoul was an honest boy, but he was so overwhelmed by the life and vibrancy radiating out from this marketplace, that he did something he never thought he would do. He aborted his employer's task of errands, and used the money given him instead, to buy the services of one of the lush, fat bellied whores with the largest breasts he had ever seen. He hardly even knew what he was buying, other than a chance to have a close-up look at them and to touch them, maybe even to kiss those big, purple tinged nipples. The whore, however, knew a first timer when she saw one, and was there to offer her expert professional assistance.

After he had spent himself, the boy laid on the soft, comforting body of the big-breasted whore for as long as she would let him. She allowed him a few extra minutes, it being his first time, so he gently twisted her huge nipples and sucked on them until she'd had enough. The movement of her rotund body dumped him to the ground. She laughed when his well-muscled body hit with a thud, destroying his reverie and bruising his dignity.

"You have used up all of your money now and I am not in this business to nurse little boys. Off, you ragged little fucker. A big cock you may have, but unless you have a big purse, get away. I have customers wait-ing," she said. Abdoul had already become addicted to women. Fat ones. The fatter the better. Only a taste, but it had been enough to make him know that there was only one thing worth living for. It was all right there in a most convenient location. He knew he would pursue this new addiction 'til the end of his life. He had no doubt that this encounter, that had taken less than fifteen minutes out of his life, would forever shape his destiny.

He knew that he would never be able to return to his employer with-out having either the money or the goods he had been sent to buy. The money had taken flight with the big, beautiful lady and the goods were still in the marketplace. While his lust had been satisfied for the time being, Abdoul was dejected, yet he was strangely elated and had a con-tented grin on his face, as he sat down next to the old camel driver.

The old driver knew that look well. Besides he had seen Abdoul come from the little stall of the whore. Since the driver, Omar, by name, fre-quented the ladies often, he knew what had just happened.

Omar was a rich man. He owned fifty camels and traded goods all over the dessert. He was a keen businessman and spotted Abdoul with his fine physical shape immediately. Such a body with such strength was a rarity in this land of little to eat. Omar wasted no time in taking advantage of the window of opportunity that he knew would be brief.

Introducing himself to Abdoul was his next move.

"Ah," he said, "Allah is good. Allah is great. Just this very morning I was asking Allah to lead me to a strong willing boy to help me in my work. Allah has answered my prayers, for here he is!"

Omar rubbed his hands together and continued to speak, "Yes, if any boy should answer my call for help he would be fulfilling a duty to Allah. Allah will be pleased, indeed. I need a strong boy to help me load and unload these great beasts, to travel with me to places to dazzle your eyes. I offer such a boy a fair wage, plenty to eat, and I carry goods that make the ladies love me and share all of their heavenly delights with me."

From the look of interest on the boy's face, Omar knew he had a new camel jockey. Omar continued to tell of tales of satisfied lust until Abdoul stopped him. "Yeh, sure I go. All I want is many ladies to enjoy and to eat well. I go. I go."

It was a done deal when the mere mention of all the joys from the ladies was assured and it made Abdoul jump to a standing position, in more ways than one.

On that day Abdoul the boy left his family and all that he had known all of his life to become Abdoul, the man. He never looked back at the poverty and degradation of his childhood. Abdoul was born again, this time with a chance at life.

All that old Omar had promised came to pass and many more times over. Abdoul learned the trading business well under the old man's shrewd tutelage. And became a very skillful merchant.

As the years went by, Omar's eyesight began to fail. His health was declining. He grew weaker and more infirm from the cruel vestiges of hard work and old age. Abdoul was very fond of the old man who had given him so much since the tender age of twelve.

When the old man died, Abdoul gave him a fine funeral and then sold all of the camels. He was, after all, the sole beneficiary to the wealth left at Omar's death.

Abdoul wanted a different kind of life now that his obligations to Omar had come to an end. He hung around the city of Constantinople for several weeks, but did not go to the street where he had been born and where his family might still live. He could not bear to see the way they lived. He knew there was little he could do to help them so he stayed away.

One day, Abdoul found himself sitting at the water's edge looking out upon the Straits of Bosphorus, mesmerized by the sight of so much water. He had been long on the dessert and had a sudden urge to go to sea that surprised even himself. He went in search of employment as a seaman, inquiring of the captain of a vessel named the "Star of Constantinople."

The captain noted the strong arms and back of the young man and hired him on as one of the "black gang" to replace a man who had recently died.

So Abdoul became part of the crew that shoveled the coal into the great maw of the boilers that made the steam to drive the ship out to sea and across continents he had never heard of. It would go to Greece, Spain, Italy, Corsica, Portugal, Crete, and many ports in between. He was anxious for the voyage to begin.

Abdoul knew there would be plenty of willing ladies in every port he visited. In fact, he would be content with such an arrangement until he would fall in love for the first time in America.

Abdoul had only dreamed of going to America, and one day soon such an impossible dream would come true. It would take a circuitous path, but it would come to pass.

Chapter Three:
Coming To America

When Bailey saw the dwarf, he thought of him as another clown, but Tico soon disabused him of any illusion that he, Teodoro De La Porto of Seville, Spain, would adjust his dignity to become a "*Buffoona.*" Teodoro Maria De La Porto was the son of an internationally known diamond merchant. His father, Emiliano De La Porto of Seville, Spain, was well known in the trade. How Tico came to the circus was through a curious set of circumstances. The De La Porto Family were Spanish Jews, and one of the wealthiest families on all of the Iberian Peninsula. They lived well. Their home was the finest in the city, and the whole town could see them riding around in their American-made Cadillacs and British made Bentleys and Rolls Royces.

The best designers from Europe dressed the De La Porto family, and their dining room table was appointed with 17th Century silverware. Gold-lined goblets were filled with wine straight from the vineyards of the French countryside, as well as from those of Italy, Austria and Portugal. The family also owned a large country estate where Tico's mother directed a staff of caballeros in the art of breeding and training the finest horses in Spain. Hazelotta De La Porto was a grand champion equestrian who competed with her equitation skills internationally.

Their servants were skilled, highly trained, and loyal to a fault. It was a distinctive honor to serve the De La Porto's, if one's lot was servant hood. Working for them showed the highest class of such an appointment.

Mrs. Hazelotta De La Porto, Teodoro's mother, was an exquisitely beautiful woman. A gracious hostess who kept a well-run household where guests from every continent were always welcomed and frequently there.

In addition to their son, Hazelotta and Emiliano had two daughters, Carmella and Consuelo, and both parents doted on their children, but especially Teodoro. He was the last and the youngest, and both parents feared they'd fail to produce an heir to the De La Porto throne.

It was a cruel accident of fate, a dirty trick of a perverse Mother Nature that Teodoro had been born a dwarf. Not a cute little replica of a full-grown man, but one with a twisted body, a hunched back and one leg an inch shorter than the other.

His complexion was rough and pitted and his nose was too big for his face. But he had a sweet and gentle look about his clear brown eyes, with long eyelashes that matched his thick, slightly wavy, black hair. He also had a sweet and gentle manner, except when he ran into some injustice against a weaker or less educated person, and then he was no one to be trifled with, regardless of his size. He had considerable resources at his disposal, and that made some fear him, while others tried to be his friend. He could always smell a fake though, and kept those at a distance that would use his family's money or influence. Never did this young man compromise his dignity, a commodity he treasured.

At birth, Teodoro's condition was apparent. At first, his parents were devastated. His mother sequestered herself within her private chambers with only her son and his nurse, spending days at a time in prayer and spilling quarts of tears in grief because of the terrible tragedy that had befallen her little child.

She hid little Tico in shame during his infancy, believing that friends and neighbors would blame her for some undefined sin for the condition of this little angel. God was blaming her for some undefined past sin, so surely would every one who saw her dear little deformed baby boy. But as he grew from infancy to childhood it became obvious that Tico was a gift straight from God.

Tico could read at the age of three. He showed a particular skill at mathematics and a special gift for learning languages other than his native Castilian and the Hebrew often spoken at home. Tico was very bright, and his tutors were astounded by his practically photographic memory. His early education was mostly with tutors at home. And being the only student, Tico blossomed into an impressive intellect. His teachers were the best that could be secured, not only in Seville, but also from around the world.

Once his intellectual gifts, his compassionate heart, his talent, and powerful personal dignity became apparent, Emiliano decided this child would no longer be hidden at home. He would be introduced with his father's pride to the world, and those that would dare make a derogatory remark against the son would face the father's wrath. It was considerable, and any person bold enough to insult a De La Porto would surely pay in some way that would be most uncomfortable. So no one dared. But Tico knew he was different. How could he not know it? The girls were always kind to him but never showed the kind of interest Tico craved. Tico had so much pride and dignity that he was able to pretend it was a small matter. But it was not. Tico knew he was destined for a life as the dwarfed son of Emiliano De La Porto. It was his preordained fate. Even when he was with friends, Tico knew he was alone. He felt it acutely at moments when he should have been the happiest. He concentrated on his studies and spent a great deal of time with his father, listening to international gem dealers doing business. Tico became a very astute trader and knew much of the world of commerce in stones of great value. He accompanied his father to Paris, Madrid, Berlin, Hong Kong and Casablanca, and was a world-class traveler by the time he was twenty.

Tico's education was high priority and the family spared no expense. He was a graduate of the University of Seville, with a master's degree in mathematics. He spoke seven languages, and was a credible gemologist. The small man's stature didn't keep him from adopting a dignified manner, and he was well liked by those who loved justice and for those who often could not buy it for themselves. His mother and his sisters showered him with love, and at school, loyal bulldog-type college mates, who protected him as his father had, often surrounded him. Not only did they genuinely like him, but usually they owed him such loyalty because most of their families were in some way indebted to Emiliano De La Porto, Tico's father.

Soon after Tico's graduation from the University, Emiliano came to his son with a very important task. He needed to deliver a sizable order of gems to the Speigelman Gem Dealers in the New York City diamond district.

Tico jumped at the chance to go to America. He had never been free to travel that far by himself, and he was more than proud that his father trusted him with such an important delivery.

Emiliano had not amassed such wealth by being naïve, and he was sending his son, not only because he trusted Tico, but also because he was sure that no one would suspect such a large fortune in gems would be carried by such a little mouse. But Tico would not be told the second part of his father's thinking. Emiliano told Tico he was the only one to be trusted, and his son believed it. Of course, it was at least partly true.

Passage was secured for Tico aboard a Turkish cargo ship called "The Star Of Constantinople" traveling out of the Port of Lisbon. Of course almost all Turkish ships were either named after Constantinople or after some star. Emiliano knew the ship would be a dirty, possibly rat-infested steamer, but he explained to his son why it was important to participate in such a charade.

Emiliano secured a very modest cabin with two beds. He paid for both tickets, so Tico would not have to share the space with anyone who might be less than desirable company. He forgot about his son's penchant for attracting poor friends, and although the dwarf kept to himself for the first few days, it wasn't long before someone who wanted to protect him, and who also owed him a favor occupied the second bed.

Tico became acquainted with Abdoul during a poker game. It was early evening and the steamer was still a few days out of New York. Abdoul was seated at the side of the room mending a pair of socks when Tico came wandering into the poker den, looking for a way to pass the time.

As he entered, a big, blowhard man from Liverpool, Percy Ferguson asked if "the bloody midget was flush enough to take in a game of five card draw with these here mates." Tico just shook his head yes, and Abdoul, shooting the man a disgusted glance, put a sack of potatoes on a chair, and hoisted Tico onto it in one movement of his muscular arm.

Tico's photographic memory and his extensive knowledge of mathematics made him a very skilled player. He was also smart enough to keep his mouth shut, and his education to himself.

Percy had the deal, and many of the men were already half drunk. But Abdoul never touched alcohol, nor did he gamble his few coins.

And while these men were men of the streets, Tico had led a sheltered life. He was over his head when it came to being surrounded by scoundrels because he never assumed that just because people were poor they were less honorable. His experience in the world was limited to his friends at the University of Seville.

When Tico raked in the first small pot of money, the others chalked it up to luck. But the second and third hand was also his, and by now he had a couple of glasses of cheap wine under his belt. His judgment was altered, and he missed the alarmed look on the Turk's face from the sidelines. Grumbling about his uncommon luck was underway, and only Abdoul noticed.

After the third win, Percy stood up and screamed, "Ya bloody cheatin' little fugger. Nobody can win one hand after the other wi' out cheatin.' I seed ya' palmin' them cards, ya was!" And he grabbed Tico and threw him against the wall.

Percy drew back his fist but Abdoul was already on his feet before his fist made contact. Abdoul caught Percy's fist in his own.

by Loma A. Phegley

"No, my friend, little dwarf not cheat. You drunk," he said. "You no hit him. You go sleep off wine. Game over!"

The game was, indeed, over, but the fight had just begun. Percy now turned his attention to Abdoul, and except for the fact that one man was drunk and the other was not, they were about evenly matched. Percy's drunken swing missed by several inches, but it only took one swing for Abdoul to make solid contact with the right side of Percy's face. The blow dropped him like a stone, but Tico was still in trouble. Another of the men, seeing that the dwarf was left unprotected and in possession of his winnings, tried to jam his hands in Tico's pockets to retrieve his losses as well as Tico's winnings. The ripping of Tico's coat caught Abdoul's ear just when Percy was going down. The dirty man from the back alleys of New Delhi was trying desperately to recover his money and Tico's winnings when Abdoul grabbed him by the lapels on his grimy coat, and shoved him across the room. By now, the rest of the players had exited the room, and no one else was brave enough to go after Tico's winnings. But when he had ripped Tico's coat the little bag of jewels hit the floor and the drawstring at the top opened, spilling the gems out onto the floor. Abdoul, attentive to every detail in the room, saw the dirty little man trying to scoop up the gems and grabbed his hand in a strong and angry fist. The man let out a cry of pain and dropped his fist full of treasure. Abdoul retrieved them all and handed them back to Tico with a shake of his head in disbelief that any one would be stupid enough to carry such a fortune on his person. The Indian had hit his head against a metal pipe and was out cold with one shove from the Turk, so Abdoul turned to Tico, pulled him to his feet, tucked the little man under his arm and threw his coat over his shoulder. He was intent on getting out of that room, although he had no idea where they'd go. With the drunken Tico still under his arm, he shoved his few personal items into a sea bag and left the room. When he got safely out he set Tico down and said, "Now what, little shit? Got any ideas?"

"I have a cabin where you can stay my friend," said Tico. "Just down this way and to the right."

Abdoul steadied Tico while they headed for his cabin. The two would share the accommodations for the remainder of the trip; an excellent arrangement, as Percy was a popular fellow among his shipmates and Abdoul had whipped his ass in front of them all. Sure that Percy and the men would be looking for their chance to even the score, Abdoul was glad for the use of Tico's cabin for the remainder of the voyage. Also, the men all knew of the gems now, and Tico certainly needed the protection Abdoul's presence afforded. The men did not, however, know of the immense fortune in premium diamonds of his father's that were in the black leather cases in his cabin. Tico was very pleased with having Abdoul in the cabin with him. He was sure his hold on life would be very fragile were it not for the big Turk's protection. Fortunately, the ship was only two days out of New York, so he stayed in his cabin with the door locked while Abdoul worked in the hold.

At first, it was a friendship born of mutual need, but grew into something stronger as the voyage continued on to New York in the United States of America. The two men actually liked each other. Soon Tico began to depend upon the big Turk for protection and they enjoyed the companionship of each other. They became friends.

When the ship reached the port of New York, both men disembarked knowing full well that neither of them would be with the ship when it left for it's return voyage.

New York!

Tico had heard from his father about this city of wonders and of the great statue that sat in the harbor. She did, indeed, lift a Golden Lamp and it affected Tico. He knew this lady represented all that was good in the world and all that was free. He knew enough of the history of Europe that he had already decided that America would be his new home. He also knew his father was apprehensive about the future of Spain and Italy, and especially Germany. Emiliano kept a very wary eye

by Loma A. Phegley

on what he saw as a frightening deterioration of the politics of the whole continent. Tico also knew that his father was entertaining plans to go to America one day, this time to take his family and his fortune with him and to stay there.

When they hit the streets of the city they were practically giddy with expectations. They wandered the sidewalks for hours, peeking in the shops, looking at the beautiful ladies, feeling the air, smelling the smells.

"Hey, Little Shit, I not read this language very good and I hungry as a camel stud been breed all day long. We find some to eat, eh?"

"*Si*," said Tico. "I see *venduro carta*. There. You see? Says he sell…holy shit! He feed peoples dogs. Sign say 'Hot Dogs' *Caramba!* I not eat dog."

"Well," answered Abdoul, "I eat camel, not bad. And goat pretty good. I eat donkey once. Taste like cow. But I not eat any dogs, I do not think."

Tico was appalled at the thought of eating dog meat. Nevertheless, they approached the venders cart and Tico asked, "This is dog?"

The vendor laughed heartily and said, "Naw. We just call it dogs. Kinda' a joke, ya' know. Here have one on the house. I'm getting ready to close up and I will have to throw all these dogs out if someone don't eat 'em."

He handed one to each man and just as Tico was about to bite down on his, the vender, who was an amateur ventriloquist, barked a pretty good "woof, woof" into Tico's hot dog. The little dwarf threw the sandwich into the air and cried out, "Aaaah hey, you big Turk. Not eat. Is dog. For sure is God damn dog to bark on me!"

The vendor, known as "Skookum" Pete Mathers, and Abdoul had a great laugh at poor Tico's expense. When Tico was finally convinced he was not eating dog meat, he tucked into his hot dog *con mucho gusto*. Neither of them had ever eaten tomato ketchup and they fell in love with hot dogs with ketchup, mustard and onion, although Tico would have welcomed some of his mother's cook's *chili tepeno* sauce.

When they had finished eating, Abdoul asked if there were any jobs to be had in New York. "Skookum" allowed as to how jobs were about as scarce as hen's teeth. But he offered a solution. "Say, I got an idea. I'm leaving about noon tomorrow for Florida. I got me a gig with a circus down there. I know they can always use somebody as strong as you, Abdoul. You, Tico? Well, we'll see. Maybe. Circuses always use all kinds of folks. You guys can ride along if you want. I will be taking my car and my little vender cart, but I got plenty of room. Whatya' say?"

Tico and Abdoul talked it over and on the prospect of jobs in a circus decided to go. "OK. We go. Where to meet you? My friend here have business to do for his father. Can do this day and be ready for tomorrow. Is OK?" They decided to do Tico's business and when finished, take a taxi to Pete's house, spend the night there and leave for Florida the next day.

Chapter Four:
Diamonds Are A Jew's Best Friend

Tico pulled out the little address book and memorized the street and number of the diamond merchant to whom his father had sent him. He hailed a cab and gave the cabbie the address. It seemed like a long way to the diamond district but both guys used the time to look at all of the fine sights of this huge city. They were impressed, to be sure. Abdoul was a bit disappointed when the ride ended and the cab stopped before the storefront of Mordecai and Abraham Speigelman. They were met on the sidewalk before the shop by four Jewish gentlemen dressed in the traditional garb of practicing Hasidic Jews, long black coats and wide brimmed black hats. Abraham Speigelman had nine mink tails covering the brim of his flat brimmed black beaver hat, denoting great wealth. His son, Mordacai, had but four on his. He was wealthy, but not so much as his father. Abraham spent some time reading the letter of introduction from Tico's father. He read it twice. Then he handed it to his son to read. From there, it was handed to a third man, who also read it. From him, it was given to the fourth gentleman who also read it, slowly and with great concentration. When all four of the men were satisfied that Tico was who he said he was, Abraham Speigelman took a ring of heavy iron keys from under his coat and unlocked the first set of steel barred gates. When Tico had been admitted, Mordecai held up his hand in front of Abdoul.

"Not you," Mordecai said rudely. "Only the dwarf." Tico was upset at this treatment of his friend but it was not unexpected. After all, there were many millions of dollars in gems behind those gates not protected

by guns or arms of any kind and Abdoul did not have a letter of introduction. Not only that, he was not a Jew. In fact, these Jews thought
Abdoul looked like an Arab. These men were just being cautious.
Abdoul remained outside and Tico was passed through three more
steel barred gates and two locked doors before he was admitted to the
shop itself.

"OK, you! Son of Emiliano De La Porto, let us see the jewels," said
Mordecai abruptly. "We will see if stones are as we have been told they
are by the great Emiliano De La Porto."

To Tico, his words had the sounds of ridicule and sarcasm and he was
not about to brook any such thing from these men, who Tico considered his inferiors anyway. "Maybe I show the stones and maybe I do
not," snapped Tico. He knew just how to deal with these suspicious
arrogant Jew bastards. Hadn't he learned at the knee of his father to take
none of their shit? Ah, yes, and he had learned well. "We shall see," Tico
continued, speaking the same Hebrew being spoken by the merchants.
"I was led to believe that this sale was already complete and all that was
needed was the exchange of funds." He made no move to open the case
for their inspection of the merchandise. The three other old men, obviously associates of the Speigelman's, stood about looking wise and saying nothing. Tico ignored them.

Tico's looked evenly into the eyes of Mordecai, and with a voice rife
with menace said, "My father has guaranteed the quality of the gems as
being exactly as he has represented them to be. Since you people and my
father have already agreed upon the price, you and I will now confirm
that price to be correct and then I show the stones."

"We do not talk money until we see the stones to confirm their quality," said Mordecai.

"You insult the integrity and reputation of my father. No, I do not
think so!" Tico would demand respect for his father's stellar reputation. That reputation was the very essence of the De La Porto family
and so, since he was doing his father's business, of Tico, as well. Tico

was angry but with a controlled anger. He remembered his father's words. "Anger, my son, is the wind that blows out the lamp of the mind." However, as he was on a roll he continued. "You dare to sully this reputation by implying that he has sent me here, his son, with inferior stones? My father has proven to you and to the world over and over again that his word is a very important and sacred bond. He is known for this on every continent. No, I go elsewhere. There are many eager to buy the stones of Emiliano De La Porto!" Tico picked up his case making ready to leave when the senior Speigelman spoke up. "You are right! We, one and all of us, apologize to your father. It was a serious breach of good manners. No one meant to insult his integrity. I do understand how you could have interpreted it as such." He shot a stern look at his son, the offender.

"Now, let us put this foolishness behind us and do business, shall we?"

Tico set the case down and said "OK. I now do my father's business."

When the deal was completed to everyone's satisfaction and the money had been exchanged for the gems, Tico declared as how he must get to the bank of his father and deposit the funds. Mordacai offered to take him to the bank in his new Buick automobile and Tico graciously accepted. Both young men were making an effort to show there were no hard feelings. Just in case the little dwarf came back one day to do more business for his father.

Mordecai was proud of his new car and he had just learned how to drive. He took Tico and Abdoul at an insane, reckless speed through the streets of New York to the bank of Tico's father. Tico and Abdoul were shaken but tried with all the manly dignity they could muster that such a ride was exciting, not scary. But scary it had been.

Tico was proud of himself. He knew his father would also be proud of the way he defended the family honor and handled the transaction. That honor was the stock in trade of Emiliano De La Porto and his family.

Emiliano De La Porto had made a wise choice in sending his son to do this transaction, but it would be a long time before he would see this beloved son again. The magic of being his own man had kidnapped the boy and held him for ransom.

Chapter Five:
Jack, The Cat Man

Jack Flanagan was a cat trainer extraordinairé. He was known in his field for his fearlessness and, yet, respect for the power, and often unpredictable cunning, of the cats, as well as for his calm control of all the animals under his care. Some men had the touch with animals and Jack had that certain quality that commanded their attention. He was known in the business as a natural. He had been on several of the African excursions of men like Frank "Bring 'em Back Alive" Buck and Ossa and Martin Elmer Johnson. He had learned a great deal from all three of them, mostly how not to capture and train big cats. He hated the cruelty of Frank Buck and he detested the fraudulent movie making of the Johnsons. It was often comical the way that Johnson would have the natives capture the animals for him, and when they were safely in a corral or a cage, he would have himself filmed doing the 'death defying capturing.' He knew Frank Buck and the Johnsons as cruel, stupid, ego driven assholes.

Jack had quit in the middle of a movie take, when a black boy of about twelve years old was clawed by a lion, and Mrs. Johnson had screamed "get that stupid little nigger off camera. He's spoiling the whole fucking scene!"

Jack knew the boy's father, and in fact, knew and liked the whole bunch of natives that had been hired by the company for the Congo Safari. But when the boy was mauled, it was the last straw for Jack. He left the company and came back home to Florida.

Jack kept his cats in Sarasota when he was on safari and he was there when he saw the ad for employment with Bill Bailey's circus. He returned home just in time to secure the job. Prior to leaving for Africa this last time, Jack had been working up a new and spectacular act that had never before been accomplished by any trainer with the big tigers.

Jack Flanagan was known to all of the people in the circus as "The Cat Man."

Jack had been one of the first children taken in by Father Flanagan at Boy's Town, and since he did not know his real name, he took the good father's surname. He never learned bigotry at Boy's Town, so he always treated the natives with the same respect as he treated white people. He could never understand the cruel manner in which the Johnsons regarded their native employees.

Jack was not a very big man, maybe 170 pounds, but he cut a fine figure in his tall boots, and light tan officer's pants tucked into them. He wore a shirt unbuttoned to the waist, exposing a smooth, muscular chest and a flat, hard belly. Around his neck on a gold chain he wore a tooth from a great white shark. A large brimmed Stetson hat with the brim turned up on one side, Australian style, and a colorful kerchief around his neck completed the "Cat Man" picture.

Inside the cage, Jack's movements were confident and economical. Much like a dancer's, graceful and smooth. He knew his job and was somewhat arrogant about it.

The ladies swooned over Jack when he first came to work at the circus, until they realized he was totally committed and desperately in love with his wife, who was far more beautiful than any of the other women of the circus. Her name was Sylvia. She painted posters, and soon began doing the posters for Mr. B's circus. Sylvia was also a beautician, and soon began doing most of the performers' hair. In fact, the Caesar girls would not go on without some attention to their coiffures by Sylvia.

Jack had begun to train twelve big tigers to do an act unheard of in the circus business. He trained them to work in close contact with each other. Then, when they were ready, he taught them how to circle a pole, side by side, so they looked like Little Black Sambo's puddle of butter going round and round the pole each black nose as though glued to the pole. It was a fabulous attraction.

The purchase of animals was often left to Jack or Ivan, but when Mr. B bought two untrained tigers from an outfit that was going out of business, Jack took one look at them and said, "No way! Those bastards are man-eaters and will never be taught to do anything but eat and shit. Get rid of 'em!"

But Mr. B was reluctant to admit that he'd made an unwise decision, yet began to look around for a buyer, nevertheless.

Jack had told Mr. B not to let any of the animal caretakers feed them, so the job fell to Ivan, who fed the tigers with a long pole. Ivan did not display any macho bravado about those tigers; he knew they were dangerous killers and treated them accordingly.

Once, Ivan caught Hiram showing off for a group of the roustabouts with the feeding pole. He was poking Barbarossa in the face with it, and the animal was roaring and cowering in the corner, trying to dodge the jabs.

Ivan stood for a minute and listened to Hiram brag about how scared the tigers were of him. He bragged that he would not be afraid to enter the cage and that Jack was just a coward. But on the next jab, Barbarossa hooked a claw into the wooden shaft and jerked Hiram off his feet, pulling him right up to the bars with lightening speed. His face was close enough to smell the fetid odor and feel the warmth of the tiger's breath. Hiram screamed in terror as he let go of the pole and fell to the ground, out of the reach of either tiger.

Ivan laughed and asked, "You not afraid to go in cage? OK. Ivan helps you in. Right now."

By now Hiram's audience was also laughing as he so was visibly shaken he had wet his pants.

"Yeah, and I'd let you too, 'cept I promised to be somewhere at…" he looked at his pocket watch, "this very minute. Gotta go! See ya later." That was one of the times when it could be said of Hiram that he was a true clown. He always left them laughing.

Chapter Six:
The Wages Of Sin

Mary Lou Franks had been perfectly normal until she was about eight years old. She was slender and quite a beautiful child until her beloved mamma died, and life for this little child changed so drastically and tragically that she could never look at anything in the same way again.

Her mamma, Tassie Lou McCorkle, had been one of the dirt poor migrants from the dust bowl, camped out along the Yuba River with her family. She met her future husband when his mother sent him out on a mission of mercy to help "those poor migrant families" who suffered not only from lack of food during the depression, but from malnutrition that often killed them. Just plain malnutrition that made them susceptible to disease and even injuries. It was hardest on the children.

Every Saturday night, Simon Franks' German mother would send her son out with some chicken meat and soup bones, and even some old hot dogs to give to the river bank dwellers, who were always one or two meals from starvation. Simon also carried day-old bread from Mr. Panatoni's bakery and wilted vegetables, too old to sell, from Mr. Brown's store. People in town didn't have much either, and although they despised the migrants, many of them felt it was their Christian duty to try and help anyway.

Simon spied Tassie on one of those missions of mercy. She was a pretty little girl of 13, and Simon found reasons to go down to the riverbanks more often than was required by the food deliveries. It wasn't long before Tassie became pregnant and Simon's mother threatened to disown her son if he didn't marry the young girl, so he did. Tassie worked hard at the butcher shop her husband's family owned, but the years of hunger and lack of medical care took a toll. She was sickly most of their married life, but she kept up the best she could, caring for her home, the business, and her beloved baby girl, Mary Lou.

A bad case of pneumonia weakened Tassie irreparably when Mary Lou reached the tender age of seven years old, and the next year her mother died.

Simon Franks had a profitable business in the butcher shop, and although he never drank on the job, when his wife died, his best friend became a bottle after work. In the bottle, he attempted to avoid facing his grief.

At first, the abuse he directed at his daughter was simply physical beatings with a wide leather belt, or pulling her long hair. But then one night, Simon Franks made his young daughter take her panties down for the whipping. But instead of the beating with a wide leather strap, Simon Franks let his fingers wander and to probe. He laid her face down over two pillows and that night, for the first time, he violated his little eight-year-old child with his ugly, out-of-control drunken cock. It was the first of many nights to come of this unspeakable abuse. He reminded her often that, "you been askin' 'fer this. It's all your fault."

Mary Lou took the burden of shame and it piled up on her shoulders like a great weight, with every encounter. Simon also set her up for when she was older, reminding her that "this is all boys ever want, so you ain't goin' nowhere." But she began to eat comfort foods in larger quantities, ironically to try and alleviate the weight of shame and guilt that was pulling her down. Food became her always-available friend. In his drunken rages that followed over the years, Mary Lou's father justified his actions by saying she was "cut out to be a whore," and he was going to show her how to be one. And when she began to gain weight over the next several years, his beliefs about her were confirmed. The sexual abuse was a nightly ritual by now, and by the time Mary Lou was 13, she weighed two hundred and twenty pounds. Her days were a cruel hell as she endured teasing by classmates, and her nights were a cruel confusion, servicing her father's depraved needs. Her only solace was food, and it was always there when she needed it. She was a marvelous cook and could make gourmet meals from the fine cuts of meat her father brought home from his butcher shop. She used the German and Alsacian recipes left by her grandmother, and her father gained weight too. There were seldom any leftovers.

Her father rarely missed the opportunity to slap her on the butt, and remark, "Yer' ass is gittin' bigger everyday. No man is gonna' want ya. Yer becomin' such a pig. No man in his right mind would ever marry such a fat pig of a girl."

Mary Lou had a greater talent that no one had ever recognized. Her father was a lover of opera and classical music, and he had a fine wind-up phonograph, with records by Madame Schumann Heinke and Caruso. His library also held some Nelson Eddy and Jeanette McDonald, even a Rudy Vallee, and other contemporaries of the day. But Mary Lou's favorite was the opera, "Carmen," and she could sing with the voice of an angel. She knew the words to every one of the operas in Italian, German and Spanish. But the *Habenero* from *Carmen* was the one she sang most often. Her range was phenomenal, and she found church as an avenue where she thought she could express herself in song. The choirmaster thought differently. He was annoyed at Mary Lou for her fatness, that failed to blend in with the group, and called her a "show off" because of her strong contralto voice that overwhelmed the other voices. And as her weight swelled, the choirmaster had the excuse he needed. He banned her from the group until she lost some weight, which she never did, and her singing days came to an end. Ended, that is, except in private moments, when she sang solely for herself to dispel the loneliness.

At thirteen, Mary Lou ran away from classmates, her father, the church, the town and years of rejection and grief. She climbed into a boxcar that was sitting on the side tracks and made it to the old

Southern Pacific rail yard in Sacramento. With her few pitiful belongings and the three dollars she had stolen from Simon, she walked up Third Street. Before dark, she had made twelve dollars. Sure enough, Simon had made his daughter a "damn good whore" as he'd promised. And for the next few years, this was Mary Lou's life.

The men who paid her rarely abused her, and they didn't seem to care that by then, she was tipping the scales at 380 pounds. Some of the men even held her close and caressed and kissed her. Others even told her she was beautiful. Mary Lou loved the positive attention, and the negative was nowhere near what she had already endured, so life was pretty good. She also loved having her own little room in the Sixth Street hotel where she could lock the door and refuse service to anyone. She was able to buy a sewing machine, and had a small kitchen where she prepared enormous gourmet meals. She ate every scrap, and shared a few morsels with some of her best customers. The occasional name-calling she endured didn't seem that mean spirited. This was her job, and she endured it, feeling better when the money was handed over. In her new life, Mary Lou even got to sing. In the summertime, when the heat was unbearable, she would step out on to her tiny balcony in the evening, and sing one of the old Nelson Eddy and Jeannette Mac Donald tunes or something from Gilbert and Sullivan. *Poor Little Butterfly* was a favorite, and almost always made someone cry at the plight and anguish of the delicate little Japanese girl. People passing by would gather on the sidewalk below and listen to the magical voice. Very few theatre and opera people passed by in that section of town so she was never "discovered."

One year, in the spirit and joy of the holidays on Christmas Eve, she went to midnight mass at the Cathedral on Twelfth and "K" streets, determined to sing. Her confidence was high, and just before mass started, she stood up and burst into an a cappella rendition of Schubert's "*Ave Maria*." When she finished, the silence was almost magical as the people in the church were struck by the wonder of the music of Schubert and the quality of the voice. They were thrilled and amazed when her strong contralto swelled to the rafters of the Cathedral and filled the hearts of the listeners. When she had finished, a priest sidled up to her and asked her to leave. She had not been invited to sing, he told her, but the truth was that he knew she was a whore. He had visited the Third Street district enough times to know some of the people who lived there. In fact, he had even visited Mary Lou and bought and paid for her services. It had been at three o'clock in the morning and he had not worn his collar. But Mary Lou recognized him, nevertheless.

Mary Lou was again devastated. Her song was silent for months afterward, taking the rejection as a sign from God Almighty that she should keep quiet. She turned her attention to sewing. She had a natural knack for putting the pieces of fabric together, and made patterns from cutting them out free hand from newspapers. She made shirts and dresses and sold them to some of her friends, and some of her customers. They were quite a bit cheaper, and just like store-bought. And now reaching 400 pounds, and in the still tough times of the tail end of the depression, Mary Lou had to make all of her own clothes, which honed her skill as a seamstress. Mary Lou was also talented in design, but she knew she could make more money "fuckin' than stitchin'," and she did both with equal skill. Trading on both talents, she was able to save a few dollars and make regular trips to the picture show at the old Fox Theatre on "K" Street. She was such a good, regular customer, the management found an old chair with no arms on it that she could actually sit in. And even though it had to be set up in the very back of the theatre, she happily bought two bags of caramel corn and a root beer float, usually more than once, and lost herself in the movie. Her fantasies of true love blossomed there in the darkened theatre, and some days she even let herself dream about marriage.

She was pretty content with life for the first time since her mama died until New Years Eve 1932. The Sacramento police had a new "vice" unit, and they were out to get all the whores off the street. She was arrested for soliciting, and badly treated by the cops. One of them tried to push a nightstick into her vagina and the other one made her give him a blowjob on the way to the jail.

Mary Lou was 18 years old and had never heard of the constitution. She had no idea that they could only keep her for 72 hours without charging her, nor that she was entitled to a lawyer. She was held for two weeks at the 6th and "I" streets jail before her court appearance.

The jail stank of urine, and Mary Lou was the only woman there. She was expected to service all the guards as well as the prisoners that could pay the guards for her service. The guards rationalized that "what the hell. She's a whore anyway so she probably likes it." By the time she appeared before the judge, she was so traumatized by threats and numerous and varied types of rape, she could barely speak. She sat silently as the tears rolled down her fat cheeks. The judge gave her what they called a "floater." So called because it was an order to "float" out of town by sundown, or go back to jail for 30 days.

Mary Lou rushed from the courtroom to her little hotel room, terrified that her things had been stolen in her absence. But they were still there, just as she had left them. Her new doll and all the pretty clothes she had made for it. Her radio, which had accompanied her on lonely nights and kept music in her life, was there. The sewing machine, with its little electric motor, the wind-up record player, her electric fan, a hot plate and portable heater were all there. She checked inside the cupboards. All her pots and pans and dishes, the new bedspread, and her clothes and shoes, were there. She sat down on the bed and began to cry. Not just crying, but great breath stealing sobs, moans and frightened keening like a wounded animal. "Oh, Mamma, why didja' go away? Why didja' up an' die? Please come back. I'm such a bad girl. I wish I was dead. I been so bad. That judge called me a 'human dreg' and I don't even know what that is. Daddy said I was bad. The judge said I should be punished. But Mamma, I been punished enough. I just want to lay down an' die. I just want my Ma-Ma-Mamma!"

by Loma A. Phegley

Mary Lou's wailings did not go unnoticed. Someone close by was about to offer her a deal she couldn't refuse. There are many degrees of slavery, but it is all slavery.

Chapter Seven:
Golden Earrings

Starshine Moonstone was her real name and she was a pure Romany gypsy. She was born in 1910 in a wagon camped only a few miles outside Budapest, Hungary. Her mother did not survive the birth, and when she was only a few months old, her father smuggled her to America in the bowels of an Ocean liner. He was a Ceygan—a gypsy who was generally despised by the rest of the populace, so his chance of getting permission to leave the country was pretty slim. But Lazlo Zaccanarro was not a Gypsy for nothing. He was more resourceful than to let anyone keep him from his destiny. Late on a moonless night, Laszlo said his goodbyes to family and friends and waded into the cold water of the harbor and, with his tiny daughter tied around his own body with a sash, he swam to a passenger liner and climbed one of the ropes to the deck. From there, he made his way to the steerage compartment.

Some of the steerage passengers that knew they were hidden there, shared their meager rations, and when they arrived in New York, her father swam to the shore with little Starshine tied in the same sash he had used to get to the boat back in the old country. Since he had no papers admitting him and the child to America legally, this was his only method of avoiding the immigration authorities of Ellis Island. He made his way to The Bowery, to the squalid little tenement walk-up cold water flat where his brother and his family lived. Laszlo Jacannarro was a very fine musician whose violin and music eventually became much in demand. But to start his new life, he played on the streets for coins until he landed a job playing his sad, sometimes wild gypsy music in a cocktail lounge in Manhattan.

When Starshine was old enough not to get in his way, maybe 6 or 7, she accompanied her father to work, but there was no plan for her to remain idle there. She was required to earn her keep by becoming part of the act, and to the delight of all who saw her, danced for them with a rhythm that kept good time with his music. She learned early to keep the beat with the tambourine, and she would pirouette, twirl, twist and sway in a sensual manner that belied her young age. She even invented her own steps, learning "the art of the eyes" along the way. Keeping eye contact with strangers, especially men, seemed to render them helpless, and as she grew older, she recognized a business opportunity to be had, simply by retaining eye contact. She could make every man weak with the anticipation of sex and wild with passion when he would look into those black expressive eyes. But the girl was no fool.

The hard times her family endured, and the tricky ways they got hold of money, taught her some good business sense. Even as a young girl, she knew what men wanted. Some of the men among the gypsies she knew wanted it too, and the older gypsy women gave her some lessons in the value of letting them have it…. for cash or trade. But Starshine was the huntress. She took no man to her bed unless he was her choice. For the most part, men got one chance to be with her if she wanted them. One night, one encounter, and he was no longer in her life. She used those encounters to learn the ways of men, but preferred to remain unattached to any of them. She was fiercely independent and saw that her sexuality had a magnetic pull that made them want to stay around. But she would have none of it, and she let them know right up front that it was a one shot deal. There were a few who thought they could change her mind, but Starshine set them straight in quick order. Star was not what the movie people called beautiful. For one thing, she wasn't a blonde, but generally, she was described as handsome and captivating instead of beautiful. She stood 5-feet-8-inches tall, with long slender legs and flawless olive-colored skin. Her face was long and oval, with an aquiline nose, a wide sensuous mouth, and perfectly straight, white teeth with a slight overbite. She kept her lush black hair in a single braid that fell below her hips, and it was thick, straight and silky.

But when the men reminisced silently about their encounter with her, it was the eyes that they remembered. They were a little bit heavy-lidded, a characteristic that made her look ready for bed at all times. The long black lashes swept her cheeks, and her eyes showed the emotion she chose at any given moment; penetrating, expressive, blank, smoldering, happy, angry...it all depended on what emotion she wanted to evoke from foolish morons whose money interested her most of all. She would have done well in Hollywood. She was a born actress, having learned the way from her mentors. She was an excellent student in the ways of people, but particularly men. She was cold and calculating in her selection of men. He must have sufficient money to pay her well, but also to treat her with respect. Her chosen customer had to agree to leave her presence as soon as he had spent himself. They knew the agreement before she ever opened her door or her legs, so if one of her lovers showed up a second time, she screamed obscenities at him so loudly that the neighbors knew him as a disgusting ravager of innocent women. Any man who tried such a foolhardy approach never darkened her door again.

Star attracted much attention with her long golden-hooped earrings, colorful velvet skirts, and swaying hips. She was the epitome of grace as she walked, and she knew just how to swing her lovely rear end, bouncing her large, wondrous breasts as she went, ever mindful of the admiring and downright lustful glances bestowed on her by the men she passed. The "respectable" women, on the other hand, were shooting hateful, jealous and judgmental scorn in her direction, and she was mindful of that too, as they pulled their husbands a little closer when she walked by. The whole scene amused her. But there was more to gypsy Starshine than sex and dancing.

by Loma A. Phegley

She had the gift of second sight and so she joined the circus of Bill S. Bailey and opened up her own business. It was little more than a red and black striped tent on the strip of ground reserved for the sideshow attractions called the Gayway. It drew those who wanted or needed to "see" the future or discover if their husbands were cheating on them. Star was a success in what she did. She was good when she did readings. She hit the nail on the head 90 percent of the time. But she was the first to admit that every gifted seer had blind spots, and readings were not infallible. They were simply based on this particular point in time, and the probable future. Sometimes when it was true, and sometimes when she chose not to reveal something especially horrible, she would say, "There is a blind spot. I am not being allowed to see all. Now and again, I am wrong. I am destined not to go there." She knew that one of the things that triggered the blind spot was infatuation with a man, or even the love of a person. She never gave readings for people she cared about, because the pictures all came out positive, and followed too closely her own wishes for her friends and lovers. Her objectivity flew out the window in those cases.

When she had joined the circus she knew it was time she found her own way, independent from her father and the other old gypsies she had known all of her life. Even though the old gypsies cried and begged, Starshine was adamant about seeing and experiencing the world on her own. It was a departure from old ways, when the gypsy bands stuck together for a lifetime, but she was determined. She felt good about securing her own employment with the circus, and she responded to an ad in the newspaper by showing up, giving Billy Bailey a reading, and getting hired on by agreeing to a 60/40 split of her take. That split did not include the occasional, extracurricular men she chose to "entertain" from time to time. That was her own business and she kept it so.

Her red striped tent was decorated in celestial designs, a folding table with a sparkly sky blue cloth covering it, and in the middle, a large crystal ball. Later Tico, who would become a fast and dear friend of

Starshine, found a very unique crystal skull at one of the gem auctions he was always attending when the opportunity presented itself.

When she knew the troupe would be leaving early the next morning, usually on the last night of performances, she would often turn a trick. She did it following her own strict criteria: Only if she liked the looks of the man, and if he paid her well and treated her with respect. A softly padded mat on the carpet was covered with a red quilt, where she would take her patron inside the tent. She undressed him, stripped off her long skirts, and danced above him so as to show him her secret places of delight. With her long legs spread wide, and her partner below her, she used her fingers to display the pink so he could salivate in anticipation. Dropping to her knees beside him, she would cradle his testicles in one hand, and stoke the length of his cock with the other. Then she would take him into her mouth, gently sucking, licking, running her tongue around the end of the shaft until he could no longer wait. At that point of no return, she would swing her leg over him and slowly lower herself into place, as he watched his member disappear inside her lovely paradise. It took mere seconds before the men were spilling into her, and no sooner did they do it, than she was off and up. "Go now," she would say. And when they protested that they wanted to spend more time with her, she would calmly recite their name and address, and since most were married, this put the fear into them. Star lifted the wallets to glean the information when the man was so absorbed in what he was doing that he had no clue as to what she was up to. She put them back intact before they were missed. None of them ever realized how she had gleaned such information. All she would say is, "Star sees all, knows all. Now scram, cockroach."

Star never considered herself a whore, and she never stole money from the pockets of her customers, only information.

The gypsy fortuneteller liked her new boss, Mr. B. She kept to herself most of the time. She had plenty to eat, men to enjoy on occasion, including other circus performers, and life was pretty good for

by Loma A. Phegley

Starshine Moonstone, the circus seer. Someday, her "blind spot" would prove to be a big one, but that would be at some time down the road.

Chapter Eight:
A Marriage Made In Hell

He was called Toby while performing, as most of the clowns in the 1930s were, and he was good at what he did. That was about all that was good about Hiram Lockstep, a name he had adopted to keep from being drafted into the army to fight in World War I. Tall and thin, and almost emaciated to look at, Hiram could be mistaken for a bucket full of antlers. Hiram was ugly, only he didn't know it. Most people figured he wasn't two-faced or he would have worn his other face. His large lumpy nose he called "classic" and his droopy eyelids he said were "sexy." He considered his wide floppy mouth "expressive" and on top of it all was a thick, unruly mop of red hair that was seldom combed or even washed and made him look like he'd been pulled through a knot-hole backwards. His skin was pale and sickly looking with so many freckles as to be uncountable. He looked like he had been driving cows with a short whip and an old cow had farted bran all over him. Underneath that head of red hair, Hiram was a surprisingly natty dresser. He still wore spats and striped trousers, and shirts starched and ironed to a "fare-thee well," as he was fond of saying. His grand swallowtail coat was one he'd stolen from a magician who had been on the same card last year at a vaudeville act in Jersey, or as Hiram pronounced it, "Joisey." He often bragged that his dapper derby hat had cost him "ten bucks in New Yaahk."

Hiram was a loud-mouthed braggart, and handled the truth with great carelessness. He was a genius at his job, and he knew it, and was usually tolerated in most jobs because he was a master mime. His

by Loma A. Phegley

superb performances created waves of hysterical laughter from both children and adults, and he was often the star attraction. When Hiram threw an imaginary ball to his audience, they could almost see it, raising their hands to pretend to catch. And when he washed an imaginary window, it seemed that the audience was truly in front of a glass. He would throw a bucket filled with confetti into the crowd, and the audience was sure it was water. Everyone would gasp, only to find it was but confetti. Oh, he was a good clown. He had a sense of what would be funny and used all of his skills in every performance. But Hiram had a reputation as a thief, liar, woman-beater, and drunkard and it was well known to every circus in the U.S. as well as some in Europe. Only one circus owner in Florida, who he heard had inherited a full circus get up, was oblivious to his past, and Hiram had recently sent a letter offering to perform for one Billy Bailey.

Hiram had a nose for situations where he could profit in some way or another, and he happened to be staying in the cheap hotel where Mary Lou was living. Coming back to his room one afternoon, he heard wailing and crying down the hall, and went to check it out. It was poor Mary Lou doing the wailing and crying. She was sitting on her bed with her head in her hands, sobbing as though her heart was broken, and it surely was. "What have we here?" he asked. "A damsel in distress?" The door to her room was open and when she looked up, she saw the red hair first. There he stood, in all his manly glory, looking like the most handsome man she'd ever seen. She fancied him the possible answer to a maiden's prayer, never mind that she was no maiden. And never mind that he was as ugly as a basket of buffalo chips. His yellow buckteeth became pearly white in her eyes, and she was focused on his dapper outfit. He seemed classy to Mary Lou, including that big, floppy mouth. She looked up and smiled broadly through her tears. Hiram sensed an easy take-over. He reckoned he could possibly benefit from the situation, but just how? He expected that would reveal itself if he played his cards right, and persuaded her with sweet words.

"Why is such a beautiful lady in tears on this fine day? Are you in need of the services of Ol' Uncle Toby?" he said. He moved in to put his arm around her on the bed. "Now just quit yer blubberin' and tell me what I can do to help." Help himself, he was thinking. He reckoned he could help himself to most of her possessions and a bit of her, as well. He sure as hell needed some walkin' around money at the moment and was not very choosy as to how he came by it. He'd already spotted the radio, the sewing machine and the fan. Those would bring a few dollars at the pawnshop. And it looked like the lady was a whore. Possible free ass if he could just pour on enough of what passed for charm, which was his specialty with the ladies. Mary Lou finally stopped her crying and composed herself. She then asked, "Who are you? You say Uncle Toby?"

"Well," Hiram stuttered, "that's my stage name. I'm a actor, ya know." He'd used that line to perfection many times with the fair sex, and it usually worked pretty well. It worked like a charm with Mary Lou.

"A actor? Ya mean like William S. Hart? In the movies? A real life actor?" She was obviously impressed. She could see how his handsome face and dapper appearance would have him fit right into such a world.

"Well, my name's really Hiram Lockstep, late of New Joisey, 'atcher service," he said, and took a deep bow. Mary Lou was breathless. A real life actor was speaking to her and he had called her a beautiful lady and a damsel in distress. She swallowed and extended the back of her hand to the handsome stranger who was now sitting right on her bed in the tiny hotel room that she called home.

"Charmed I'm sure," she said, just like she'd seen the ladies in the picture show do it. He took her outstretched hand, but instead of kissing it, he turned it over, palm side up, put his tongue out and licked it.

Mary Lou nearly swooned. She felt butterflies in her stomach and in her tits and in her crotch. Hiram, as he continued to survey the booty he could get his hands on, had a few flutters of his own. It was obvious she was a whore, but Hiram wanted her practiced services free of charge.

by Loma A. Phegley

"Now tell Hiram all about your problems, so I can help." He knew that being a good listener made women weak, and also gave him the advantage. Mary Lou laid out her sad tale of having to get out of town by sundown, about the horrors of the jail, and about her inability to get all her stuff out of town, not to mention having nowhere to go. Hiram himself was on a floater, which had expired three days earlier. He was supposed to have gotten out of town already, but he failed to mention that. But neither of them wanted to run afoul of the law. Hiram's next brush was likely to cost him 6 months in jail, and especially if he was unlucky enough to get Judge Springer again.

But there was still the matter of sex. Why give up a perfectly good room right away when it would just take a couple of minutes to relieve his present state of tumescence? He thought to himself, "Damn. A stiff prick ain't got no sense. No sense at all," as he started to make his move.

The ass was easy, and it was good. It was also quick, as he figured it would be. But when it was over, Mary Lou began to cry again. "Now whatsa' matter? Me dick too long? Are ya' hungry…what the hell…" Between sobs, she told him she couldn't bear to think of leaving all her worldly goods behind. Hiram had no intentions of leaving her things behind either. Those possessions were about to become his traveling money, but just as he was about to tell her to go on ahead and he'd follow her with her stuff, she said the magic words. "An' besides, I gotta' go to the bank and get my savings before three o'clock. It's eleven now, and oh lordy, how am I gonna' get all this done?" she asked.

Now it was Hiram's turn to grow faint and nearly swoon. He pulled up his pants, pulled himself together, and managed to sound disinterested. "Well, you could leave the bank money if it ain't but a little bit. Course, if there is more than two or three bucks…" he baited her. Mary Lou screeched, "Two or three bucks? Why there is more than four hundred dollars in that bank. I am not leavin' it. No sireebob." The mere mention of such a sum made Hiram revise his whole plan from start to finish. While he was grateful for the ass, he was sorry now he had wasted the time. Plenty of time for that later. Plenty of ass, too. Hiram was so excited he began to drool. The spittle dropped off the point of his chin, and when he spoke it sprayed around the room like a lawn sprinkler.

"OK, honey doll," he called her, thinking, 'that'll get the stars shining in her eyes,' and it did. "Tell ya what. I got a friend that'll loan me his car." He neglected to mention that the friend was someone he hadn't met yet and would not be predisposed to loan him the car if they had been twins.

"You go on down to the bank, and get the money. I'll go down to the grocery store and get some empty boxes. We can meet back here, git yer' stuff packed and carry it down to the alley. You can sit with your stuff and I'll go git' the car. Does that sound like a plan, or what, sugar plum?" Hiram was smart enough to know that about one or two more honey pies and sweeties and maybe a kissy lips or two and that money and that free ass was as good as his.

He got the boxes, and as he was on his way back from the store, stopped by the front desk and asked if he had any mail. The old clerk cackled and said, "Why hell, Hiram, I didn't know you could read!"

Hiram was his usual cheerful self and answered, "Fuck you, you toothless old cock sucker."

The old man was feeling frisky, so he told Hiram, "If I could do that, I'd put you plum out of business," and he laughed uproariously at his own joke. He handed Hiram a letter from Sarasota Springs, Florida, which he tore open and read right there at the counter.

Hiram was ecstatic at the letter's contents. He could hardly believe that so much good fortune could smile upon him all in one day. Pussy, possessions, money and now a job with Billy Bailey's circus. He carried the boxes and the string he had gotten to tie them shut back to the room. Mary Lou wasn't back yet so he began to pack all of her worldly treasures into the boxes. He even packed the food-canned soup, crackers, peanut butter, peaches, and coffee. Pancake syrup, mayonnaise, mustard, matches, and even mousetraps. But there was more stuff than there were boxes, so Hiram sneaked down the hall to the lumberjack's room and jimmied the lock. He knew the logger was up at McCloud River on a job for a few days, so he helped himself to a nice, sturdy, trunk, two Gladstone bags, a few undershirts, socks, and a new fedora.

When Mary Lou came back, they carried all the boxes and bags downstairs and took them in the alley. Then Hiram set off to "borrow" his "friend's car."

True to his word, which was unusual for Hiram, he returned about an hour later with a very respectable 1928 high wheel Dodge touring car with roll up window, a rear trunk, and a spare tire. Within minutes, they had crammed all of Mary Lou's things into the car. Hiram even managed to get her lovely rosewood rocking chair into the cavernous back seat. He knew he had very little time, so they set off in a hurry down Highway 40 toward Reno. They'd barely made it through the 16th Street underpass in North Sacramento when Hiram put on his concerned voice.

"Ya know darlin', I only knowed ya for a short time, but I believe I'm in love with ya. I just feel like I've always knowed ya' and I want to take care of ya and protect ya. I don't think it's safe you walkin' around with all that money on ya' bein' a weak little woman and all," he said with his most nurturing voice.

Mary Lou shot him a cutting glance.

"Weak little woman, my ass! I been on my own since I was 13 years old. This here money stays right here between my tits and you ain't gittin' yer hands on it. It represents a lot of my time a gruntin' and a humpin' and pretending to just love what those smelly old ruttin' backs was doin'. It's mine," she proclaimed.

Hiram looked hurt. "Ya mean after all I done fer ya! Saved yer damn life. Saved all yer stuff. Kept ya from goin' back to the Sheriff's Hotel. Hell, girl. That really hurts to find out ya' was only usin' me to do all yer dirty work. So ya' don't trust me! Well, I could just stop this car and let ya off at the side of the road. Then where would ya be without ol' Hiram the lifesaver? Ever think of that?" he threatened.

But he knew it was time for a little sweet talk to go with the threats, so he continued.

"I thought ya loved me. And here me thinkin' you was the best lay I ever had and not carin' that you ain't no lily-white virgin."

Hiram was picking up steam and continued, "Golly, darlin', I was thinkin' maybe if ya' played yer cards right, me an you could git married when we get to Reno."

Hiram knew marriage was the dream of every single girl, and especially if she'd been a whore, but the minute he made the offer, he realized he'd made a major error in strategy. After all, Reno was only a little over a hundred miles away and it was on the route to Florida too. There was little chance of escape, as Mary Lou shrieked.

"Married? Me a married lady? Oh, God, me? I can't believe it! I'll be a married lady. I won't' have to do no more whorin'! Oh Lordy. I'm in heaven. Oh, Hiram, I do believe I love you too."

This was one of those rare occasions when Hiram nearly panicked. He almost stopped the car and bolted across the farmland that was laid out on either side of the highway. But the thought of $400.00 nestled there between Mary Lou's overly abundant tits brought him back to his senses. His mind began to hum like the engine of the stolen car he was driving, as he began to rationalize his decision. He said to himself: "This could be good. I'll get the money, I'm headed to a new job, and maybe they could use a fat lady or a seamstress, so I'll put my new wife to work." He also considered pimping her out now and then for extra cash. And he knew he could talk her out of the money, especially once he was her husband. Hell, those dollars would be rightfully his once the certificate was signed. The more ol' Hiram considered the deal, the more he realized that in spite of all the pitfalls of marriage, the benefits seemed to outweigh the negative aspects. In fact, outweighed by all of her possessions and two wheels on the car. And of course, she would always be a ready piece of ass and she says she can cook…what the hell he rationalized. If I get tired of her I can always give her the boot.

So Hiram Lockstep resigned himself, and even congratulated himself on the deal he was about to make. He had a new car, stolen, but to him, new, a rich whore, a new job on the horizon, a steady source of extra income, and Mary Lou even said she could cook. Now he was ready to break the news to her about where they were headed.

"Looka here, Muffin," he began. "I got this here letter in my pocket from a very famous circus beggin' me to go to work fer 'em. They want me as the chief clown. Now I'm thinkin' I can do better with Ol' Barnum, but I'm willin' to sacrifice a job with the big time. And although the big time is where I really belong, I think I can git you a job with this small-timey outfit. Ya' know. Start ya out small. The entertainment business is pretty tricky to break into unless you know a big shot like me who is on the inside."

Mary Lou was skeptical. But then hadn't he come through with the car and helped her blow town with all she owned? And besides, he was about to marry her, and make her a respectable woman, and that was her fondest daydream. She repeated the word over and over, "Mrs. Hiram Lockstep. Mrs. Mary Lou Lockstep. Good morning, Mrs. Lockstep."

And Hiram loved her. He said so. Fuck her old man. She was about to prove Simon Franks wrong. At least partly wrong. He'd said he would make her a damn good whore, and he had. But he also said she would never amount to a pinch of snuff, and that no man would marry such a fat pig of a girl. She knew now that he had said those things to destroy her confidence in herself so he could keep her at home to be his slave. Now her dream was about to become reality. Mary Lou had been a happy whore when she knew there was nothing better. Now she had found something better. She just knew it. And Reno was just 85 miles away. She felt lucky. Little did she know that there were degrees of slavery, but it was all slavery.

Chapter Nine:
Broken Dolly

The deviant that raped and murdered little Becky Bailey was among the frantic searchers two days later who found her two miles down the river, her body caught in the dead stumps along the banks. Only one person knew who that individual was, and that was the murderer himself. It was the summer of 1933, and the circus had only been in town two days when the Bailey's only child was found dead, her little body dumped like a piece of garbage into the rushing currents. People in the search party wept, and spoke of what kind of a monster would do such a thing to a sweet, innocent child.

Maude Bailey, little Becky's mother, bathed her daughter's lifeless corpse, washing and combing the mud, leaves and twigs from her silky blond hair. Her little face was blue and withered from the water, and Maude sobbed inconsolably as she took care of the child for the last time.

Becky's father, Billy, the circus owner, gently wrapped her in a pink blanket before they allowed the mortician to take her away.

The funeral was brief and sad. Becky's parents were accompanied by all the circus performers, even those who had recently joined the cast of characters, including Mary Lou, now called "Tilly the Fat Lady," her husband Hiram, now working as "Toby Toontuck the Clown," the little Spanish Jew, Tico Tico, his buddy Abdoul, now acting as "Ivan the Strong Man," Ringmaster Charlie "One Shoe," the Gypsy Fortune Teller Starshine Moonstone, the Caesar Family, trapeze artists, and all the concession operators. Each person shook his or her head in disbelief and bewilderment as to who and why such a thing could happen.

But justice was elusive for Becky. The town was so small, and the police chief so drunk, along with the fact that the child of the circus was not a regular town citizen, nor her parents local voters, not even a coroner's inquest was held.

If the mortician knew little Becky had been raped and strangled, he didn't say a word about it. It was a political time bomb he didn't want to have go off in a town he practically owned. To his way of reasoning, too many crimes in his district could weaken his reputation as a good sheriff, so he was inclined to make this a non-crime. The mortician was the mayor, the shopkeeper, the Postmaster, the Coroner and the Police Chief. To his convenient way of thinking, a child had fallen into the river and drowned. That was the end of it, and besides, this child belonged to the riff-raff that made up a traveling circus. The likes of those folks were not even worthy of any special kind of attention, no matter what the circumstances. It was over and done with anyway, and the child was gone.

Thus the fragile life of the only child of Mr. and Mrs. B had ended. But it was just the beginning of the grieving process for the child's devastated mother, her saddened father, and the performers who loved her. And even the clowns, who had made funny faces at the bright child, wept.

But the child killer was still at-large, and so far, no one was even looking for the sadistic monster.

Chapter Ten:
Taking The Show On The Road

The moment Bill Bailey saw Abdoul he knew he had his strong man. Every circus has its strong man, and in this one, it was Abdoul, the Turk. But right at that moment in time, Turks were not very popular, so Bailey transformed Abdoul into Ivan, a Russian. He would call him "Ivan The Terrible." Of course, he was neither Russian, nor was he very terrible. Nevertheless, Bailey declared that Abdoul would become "Ivan The Terrible, Strongest Man in The World" and would be magically changed from a Turk to a Russian. That was fine with Abdoul, since the pay was decent, and the housing was included. He even liked his new name. "Ivan," he said to himself. He was thinking about a song he had heard one of the American seamen singing about 'Ivan Skavinsky Skavaar' and 'Abdoul Aboul Boul Amir.' "Yeh," he laughed, "that be me."

Ivan was about six-foot-seven and weighed a good two-hundred-and-thirty pounds of well-put-together muscle. He was billed as the "Strongest Man in the World," but Ivan knew he was not, by far, the "Strongest Man in the World." He knew that many of the patrons at the circus were stronger than he, yet from time to time he was challenged to arm wrestling matches or some other kind of test of strength. Ivan almost always good-naturedly told these fellows that his contract with the circus forbid him to engage in any contest other than as a performer in the act. This was not true, but he had no wish to embarrass any of the challengers if he beat them, and then it would do his reputation no good if he were beaten. He knew also, that many of these farmers and foundry workers and oil field roustabout might very well whip his ass in

by Loma A. Phegley

a game of their choice, not his. Now and again jeering and insults to his manhood forced him, to engage in some of these feats of strength. Ivan always won, but he knew that one day he would encounter one of the 'red neck' farmers who bucked hay for a living, or an oil field worker or a foundry laborer who would kick his ass. He had, so far, been lucky.

But as a showman he was a hit. He lifted weights marked five hundred pounds, wrestled the aging Russian Sun Bear, who was called "Peter The Great" and delighted the children with his antics of pretending that old Peter had wrestled him to the ground in one of these play matches. When he would strut about the ring flexing his muscles as Charlie touted his magnificent abilities, he was cheered and even booed by some of the men. Ivan loved it all and so did the audience.

Tico Tico arrived for the interview with the new "Ivan" and Bailey soon discovered that this was a man of great pride and dignity and would never become a clown, as most circus dwarfs were in those days. The little man's business acumen and ability with figures became immediately apparent to Bailey, so he was hired as the new accountant and business manager to assist Maude, who had an overwhelming job just arranging bookings and seeing to the advertising, costumes and all of the other many task it took to operate a circus.

Bailey saw the potential in this sweet fat girl and Mary Lou didn't mind the work. She was a respectable woman, having been married in Reno, and was through with whoring. She was known to make the crowds gasp by lifting her skirt a bit, to show off those massive thighs. Somewhat scantily clad for that day and time, "Tilly" showed off the body so many men had already seen to thousands of others, who would not be able to touch, but only look. It was a step up, and she considered her job educational. Her attraction was very popular with the immigrant men, especially those who considered extra weight a sign of opulence.

But Mary Lou's real joy, other than when she was singing, was when the main attraction took place in the big center tent. There was all kinds of action, with teams of dray horses prancing, elephants bowing, and clowns clowning, white horses galloping around and around with trick rides on their backs doing their "Death Defying Feats." Many of those performers took to the ring in costumes she had sewn herself, and there was a sense of pride she had never felt before in watching them. She had even made some of the trappings for the elephants and the camels.

On opening night Mary Lou got to sing "God Bless America" dressed in a magnificent costume she had designed and sewn herself. It was of rich, watermelon red satin, in fact about fifteen yards of it. The neckline was cut low enough to be modest and not only the neckline, but the edges of the bell sleeves and the hem were trimmed by a wide band of bright blue satin on which she had embroidered dozens of randomly placed and sized white stars. The gown had no waist and hung straight down from the neckline in voluminous ripples and folds of the abundant red satin. When this lady, of an easy four-hundred-plus pounds, stepped out onto the bandstand in all her fashionable glory, there was laughter and giggles. But the moment her glorious voice began "God bless America..." the laughter stopped and the listening began. Her voice swelled into thrilling musical magic and everyone who heard her knew they were listening to something unique. Tears of the listeners were not uncommon, and when the last note died, the applause began and Mary Lou was in her glory. It truly was her finest hour every performance.

But Saint Patrick's Day was when she really shined. Her rendition of "Irish Eyes" and "Danny Boy" or "Mother Macree" had every Irishman weeping tears of homesickness. After the show they would come to her and press dollar bills into her hands. She was always reluctant to take the hard-earned money of these Irish immigrants. She knew it had come hard from working on railroads and road gangs and coal mines, and the singing was her pleasure. But they insisted and finally they convinced her that it had been more than worth it just to hear a bit of the auld sod.

by Loma A. Phegley

Mr. B, the name the troupe had adopted for Billy Bailey, saw the effect Mary Lou's singing had on the crowd and he knew he had a multi-talented jewel as a valuable employee. She was not only kind and sweet tempered, always ready to help when she could, she was an excellent seamstress, had a fine sense of design and could cook like a French chef, she could sing like an angel and doubled as the Fat Lady attraction. "Lucky me," thought Mr. B.

Her stupid husband, the drunken clown, Hiram, insisted that she be renamed "Tilly." He said it was "…more fittin' for a fat lady to be named Tilly." She did not oppose Hiram. It seemed that she loved him. "Love really is blind. And stupid as well," thought Mr. B.

Although Mary Lou had many talents, the one she had been the most noted for was her ability as a whore. Nobody paid much attention to her other skills. Most of them just took her help and kindness for granted and used her when it was to their advantage. But now she had a real job and was really appreciated for herself and for her talents.

She was now a respectable married lady, through with whoring and, not only that, she had a job and a new found respect. She also had many new friendships. She enjoyed meeting all the people, customers and fellow workers, alike. None of them knew of her degrading past so she could be anything or anyone she chose, but she chose to be just herself.

Her only sorrow centered around her new husband. He was both physically and emotionally abusive, calling her degrading names, and using every opportunity to pinch her or thump her on the head. He proved to be a drunk; a sloppy, stupid drunk. Of course, he wasn't too bright sober. But at least she was married. Whatever she was forced to endure from Hiram, she figured it was part of the deal to be married. That was just how it was supposed to be. She did not know any different.

The Caesar Family was already part of the troupe when Ivan and Tico arrived. A group of talented trapeze artists from Sicily, the patriarch of the group was their father and grandfather. He had the unlikely name of Julius, but everyone called him "Papa Primo." It seemed that the circus was blessed with fine cooks. Not only Tico and Mary Lou, but Papa Primo as well. Papa was an excellent chef, especially where pasta was concerned. He was also a very good vintner, and could make wine out of whatever was handy. Often, that was peach pits and peelings from the canneries. Sometimes it was plums, dates or figs, even watermelon, and when he stumbled upon an unguarded vineyard, it would be an excellent "fruit of the vine."

The circus was a transient group that moved around a lot, so Papa Primo would sometimes stash a few barrels of wine by burying them in a vacant field to keep from insulting the delicate balance of the finished product by disturbing its "sleep." Then later, when the circus would again be in the area, Papa would retrieve his treasure, sell some, and drink some. The old man was very valuable to know, especially during prohibition. Everyone in the family, including 5-year-old Nicholas, worked in the show.

Charlie Wonshu, who everyone called "Charlie One Shoe," was the very talented ringmaster. He was an immense man, 6-foot-7-inches tall, and had a round florid face that was not handsome by any stretch, but certainly commanded attention. His Irish tenor voice was nearly melodious as he sang out his "Ladies and Gentlemen...." so Charlie became the Ring Master. He was an excellent choice and was one of the very best Ring Masters in the business. He also drove one of the trucks, played the calliope, and fixed whatever was broken.

By the time baby Becky was born to Maude and Billy Bailey, the circus was doing rather well. Billy would travel out ahead of the troupe, and make arrangements with some local landowner in whatever jerkwater town he could find with enough people in it to get a crowd up.

Then, he'd plaster up some exciting looking posters of grotesque performers and wild animals, some that he didn't even feature, to announce the impending arrival of the circus. The buzz began on it's own after that. Bailey would then hurry back to the business of closing a show, and moving along to the town that was waiting.

by Loma A. Phegley

After Hiram joined the troop, and Becky had been murdered, Billy gave the job of scouting out locations and getting the advertising going to his chief clown. Hiram was supposed to dress in costume, and hype the show a bit while he was out there, but he rarely did it. Usually, he put up the posters, got drunk, and spent some time with the local whore before returning to his job with the circus. Billy and Maude usually spent a few days, if they were in the area, to travel to Becky's grave before initiating a new show.

The little girl had become Mr. and Mrs. B's life. She was bright and lively, loving and beautiful. Her parents were sure no other child had ever been so cherished.

All the performers knew Becky had not wandered from her bed and fallen into the river to drown. Some of them had seen the giant bruises on her stomach and the look of horror still on her face when she was pulled out of the water. They knew it had been rape and murder. They also knew that a traveling circus was seen as unworthy of any investigative efforts, and they suspected that the perpetrator could be within their own troupe. Many gossiped about it, and most felt it was one of the laborers they'd hired to help erect the big top. But there were at least half a dozen of those men, and they were there, then they were gone. Most of them had no address at all, so tracking them down would have been impossible. But in the minds of those who loved Becky the most, hope for justice was still barely alive.

Chapter Eleven:
The Great Grape Robbery

Where once he had been a square block of a man, gifted with grace, balance and beauty, the trapeze days of Julius Caesar were long over. Now crippled with arthritis, and less-than-perfectly-mended broken bones from high-wire falls, the man they called "Papa Primo" was stooped with age. But he was still a man to be reckoned with, partly because of his large Sicilian family that would vehemently defend one of their own, and partly because Papa Primo was not one to let a slight go unnoticed. The Patriarch of the Caesar family, Papa ruled "the Flying Caesars" with an iron fist. Nobody disrespected the old man, and his seven children, their children, and their spouses, not only obeyed his words, they were fiercely protective of him.

The Caesar family was a group of talented trapeze artists. Papa had four sons and three daughters, three sons-in-laws, and six grandchildren.

Papa Primo did all of the cooking for the family. He also coached the younger Caesars in gymnastics, while watching after the tots that were too young yet for the business. Not one child was ever out of Papa's sight while their parents were otherwise occupied.

He hated Hiram. Everyone knew that Hiram abused his wife. Papa Primo in particular wanted to come to Tilly's rescue, but he knew it would do little good. So he just hated Hiram, daring him to even touch any member of the Caesar family. To say he "didn't like Hiram" was too mild a way to put it. He hated that man with a white-hot Sicilian, long-lasting hate. He told Hiram, "if I ever catch you within ten feet of any of my family," then he drew an old crooked arthritic finger across his throat in a gesture no one could mistake. Hiram understood it, and very well.

When Papa Primo cooked, the whole circus camp could smell the wonderful aromas of a master Sicilian chef deftly working on tomato sauces, pasta dishes, and rich spices. That skill, coupled with his considerable talent as a vintner, made him a most valuable man to know.

Papa made an excellent sipping whiskey, and he had plenty of buyers always ready for the next batch to mature. The only mistake he had ever made in brewing was the time he was given five hundred pounds of culled potatoes by one of the valley farmers. Primo had never made potato wine, and knew nothing of vodka. But he reasoned that if it was not animal nor mineral, he could somehow turn it into alcohol.

Papa consulted with Ivan, who was a teetotaler. But Ivan just threw up his hands and said, "Maybe if I am Russian I know about some Russian drink. No Ruski, only Turk."

So Primo spoke with Tico, who was of little help. "Huh, sound like bad shit. Potato not fruit. Eat them, not make booze," was all Tico had to offer.

Mr. B said he was sure the Russians made a liquor out of potatoes, but he had no idea how they did it. He suggested that maybe it was the same way gin was made, and advised Primo to ask "Doc" Brady. But Doc said Primo should leave that idea alone since no one knew how it was done. The only person that didn't discourage him from the task of turning potatoes into booze was Charlie "One Shoe," the ringmaster.

Charlie volunteered to help. He said he'd had considerable experience in making a pretty good grade of bathtub gin back in the prohibition days, so Primo and Charlie made several gallons of "hooch" that was at least two hundred proof. It tasted like pure, unadulterated cat shit.

One quart exploded and set fire to a field of grass that burned nearly an acre of a city field until the fire department put it out. It took four gallons of Primo's best sipping whiskey for the Fire Chief to keep him out of jail on arson charges.

Charlie tried some of the potato booze out on Hiram.

"Aw, it ain't so bad. I've drank a lot worse back in my drinking days," said Hiram, although everyone knew his drinking days were not exactly a thing of the past. Hiram was likely to drink most anything he could get his hands on.

"When was that, Hiram, yesterday?" Charlie asked sarcastically.

Papa Primo made his good wines from whatever he could find. Sometimes it would be peach pits and peelings from the valley canneries. Often times, the sweepings from the floor of the local grain mill, or surplus fruit from farmers who were willing to exchange a bit of it for a bit of the finished product.

Papa, of course, preferred the fruit of the vine, but he found that he would have to actually purchase the grapes to get them at the right time for the fermentation process. That was unacceptable to the old man, and no unguarded vineyard was unknown to him.

Primo would make his creations in whatever locality they were performing at the time. Papa sold several gallons of his potato disaster to a Chinese grocer who had a small store on Skid Road in Sacramento. Tico, whose family drank only the most refined wines, made the sign of the cross when he heard about the sale. He pitied the poor winos who would buy it, and worse yet, drink it.

In 1936, Mr. B. bought a new Ford Convertible that he loved to show off. He was very proud of that car. Things were going well that year for Papa Primo too who had spotted a vineyard of the finest Zinfandel grapes unguarded just seven miles from where the circus was camped. Papa's eyes sparkled when one of his sons, Angelo, came back with a sample. Papa could not, would not, leave such a prize unmolested.

He assigned family members to watch the grapes for days, until he reckoned they were ready to crush into the finest wine of the season.

by Loma A. Phegley

Late one night, Primo and his boys pushed Mr. B's new car out to the road without starting it, so the circus owner would not be awakened. They drove to the vineyard, hid the car, picked box after box of the fine fruit, and then loaded them into the open seats of the car.

Laden with their late-night prize, they drove back to the circus grounds and unloaded the stolen goods into one of the tents used to store the feed for the animals. Just after dawn, as the performers started milling around in their tents and trailers, the circus grounds were already crawling with the local constabulary. Ten cops and deputies were rousting everyone in camp, searching for the stolen grapes.

Papa Primo came forward ready to defy the cops and do battle if necessary. Not one person in camp would even speak to the law. But they kept searching until they came to the feed tent. Instinctively, Papa grasped his old switchblade knife and held it in readiness behind his back, but to the amazement of every Sicilian present, the officers emerged from the feed tent empty-handed.

"There's nothing in there but an elephant and some empty boxes and feed sacks," was the declaration of Chief of Police Bill Elliot. So Sacramento's law enforcement community was at a loss to find their thief.

The Caesar family quietly turned their backs to the cops, and there were at least a dozen whispered Hail Marys and a group of relieved Sicilians hastily making the sign of the cross in gratitude, while rosaries appeared, seemingly from nowhere.

Papa was thinking he'd gotten away clean after the police rolled down the dusty road in a procession, but Mr. B was furious. He'd seen the grape stains on the seats of his new car, and knew exactly what had happened.

"Papa! I wish to talk to you in the feed tent!" Mr. B hollered as Papa was making what he thought was a smooth getaway.

There were too many Caesars in on the grape-stealing adventure to ignore Mr. B's call, and when you called one Caesar in for a talk, they were likely to be accompanied by several others. So a procession of Sicilians turned around and headed for the feed tent to take their licks.

The feed tent was still occupied by eight-thousand-pound Arnold, the baby elephant, as the crowd moved in. Arnold was looking way too happy and satisfied, all 4 tons of him, and Papa Primo said, "Mama Mia! Look at him! He's licking on his lips. He ate my beautiful grapes. My *vino*. No, no, no. My *vino*. She's gone!"

"Yes, and you should be damned glad he did," said Mr. B. "Get him out of there and walk him around before he founders. Elephants do founder, don't they?"

One of the trainers exclaimed, "It ain't my fault. I don't know how he got loose. Probably smelled them grapes. Damn you, Primo. You ought to have to take care of this elephant. If he dies, it'll be all your fault!" And he led Arnold out of the tent.

Parked just outside the tent was Mr. B's Ford Convertible, still beautifully gleaming on the outside, with a few grape colored stains on the fine new upholstery inside.

Arnold was apparently attracted to the new car too, as to everyone's horror, he backed up to the vehicle and sat his giant ass on the side of it. While Mr. B waved his arms in a futile attempt to stop what was inevitable, Arnold let out a great ball of methane after his bacchanalian night of overindulgence in several hundred pounds of fresh fruit. There was no moving the elephant, as he lifted his tail and unloaded at least a hundred pounds of crushed grape pulp, seeds, peelings and juice onto the seats of Mr. B's new Ford Convertible. The stench of the digested fruit was surpassed only by the sight of the purple, green, brown slimy mess of elephant diarrhea.

Mr. B was beside himself, head hung in his hands, muttering something about explaining it all to the insurance company.

"I'll bet elephant shit in your car is not covered," he was heard saying.

Tico, normally sympathetic to a person's plight, was rolling on the ground with laughter. Hiram was in stitches too.

"Hey, Mr. B," he called across the lawn, "you got something to be thankful for. You wasn't in it when 'ol Arnold let loose!"

Even Mary Lou, through her tears and giggles, couldn't help but needle Mr. B just a little.

"You could plant flowers in yer car, Mr. B, and make a planter out of it," she suggested.

Meanwhile, Papa Primo was thinking of a way he could still use the juice to make a new kind of vino, but his boys vehemently nixed the idea.

Ivan had a plan for Mr. B. "Look, you tell everyone they no tell nobody about this. We tell insurance company some dirty, no-good thief stole your car. We put it in the water, up at the quarry. They pay. You happy, get new car. Look like big shot again. What you say to that?"

Mr. B said yes to that, and that's exactly what they did. And when he bought his new car with the insurance money, it was a nice 1936 Chevrolet custom built gunmetal gray sedan with four doors and a hard, unmovable top.

Arnold the baby elephant did not flounder, as Mr. B had feared. But Arnold had made a mortal Sicilian enemy and from that day on, the warning Papa Primo had given Hiram and to his philandering son-in-law, Phillipe, was also extended to Arnold. Under his breath, he muttered to Arnold not to come anywhere near himself or his family and he made the sign of cutting his throat as he dragged the old arthritic finger across his throat.

Chapter Twelve:

Philandering Phillipe

Papa Primo's daughter, Appaloosa, was married to Phillipe, who was not a Sicilian, but a Frenchman. Phillipe was a handsome man, who made the hearts of all the ladies go pitty-pat. He knew it and like most of his countrymen, he loved the ladies. But Appalonia's father, and all of her brothers, kept a very close watch on Phillipe to prevent him from straying too far. There was also a threat involving the sign Papa reserved for serious enemies. The sign of the crooked old arthritic finger being drawn across the throat. No one took such a sign lightly when it came from a Sicilian.

Phillipe was not a coward, just wise enough to know when he was well off. He had very little real manual labor to perform, as the husband of Appalonia he was considered part of the Caesar family and his devoted and loving wife served all of his meals, prepared by Papa Primo himself, and catered to his every whim. He honored his marriage vows for as long as he could, but he slipped up from time to time. He was a Frenchman, after all.

World War I found Phillipe manning the controls of a sleek little French fighter plane where he made a name for himself by his skillful flying and by shooting down a number of enemy planes. The exact number was always in question because many of his "kills" occurred when he was all alone in the wild blue yonder, so no witnesses. But Phillipe was not a coward and he had enough witnessed "kills" to be declared an ace and a hero. He had a chest full of medals and hoped no one would look too closely at them for some of them he had not really earned. No matter, he only wore them when he was sure no French war aces would see them. But they were impressive. But when he married the exquisite Appalonia, and joined the circus with her family, it was not possible for him to give up the first love of his life, flying.

Anytime Phillipe had a few extra dollars in his pocket and found himself near a small airport where flying machines could be rented, he would indulge. And he indulged in more than that. The escape gave him a chance to show off for the ladies too.

He would fly his rented plane to the next town, visiting the nicest cocktail lounge there, and proceed to impress one of the fairest with his war stories. He told stories of his adventures with the Lafayette Espadrilles, his friendship with the great American ace Harry Thaw. He would say things like, "And so, I said to General Pershing, Black Jack, I *said…*" They ate it up. His next move toward romance was rarely without reward, as he almost always scored.

Phillipe drank more than he should have, but like the French, he held it well, and many times he flew the rented rig back to it's base drunk on his ass. It was during the summer of '36 that he rented a sweet little 2-seated Maul with a door on the pilot's side and a door on the passenger side. Phillipe found exactly what he was looking for in the hotel bar.

Clara McMillan, a pretty telephone operator from Detroit, was the lucky object of Phillipe's affection this particular day. She was an adventurous girl, always ready for a new and dangerous interlude to spice up her mundane life and to provide her with stories for friends to "oooooohh" and "aaahhhhhh" over. After many glasses of wine and about a dozen martinis and after a session in Phillipe's rented room, Clara insisted that Phillipe take her flying. Phillipe knew better. He'd had too many unexpected and unexplainable events come to pass in the business of aviation. But her sweet pleas and adorable coaxing overwhelmed his better judgment, and he succumbed to her charms, just as she had succumbed to his a few hours before.

The two tipsy travelers drove back out to the little country airport where he had left the plane he had rented earlier. Naturally, Phillipe told Clara the plane was his as he hoisted her into the rig by boosting her up with his hand on her bottom. Then he handed up her little dog, a white poodle named Yvette, that would ride in his passenger's lap.

Phillipe was drunk. Plenty drunk. He had trouble finding the switches and remembering where all of the controls were.

Clara wanted the Frenchman to do barrel rolls and dips and all sorts of acrobatic maneuvers. At first, he refused, but his ego, urged on by a goodly dose of flattery and the effects of the wine and martinis, again presided over his good sense. He made a few fairly safe dips and swoops, but when he banked the plane to one side, the passenger door flew open. Phillipe had failed to secure the door in his state of altered sobriety.

As it opened, Clara grabbed for him, letting out a scream that she didn't want to die, and she could easily have fallen out. Grabbing for Phillipe caused Clara to let go of Yvette, her beloved toy poodle, who fell off her lap, and flew out the open door, yelping as it plummeted toward earth.

"Oh my God, my God! Yvette, my sweet doggie. What have you done, you bastard?" she screamed at her pilot between tears.

Clara was inconsolable, as Phillipe shakily brought the plane in for a landing.

The hysterical Clara cursed him for a no good bastard, as they taxied to a stop, but before they even got out of the rig, the owner of the airport came running up to the side of the plane yelling obscenities. He was almost as hysterical as Clara, having seen some of Phillipe's acrobatics in the air.

He yelled, "You dumb son of a bitch. I should have known better than to let a Frenchman in a rented plane fly out of my airport. By God, you're drunk! Get out of here before the police get here. Some lady just called to say a white poodle fell out of the sky and landed right on her picnic table where her guests were having lunch. Damn dog exploded guts and blood all over everyone and everything."

Clara increased the volume of her raging, making Phillipe nearly hysterical himself. He headed toward her car and tried to drive off without her, but she got in at the last minute. She threatened to have him deported, put in jail, castrated, beheaded and hung by the neck until he was dead, all the way back to the bar.

When they arrived, the cops were waiting and they took Phillipe in for public drunkenness after a tip-off from the airport owner. He spent the night in jail, finally making it back to his frantic wife and suspicious father-in-law the next day. He was armed with a dramatic story of a plane crash, but could not explain how he avoided injury.

Phillipe bought a newspaper the next day, where the "dog that fell from the sky" was featured in a story on page two. The reporter quoted the airport owner as saying he knew nothing about the incident, and the connection between the Frenchman arrested for public drunkenness at a local bar, and Yvette the toy poodle splattered on the picnic table, went undiscovered by the Caesar family.

Well, Phillipe made an honest effort to be a faithful and doting husband to Apalonia after such a close call. But from time to time, he strayed from the path. Phillipe was a Frenchman, after all.

Chapter Thirteen:
Tico Tico And The Angel

Tico Tico rubbed the sleep from his eyes, slapped his hat on his head, pulled out his weenie and took the first piss of the day. It was a fine morning. The sun was just coming up and making him warm and content. After peeing and dressing, he went into the feed tent to get the buckets and grain since he promised to help out while the feed crew was shorthanded. He liked the feed tent. The smells and the animals never failed to make him think of his mother and her ability as a champion equestrian, and of the huge barns on her country estate.

As soon as he got inside the tent, he sensed that he was not alone in the giant canvas structure. He looked around to see who might be there, and then he saw her. The sun was bright and provided back lighting behind her, so he could only make out the thin outline of her body and the golden halo of tangled hair that surrounded her sunlit head.

"*Mama mia!*" he said. "*Es un Angelica! Si, es un Angelica,*" he exclaimed.

He moved a little closer to the ethereal figure to see if it was real or just an illusion.

When he got close enough to see the figure without being blinded by the sunlight streaming in, Tico realized the figure was very real. It was a very tiny, pitifully thin girl of an uncertain age. He reckoned the fragile creature was about fourteen, and she was so beautiful he had to pinch himself to find out if it was just a dream.

She had enormous golden flecked brown eyes, a thin heart-shaped face, and her mouth formed a small, frightened "O." She had a rather slight overbite, which Tico found endearing, and her skin was like milk. The fabric of her dress was a cheap, blue and faded dimity, and it was old and tattered. She was barefoot, and although she didn't run when she saw him, it was obvious she was on the verge of fleeing for her life. Instead, she fell to the ground in a heap and began to cry in such a way that she sounded more like a little mouse squeaking. These were not sounds a crying child should make, thought Tico, as he stood for a moment mesmerized.

Seconds later, Ivan entered the tent to help with the feeding of the animals, and saw the whole scene including the young girl sobbing and Tico standing there in awe.

"Tico, go get Mr. B," said Ivan, shaking Tico from his trance.

But Tico made no move to do his friend's bidding. Instead, he approached the girl and put out his small stubby hand. With soothing Spanish words, Tico coaxed and encouraged her to take his hand. He knelt beside her and pressed her face against his chest with soothing tenderness. Instinctively, he began to sing a Spanish lullaby that had calmed his own fears as a child. The girl melted into his caress as he put his arms around her and rocked her in a slow rhythmic motion until her crying subsided and she nestled quietly into the circle of his arms. Ivan stood by silently watching.

When the girl calmed down, Ivan said, "OK, I go get Mr. B then. You wait here. Right here. You hear Ivan?" But neither Tico nor the angel girl had any intent to go anywhere.

As he held her, Tico was carried back to his years of loneliness as a broken, wounded little child, alone, knowing and feeling how different he was from other children.

It was only a few minutes before Ivan returned to the tent with Mr. B. Mr. B had just tumbled from his bed and was still adjusting his trousers and trying to get his glasses on and his eyes focused, but Ivan's urgency had made him hurry. The two men regarded the scene when Mr. B broke the silence.

"Who is she? Where did she come from?" he asked.

"*Es un Angelica*" said Tico. "She come from heaven, that is what, and I will take care of her!" His arms were still protectively around the girl as they knelt on the floor in the fresh straw and Tico adopted a defensive stance.

"Not to scare her, no more," added Tico. "Tico make her safe and don't let no one hurt this *Angelica*. No more. Never. You hear Tico?"

Mr. B and Ivan were somewhat taken aback by the fierceness of Tico's response as all his protective instincts rose to the surface. They respected him nevertheless, and took him seriously.

Without being told, Tico knew this child had been abused and was running from her tormenters. He just knew. He too had been the victim of much silent torment all of his life. Only one such as Tico, a misshapen, deformed dwarf could know so instinctively.

He turned to the girl directly.

"You want tell me your name, is OK. You don't is OK too. I call you *Angelica*."

The girl did not answer, but stared mutely at her three new captors.

"Ah," said Tico softly. "She no talk. Can not talk. She no hear, either."

"How the hell do you know that, Tico?" asked Mr. B.

Tico cast his eyes to the ground and said, "Tico know. Tico know."

Mr. B believed he did, since he knew Tico was intuitive in business matters, why not in matters of the heart.

"When someone hurt so bad, maybe do not want to live where all the mean peoples live. This is little bird that no one care for. Probable no mama. Tico know. Tico understand."

Ivan and Mr. B were stunned, as Mr. B told Tico, "Right you are. You'll be in charge of her care then. Now, where will she stay?"

Before the words were out Tico said, "With me. I have extra bed in my trailer. I have Tilly make her new clothes. I comb her hair. I make her *paella* and *sopa* and *flan* to eat. Make her *gordo*!"

Mr. B was skeptical, partly because the girl looked so young, but he didn't want to ruffle Tico's sensibilities and extreme protectiveness when it came to the tiny mouse of a girl. "Well…" Mr. B began, but Tico interrupted his skeptical thoughts.

"Why you worry? Because it no look right for young girl to stay with funny little dwarf? Maybe evil monster? You think peoples talk? Well fuck them peoples. Maybe I am ugly, but I am honorable. Yes, I am honorable. Just look at Phillipe! He soooo handsome, but he has no honor. He is cheat, drunk, gamble and fuck all the womens he can while nice little wife cry at home. I tell the world that I, Teodoro De La Porto, I honorable guy! So shut up you mouth, all you dumb guys!" And all the dumb guys shut up their mouths. With that, the little dwarf led his new charge home by her tiny, willing hand, as Ivan and Mr. B looked at each other in disbelief. Tico told Ivan to go and get Mary Lou and send her to his trailer.

Tico busied himself immediately in his trailer. He got his *paella* pot, his spices and some canned shrimp. From his tiny icebox, he produced fresh celery, tomatoes, green peppers, onions, cheeses and all the secret ingredients he would need for his great production. When Mary Lou squeezed into his small trailer, he welcomed her with open arms, set aside his cooking utensils and ingredients, introduced her to the little deaf girl, and inquired as to whether she'd be willing to help sew some new garments for the tiny girl.

Mary Lou was delighted to be of service. She said it would be just like making the doll clothes she had always loved to craft for her dolls.

Packed into the small space, Mary Lou managed to take Angel's measurements with delight, as she planned the patterns, fabrics, thread and style of clothes she would put together.

"First, I think I'll make you a slip. I got some pink satin I made Juliette's costume outa'. Then, I got this pink silk. You like silk, honey?" she asked, but didn't wait for an answer as the girl read her lips and began to nod. She went on.

"Then these pink ribbons…a little darker than the silk but they could make a nice sash." While Mary Lou chatted on, she measured and planned, and the girl picked up a pencil and a writing tablet off of Tico's shelf. She began to sketch, drawing the dress she wanted. It was an exquisite design and the sketch itself had a certain artistic flair that impressed both Tico and Mary Lou. It looked professionally drawn.

"Why, will ya look at this! Tico, this girl's an artist, and a damn good one. Now where did she learn all of this? Ya know Tico, if she can draw like this, she can write I just betcha.' She could write a note and tell you where she comes from," said Mary Lou.

But Tico, instead of agreeing, took the pencil and tablet from the girl's hand and said, "Is nobody's business where she came from, she here now. I think she gonna' be happy here with Tico. No persons who treat child like this can have her back. She stay here with me now."

Mary Lou protested. "But Tico, she ain't a stray dog. She's somebody's baby girl. She got a mama someplace that's probably worried sick."

The girl, reading the lips of the two strangers, and knowing she was no one's baby girl, shed a silent tear. Tico was visibly angry, and the conflict she had brought to the two kind performers made her sad. She had no wish to be a burden or to cause disharmony. She held up her hand to stop them, and took the tablet back from Tico to signal that she would be heard in the matter. She began to write.

I am called Katerine. I ran away from the big house for crazy folks over at Fort Smith. I have been there most of my life. I do not know who my mother and father are or were. They said an old lady brought me there. Madame Zia thought she might have been my grandmother.

Tico and Mary Lou looked at each other, then at the girl, and urged her to go on.

The old woman left me at the asylum when she found out I couldn't talk or hear. They thought I was simple minded. I am not. Some of the crazy people were good to me there, and taught me to read and write. An old man, Pietre Van Der Hoosen taught me to draw. But that place is a bad, bad, bad place.

Her eyes were cast downward as she continued to write.

It is dirty and smells like pee and worse. If you take me back, I will only run away again, she wrote, and the tears streamed down the girl's face.

"Well you come to the right place," said Mary Lou, reaching out to hug the girl, who collapsed against her giant bosom. Mary Lou's mass was comforting to young Katerine.

"Most of us here know jest what yur' talkin' about," continued Mary Lou as she patted the blonde mass of matted hair.

The girl did not catch the specifics of what Mary Lou was saying, but she knew the woman was empathetic and comforting, just like Tico had been.

Tico took up the tablet and wrote back to her.

Not to be afraid. We leave this place tomorrow. You come. How old are you? he asked.

She penned back, *I think I am nineteen. I am not sure.*

Mary Lou looked concerned.

"Tico, that puts a different light on her staying here with you, don't it? Her being all of nineteen."

Tico smiled. "Yes my good friend, it does change much."

"That ain't what I meant you lecherous little rat!" she shot back. "What about all that honor you was talkin' about?"

Tico thought for a moment. "I will not be in charge of whether or not this *Angelica* will be anything more than my little friend. I am still an ugly dwarf. She will not see anything in me except a benefactor. That is all. The end." He was wistful.

The girl laid her hand on Tico's head and smoothed it through his thick, black hair. A small gesture, but it spoke volumes to Mary Lou.

"Humph," she snorted. "Don't be so sure. She sure don't seem bothered by how you look. Besides, caring about someone ain't got nothin' to do with looks. Lookie how I always loved my Hiram, no matter how bad he treated me. In my eyes, he's the most handsome man in the world, but others don't think so. And he ain't no good. Bein' good lookin' didn't make him the greatest catch in this here world. He's a bad husband, so bad I'm gonna' leave his sorry ass one day. You'll see."

Tico smiled to himself thinking of big-mouthed Hiram and what Charlie had said about him. 'Why, he could eat a punkin' through a picket fence with that set of chompers!'

Yes, he thought, if love can make a woman think Hiram is the most handsome man in the world, it is indeed blind…and stupid as well. But he kept his thoughts to himself. Still, he was glad that someday Mary Lou might leave his sorry ass behind. She was such a good woman, and a dear friend. He hated to see her treated so shabbily.

Tico was afraid to harbor any hopes that his *Angelica* would consider him as husband material, though his heart held out a little. In the far reaches of his heart, he hoped. But he knew the likelihood of such a beautiful woman ever loving him was remote. It was a beauty and the beast fantasy, and it encompassed every dream the little Spanish Jew had ever had. Soon, he expected it would evaporate. The sadness enveloped him and he felt like crying, but he put on a happy front as Mary Lou left, and he wrote to his Angel that he would cook her something special.

In the next few minutes, the wonderful smell of *paella* was drifting over the camp. Tico was an excellent chef, and his *Angelica's* mouth watered with expectancy. The dwarf's reputation with a cutting knife and a cooking pan was well know in camp, and an invitation to eat his delicious meals was a sought after reward after a hard day's work.

Outside the culinary nest, Ivan was curious and seeing Mary Lou on her way back to her own trailer, he intercepted her just before she went in. He drew in a deep breath and smelled the enticing odors coming from Tico's place, and Mary Lou nodded in agreement that the fragrance of supper was enticing. She filled Ivan in on what had taken place, highlighting the fact that the girl was all of nineteen years old, and the wheels in Ivan's brain began to turn.

"Love feast," he said as he sniffed the air. "Yes, love feast, I think."

Ivan knew Mary Lou had not noticed that he was talking both about the fragrance of the *paella* and about what he thought of when he looked at Mary Lou, an abundant feast. When men were attracted to her, Mary Lou never noticed. It wasn't even a remote possibility to the rotund woman, so her thoughts never wandered there, and the look on Ivan's face as he regarded her lustily went entirely over her head.

She smiled. "You could be right. You could be right," she said, as she bid him goodnight and went inside her trailer.

As he cooked he poured himself a few glasses of a fine red wine and poured Angel several, as well. By the time the meal was ready and they were preparing to sit down to this grand and glorious feast, both of them were a bit tipsy. Angel was unused to drinking anything at all, was giggly and lightheaded.

Her eyes danced with joy at the abundance of food as she lifted the first forkful. Tico watched in anticipation as she tasted it and began to chew. The look on her face at the wonder and taste of such a new and excellent food told Tico everything he wanted to know. "She like it!" he whooped. "Yes, she like it! Eat, eat!" he encouraged.

She understood his expression without having read his lips, and she smiled and giggled at Tico's antics for he was dancing around the kitchen and singing a bar from the opera *Carmen* "*Toreador. Toreador...*" He warbled in his gravely voice. She felt the vibration of his singing through the floor.

"*Figaro, Figaro,*" he sang after climbing up on the bed, then he followed it with "the Spanish cavalier, stood in his retreat..."

He did not even try to contain his happiness because he could not. Feeding someone who was hungry with his magnificent culinary talent was one of Tico's most prized moments. And Angel was eating vigorously of the succulent meal while Tico entertained her, and hardly touched his own plate since he was so busy dancing and singing for the hungry girl.

When she finished, she rose from the table and to the delight of Tico, began to do a very skillful belly dance. She had no music, but of course it didn't matter to her. The effects of the smooth red wine and the magic of the moment had captured her sweet soul and she lifted her golden hair and let it fall in all it's disarray, a gesture in the universal language that all women know and understand. She tipped her tiny chin down an looked at Tico from under her long lashes and then, slowly, sensuously she rose to her feet

She lifted the hem of her tattered dress, and tied it under her tiny breasts, pulled her panties down to below her belly button, and undulated her hips. She moved with a dancers precision, performing intricate gyrations and hip thrusts Tico had not seen since his days in Morocco. The sensuality of all that movement coupled with so little clothing on the beautiful, petite, creature made Tico weak and he felt faint. He was wild with desire, and yet determined to keep his vow of honor. But the effects of the wine and the mood of the night began to erode his resolve. Tico fastened his gaze on her beautiful body dancing before him and allowed himself to entertain the remote notion that something might be possible between them. After all, she was dancing just for him, and his ray of hope was spreading into a bright beam of swirling pale blue fabric. She moved toward him. He held his breath.

His *Angelica* placed her hands on his cheeks, pulling him toward her so that he was touching her sweet belly with his lips. He moaned and she felt his vibration and a slight quivering. He was too afraid to move and more afraid she would reject him.

The young girl made the next move sensing his frozen state, and pulling the dress over her head, she guided an erect, pink nipple into his mouth. Tico thawed out immediately and slowly slipped her panties off. She stood naked before him as he made small circles around her other nipple with his tongue and fingers. He pressed his face against her belly again, and held her body closer to him as she embraced his head of thick black hair to her breast.

The bed was only a step away in the small trailer, and she lay down on it, parting her thin thighs. He struggled with the fly of his pants, and before he knew it he was inside her. It had been such a long time since Tico had made love to a woman. He came with an *"Oh mi Dio!"* as soon as he had entered her. He stayed atop the lovely girl afterwards, drinking in the beauty and sweet compassion on her face. Tico made love to her again before his magic wand dropped like the mercury in a thermometer from her lovely garden of delight.

He rested then and rolled over, as she snuggled into the hollow of his shoulder.

"Oh God," he said, directing her face to look at his as he spoke. "Where did you learn to dance like that? To make love like that?"

She read his lips and laughed, and Tico, being a man of the world, did not really care where she had learned it. He was only grateful that she had shared it with him, but the sadness was returning as an emotional wave of potential abandonment swept over him.

As they lay quietly together, a tear escaped from Tico's eye. He imagined the dream was over, especially now since she'd seen his twisted body up close, touched him caressed him. She would soon leave him for a normal man, and all he would have of his *Angelica* would be a memory of her tenderness and sensuous dance. She felt the wetness of his tear on her breast and brought his face to hers to look closely. He tried to hide the tears, but she saw his eyes and grabbed the writing tablet to ask what was wrong.

"My dream of having you is over. I know you will leave me now for a normal man," he mouthed to her. She understood, but shook her head "no." He went on.

"I am ugly and deformed," he said as he looked down at his own body. But she continued to shake her head "no."

Angel took his head in her arms and stroked his pockmarked face so tenderly and lovingly that he burst into sobs and the tears rolled down his cheeks. He pulled away from her so she could not see his weakness, but she pulled him back to comfort him as she stroked his hair.

She arose from the bed and poured him a glass of Papa Primo's very best port, and picked up the tablet and pencil. She began to express herself to Tico in the only way he could hear her.

Tico, my beloved, it began. *You think I did that because I am grateful to you. Maybe some, but no. Because you are kind and I want to trust you. I have no one in this world. Maybe you have no one. Maybe we can love each other some day. I know you are wondering where I learned the dance. Madame Zia was crazy at the crazy house, but she could dance. I heard that she killed men just for the fun of seeing it, but to me she was good. She had nothing to give me and she thought of me as her daughter. So she taught me to dance like they do in her country. I had many good teachers.*

Tico was drying his tears with a tissue and reading. When he read 'maybe we can love each other someday,' his hope was renewed a little. The girl went on with her story.

I am not a virgin. No girl in that place could stay a virgin. I was only ten the first time. One of the men who took care of the people. He was a pig. One day he just disappeared. I heard that Madame Zia...well, I really do not know what happened to him.

Tico stroked her hair and grieved for what she must have endured as she continued to write.

The director did not care what happened to that pig nor to me. I am not a bad girl. I just wanted you to know that I like you, and I want to stay here with you.

Tico gulped the wine down and she indicated she would pour him another, but he shook his head and said, "No more vino, my Angel. Another glass of you. I will never get enough of you. Never, never."

This time it was Angel who was surprised. Tico was a skillful lover, and an excellent student who had read the medical journals and knew all about female anatomy. Angel had never experienced such talent and tenderness since she had never been made love to before. She had only been taken and used for the depraved gratification of lustful men. She felt things she had never felt before. It was a new experience for her.

Across the grounds, Mary Lou spent the day measuring, cutting and sewing for what seemed like her new doll since the garments were so small. She cut out three print pinafores, the pink slip, and a pink satin dress.

As the sun set, Angel was tired, but willing to eat a bit more of Tico's *paella*. He heated the dish for their supper, and both of them ate hungrily from the day's lovemaking. Angel fought with him over who would do the dishes but she finally won, so she washed while he dried. When the clean up was done, the two lovers fell into bed.

For the entire night, Angel lay snuggled and secure in his arms. When dawn came, he did not get up to go to work as usual. He did not wish to wake her and he wanted to savor the moment. Besides, he knew Ivan would understand and would cover for him.

Tico's emotions ran wild as Angel lay in his arms sleeping. He went through misery he'd not known in this intensity before, recalling the days when street people made fun of him, and times when he was rejected over and over for his deformities. Wracked with doubts and questions, he asked himself if he could keep her, and calculating how long it would take her to leave him for a normal man. After all, she had said, '*Maybe we can love each other someday*,' so it's not as if her love was totally unattainable.

He struggled with questions about whether this depth of love for her could be real at such an early stage, and whether she was just loving him to make him feel good or because her love was genuine. Was she really just grateful or was he a safe haven until she could make other arrangements? How long would he have her? Would she be gone in a few weeks, days or months?

Tico knew that no normal girl, especially one so beautiful, could love such an ugly, misshapen little mutant. But when she awoke, he shared none of his doubt with her as he put on a smile and got up to make her some coffee.

As Tico moved around the little kitchen, the girl who was known to him as *Angelica* watched him with eyes he hoped were filled with love.

"No," he told himself. "How could it be. Not possible, not for you, Teodoro De La Porto. Never for you."

As he handed her the steaming cup of coffee, she smiled and drank in the strong smell of the dark, rich liquid. She warmed her hands on the cup, but then put it aside and took his hand and kissed it. Tico glowed with affection, but his mind was still twisted with doubt.

"My *Angelica*," he said, and he wrote the name down for her as his mouth made the words. She liked the name and was pleased when he called her that.

Their reverie was interrupted by a knock on the door, and Angel felt the trailer shake. It was Ivan.

"You little shit," he said in greeting to Tico. "We got work to do. We leave here in few hours. Can't sleep forever," he chuckled. "Can't fuck forever too. You gonna be too tired for work?" he asked, noticing how disheveled Tico appeared after a night and morning of bedroom gymnastics.

"OK, you beeg ugly Turk," said Tico as they both smiled knowingly. "Tico coming. Tico be there to help. Too tired? *Nunca*. Tico good strong man. Who say I can no fuck forever? I can do it forever and ever and…" Angel was out of range to read their lips, but she imagined there was some ribbing going on at the door of the trailer.

Ivan roared with laughter. "Hurry up little friend. Drag what is left of you out here to help with work."

Tico turned inside and scribbled a note to Angel, telling her where he was going and pointing out the towels and soap. He pointed to where he was headed in case she needed him. Then he wrote that since he would be moving the little trailer, could she secure some of the items that might tumble around during transport. She nodded "yes" and Tico set off to help get the circus packed up for their next venue.

The dwarf was embarrassed when Mr. B said, "Honor, my ass. More like inner!"

The crew guffawed and made a few more lewd remarks, which Tico took with good nature, knowing it was the price any man paid to have a woman in his trailer all night long. "Christ aw'mighty Tico. You look like you was rode hard and put away wet," joshed Charlie. It was worth it since he'd made love to his little Angel four times last night and his movement was slowed down. He tried to pretend there was still a spring in his step and did his best to keep up, but the crew watched him for the first half hour making comments.

Mr. B noticed too, and called Tico off the job to go into the office and work on the books. Tico was grateful for his boss's consideration.

As he worked on the bookkeeping task, Tico tried to make peace with the situation he was in.

"OK, maybe all the doubts I having be true. Maybe it all like smoke and will go soon. So Tico be happy for what it been while it last. Be sad when it is gone. Been sad before. Lose much before."

His thoughts drifted to his lovely mother who had hoped so much for Tico to find the right girl. "But I would like to take my Angel home to see my mama. Yes. It been too long and Mama would be so happy. If she agree, I take *Angelica* home soon."

Chapter Fourteen:
Kidnapped

Tico's *Angelica* sat outside the trailer drawing pictures on new sketch pads while the crew was packing up in preparation to move on to there new job site in another town down the road.

It was bright and sunny and she enjoyed the sunshine's warmth while she happily sketched away at her little designs and cartoons. She was paying very little attention to much of anything but her sketching. She never saw the two scruffy looking men watching her.

"Hell, yeh, that's her. Seen her lots of times over there at that old insane asylum in Fort Smith. I know damn well that director is looking for her. She run away about two-three days ago. He wants her back. He sells her paintings and drawings to some art gallery over in Chicago. Makes himself a pretty penny on them. No, he ain't wantin' to give her up. I know for a fact he'll pay to get her back. Maybe a whole fifty bucks," said the one called 'Cooter.'

"Fifty bucks? Hey that's a lot of money just for bringing a gal as little as that one back. Let's nab her. Ain't no one around. Let's go," said his companion, who was known as "Gator."

Now Cooter and Gator were two good old boys from the South, who sometimes went to church on Sunday, Klan meetings on Friday night and could be found at Noodles Huffman's bar and drinking establishment most other times. Their drinking money came from whatever source came handy. Stealing chickens was a favorite, but hunting Coon, Possum, and Skunk to sell the pelts and squirrel, rabbit and catfish to eat. So to them a fifty-dollar reward seemed like just about more money than either one had ever seen all in one place in their lives. Of course, there was that time they stole ol' Grimshaw's moonshine and sold it. They got a lot of money for that, but Cooter also got to carry a lead bullet in his ass for the rest of his life.

But the main occupation of these two scalawags was selling cut firewood. Their biggest customer was the insane asylum, as all the area residents knew it by. It was actually the "Arkansas Hospital for the Insane." The director was an unscrupulous character named Dr. Porter. That is where Cooter had seen Angel and knew who she was and why she was so important to Dr. Porter, so when Cooter saw her at the circus he saw his chance to make a few bucks. No, lots of bucks, for fifty dollars was a lot of money in Arkansas in the thirties.

Before Angel knew they were even close by, the two men had grabbed her and carried her to their car. Cooter got in the back seat and held her while she struggled and tried to be heard, to no avail. She could not make any sound loud enough for anyone of the crew to hear, but as the car left the grounds Skookum was standing on the top of his little hot dog stand closing a vent. He could see down into the cars as they passed out and he saw Angel being held down by this big brute. Angel managed to make eye contact with Skookum and he could see the terror in her eyes. He climbed off the cart and ran for the office trailer, screaming for Mr. B.

"Mr. B. God Damn it. They got Angel. She got stole. I know it. Hurry up. Let's go chase 'em."

By this time the car was out of sight down the dusty road.

"I seen 'em. A old black Chevy. About a twenty-nine model. Two guys. Had a Arkansas license plate on it." Every thing was in chaos. Mary Lou was crying, Ivan was swearing. Doc Brady was sputtering and Tico was screaming, crying, and praying to every Saint whose name he could remember. When Mr. B and Charlie were found and joined the group, they all seemed to feel better, except Tico. He was hysterical.

"Whoa, everyone. Let us calm down and regroup. These people are long gone into Arkansas by now. We must devise a plan. A strategy."

"They took her back to that place. I just know it. How we gonna get her out?" blubbered Mary Lou.

Jack was standing nearby and said "OK, listen up. Two of my white tigers are in the back of my transport truck. There is plenty of room for all the men who will go after Angel up in front of them. Mr. B, Ivan, Charlie and Tico, Skookum, too. We better take Doc Brady. He can gain access to that place as a medical person. They don't know him."

Thanks to Mary Lou everyone in camp knew where Angel had come from. She had told them all that Angel had told her about the evil place she had been kept for all those years.

Mr. B spoke up, "But Jack, how come we are taking the two white tigers? You have a plan?"

"Maybe," said Jack. "I saw one similar to my plan work once. We can only try. We will need all the help we can get."

And so they all left in Jack's unmarked transport van with Jack driving. Mr. B and Doc sitting in front beside him and Ivan, Charlie, Skookum and poor little Tico, nearly mad with fear and worry, trembling and crying, all in the back behind Jambo and Kuki, two of the most beautiful White Tigers in captivity.

These tigers were barely more than cubs, but because of the excellent attention, care and feeding, they were big and strong looking, with heavy bone structure and thick coats. Their teeth were exceptionally long, but there was one problem. Jack had been handling these cubs since infancy and they had lost their fear of man. However, man had not lost their fear of them. That was what Jack was counting on. He had a plan, but was just not sure how he would put it into play. He knew one thing about the insane in these institutions, and that was if something went amiss, like a death, fight or any other confusing happening, that it was bound to create such chaos that the staff would be overwhelmed in trying to restore any kind of order. He had heard of it happening in an institution in England. He knew one of the staff nurses and she had told him about a time when two of the inmates got into a fight and blood was spilled. She had said that the patients screamed, babbled, threw furniture, attacked each other and sat in corners and rocked themselves and moaned until the noise was unbearable. Jack knew that if anything could strike fear into a group of people, sane or insane, two fierce, striped tigers could do just that. Never mind that these two were far from fierce. They damn sure had stripes and looked like the tigers in picture books.

As they traveled along, Tico, speaking through the opening into the driver's cab, told of all that Angel had revealed to him about the place she had been confined for so long. He told them of Madame Zia, who he believed was Turkish, and about the director, and some of the staff. He did not know much, but what he did know about Mr. Van Der Hoosin, and Mr. Aramis was all as good as the information was going to get. He wished that he had a map of the interior of the building, but who would have ever thought that it would be needed.

Fortified that his friends were determined to rescue his dear little Angel, Tico had become much calmer, but the words of Mark Twain kept repeating themselves in his head: "Faith is believing in something you know is not true." This was so important that his fear of the failure of his little troop of loyal friends just seemed immanent. After all, his luck in finding Angel was too much to hope for to this deformed little man. If his luck had been good he would not have been born a dwarf, he reasoned. He alternated between despair and hope, between tears and hysteria. He thought of his dream to take Angel to his mamma, the incredible times of unbelievable joy he had experienced in just the few hours with Angel, how he had truly believed that his loneliness was at an end. He was a basket case. Charlie wanted to tell him that he was in no shape to help with this rescue attempt, but he had no heart to do so.

Instead, he said, "Don't make no difference how high a guy builds his nest, some sun of a bitchin' bigger bird will fly over and shit in it." Small comfort, in fact none.

Charlie, an old time bootlegger from the prohibition days, on the other hand, seemed right in his element. So did Skookum, a one time New York rum runner and petty crook, recently gone straight after a year in jail. They were busy planning tactics, alternative moves, signals and all of the other elements of an illicit operation. Skookum had made so many runs between Cuba and Miami that he looked upon himself as an experienced seaman. He allowed, as how most of the poorly paid attendants at the asylum would be as stupid as the inmates were crazy. He counted on it.

When Jack drove into Fort Smith, he stopped at a gas station and told the attendant that he had some deliveries to make to the institution and needed directions on how to get there. The guy was accommodating and Jack drove by the place once just to reconnoiter.

The place sat on a slight hill. Not good, but manageable. It was a huge brick structure of many wings, with concrete buttresses arranged all along the sides. There seemed to be but one entrance and it was a large double-glassed door at the top of a short flight of granite stairs. Jack counted four stories and a daylight basement.

"Man, oh man. How do we find one little ninety pound girl in all of that?"

Skookum spotted the old Chevy he had seen Angel being driven away in. He said, "Well, she's here. I suggest we drive on down the road towards town and wait for those two yokels and stop 'em. Drag their asses out of the car and whip 'em into shape 'til they tell us where the little one is at."

Charlie agreed and so did the rest of them, except Tico. "Then we kill them," he said. "No let them go anyplace."

But Mr. B's calm head prevailed and he vetoed that idea. "No, we will let them go after we have Angel back."

But Tico insisted that at least he get to permanently cripple them both. In an effort to appease Tico, Mr. B said, "We'll see, Tico, my friend. We will see."

Jack drove the truck to a small roadside park where all seven of the guys got out to form some kind of plan. Doc Brady was the first to speak.

"Now, I have some understanding of the workings of state hospitals, I will go in and request to see Mr. Van Der Hoosin, since that is one name we know. I shall tell them I am a doctor sent by the state of Arkansas to re-evaluate Mr. Van Der Hoosin for possible release. He will demand paper work, so I have brought along my little portable typewriter. I shall sit here at this picnic table and formulate a letter of introduction and an order from a Doctor Elmer Pritchard, who by the way is a real man and a real official with the state medical board. I suspect that if this director does not telephone the good Doctor Pritchard, I will receive at least some kind of interview with Mr. Van Der Hoosin. I hope I shall be lucky enough I will get to speak to him in private. I also hope that this gentleman knows of Angel's whereabouts, or at least can find out."

Doc looked very thoughtful for a moment. He appeared to be pondering something very deep. Finally, he said, "You know, gentlemen, I believe I have hit upon a better idea. Very few people understand the working of the U.S. government. Most people even fear it. I think it would be a more productive plan if we were to go in to see Madame Zia instead of Van Der Hoosin. I believe I can baffle them with bullshit and tell this director that I am from the Turkish Embassy working on deportation proceedings for her, an illegal immigrant. Now I am counting on the fact that this director will be unfamiliar with such matters and will not object for fear of showing his ignorance or out of his natural fear of the government. What do you think, Mr. B?"

"Yes and that will give you an excuse to take Ivan along as an interpreter. Yes, I can see a great advantage to such a plan. Yes. I agree."

"Sure, then if this lady is Turk I can tell her plan in my language and no one understand. Yep. OK, we do."

"OK," spoke up Skookum. "We gotta' wait 'till morning. Just before first light I will go in and cut the damn phone line."

Tico was beside himself with anxiety. "No. No!" he said emphatically. "Not to leave my baby in that place overnight. No, never. Go now! I go now!" But Doc Brady calmed him down by reasoning with him. "Tico I am surprised at you. Usually it is you who sees the value of a strategy and a plan of action and the wisdom to adhere to it. You are always the cool and collected one of us all. Be calm. This is one of the most important ventures of our lives. We have a one shot deal on it and must not blow it," Doc pleaded.

Tico, properly chastened, said, "Yes, Tico scared. Tico too emotional when come to my Angel" and he calmed down as best he could.

"Oh, oh," said Jack, "here comes that old black Chevy. Let's go after them." Everyone got back in the truck and when the car went by, Ivan stepped out in the road and flagged it down. When the driver stopped, Ivan, a big smile on his face, said, "Hey, we outa' gas. We pay you fellas you get us some gas?"

"Sure," said Cooter. "We do anything for money. Hop in big fella.'"

Ivan opened the door on the driver's side and before Cooter could react he had him on the ground and the keys to his car in his big fist. Skookum was on the passenger side and opened the door and dragged poor ol' Gator out and threw him to the ground, too.

Jack got in the car and drove it over to the side of the road into the brush. By now, both Cooter and Gator were yelling their heads off. That is until Tico stepped up to Gator and smashed him in the face with a fairly good-sized rock. "Shut up you noise, you fuckin' asshole. I hit again! Next time in balls."

It took a smack or two from Ivan to guarantee silence from both men so Mr. B and Doc could get the necessary information from them.

by Loma A. Phegley

"OK, maggot," Mr. B began, "tell us where they put the little girl you kidnapped. By the way, you are familiar with the Little Lindbergh Law as regards kidnapping. Federal offense, you know. Especially when you transport a victim across a state line and you did you know. Well, you know how the feds work. Very efficient. It will mean the rest of your miserable lives in a federal prison in Kansas."

"We ain't tellin' you guys nothin,'" Cooter said. "You ain't the law. Gator, you keep your dumb mouth shut, ya' hear me?"

Gator wasn't talking because he was still trying to get the broken teeth out of his bleeding mouth.

"Well," said Jack, "we may not be the law but we will do until the law gets here. Besides, we have a surprise for you two. Ivan, could you please assist them over here behind the transport truck? I want to show them what I have here for them."

Ivan's assist was accomplished by grabbing them both by their shirt collars and dragging them to the back of the truck. He then pulled them to their feet while Jack opened the doors.

With an exaggerated and dramatic bow, Jack said, "Let me introduce you to my friends, gentlemen. My two very hungry friends, I might add. And…" he said to Kuki and Jambo, "let me introduce you to your dinner."

Both tame cats growled in greeting to Jack and of course, Gator and Cooter took it to be a menacing growl directed at the prospect of getting to eat a couple of fat rednecks for their dinner. They were terror stricken. Their faces were white and they were trembling uncontrollably.

"Skookum," said. "I thought they didn't like eatin' them Rednecks."

Jack replied, "Oh, they don't usually eat them. They just drag them around until they're dead and leave 'em for the buzzards."

"OK, God Damn it. Whatda' ya' wanta' know?"

Doc said, "For openers, where did they take the child when you brought her in?"

"Hell, we don't know. Some ol' wild looking woman came in and took her away. I think she's the one who is the dancer."

"Ah, yes, Madame Zia?"

"Yeh, I think so. They told us to keep away from her 'cause she likes to kill men."

"You filthy pukes," said Tico. "You not touch my Angel, do you? Not hurt her or you die and I feed you to those tigers myself. First cut off feet, let you watch while them eat you feets. Then you balls."

The surliness had left the two hayseeds. They were downright respectful of those two tigers.

"OK," Doc said, "I will do this typing and we will go get a place to stay tonight. As a matter of fact, right here seems pretty good to me. We have good view of the asylum from this vantage point and can see if they move her to another location. Jack can drive into town and get us some hamburgers and Coca-Cola. We can sleep in the truck. We can put these two miscreants into their automobile and tie them up securely. Come morning I shall do my 'official visit' and we will act accordingly."

"Man," said Jack, "I can hardly wait until I can turn my two kitty cats loose in those hallways to do their jobs." Laughing a little, he continued, "Wow, some scene."

"Some scene, indeed," said Doc. "It will be Bedlam for sure" and he chuckled to himself.

By now, night was approaching and Jack had gotten some hamburgers while Ivan and Skookum tied up the two kidnappers and placed them securely in their old car. Skookum lifted the hood and pulled the horn wires loose and said, "Just in case they can get to the damn thing and try to signal someone."

After dark the men tried to settle in to sleep. Ivan and Skookum knew they would have to be up and at 'em in the wee hours to sneak onto the grounds of the asylum to cut the telephone wires, so they positioned themselves near the side door. Kuki and Jambo were the first to go to sleep and their snoring was a gentle purring that wasn't at all unpleasant. Their sleep was not comfortable but nobody complained. At the appointed time Skookum kicked Ivan's foot and woke him with a single word "Time."

Quietly and with care the two men exited the side door and began to trot back down the road towards the asylum. They entered the gate and Skookum began to search for the overhead wires that would lead them to the place where they would connect with the inside telephones. It did not take long until he grunted and pointed to the side of the building where the wires ended at a control box. Skookum was extra quiet but the hinges on the metal box were rusted and squeaked like a banshee when they were opened. Skookum paid no mind to the noise and with his wire cutters, severed the wires. Without a word, he signaled Ivan the deed was done and both men trotted back out the gate and down the road to the truck. Unseen, unheard. A good job by any standards.

At precisely eight o'clock, Doctor John Brady M.D. walked briskly back toward the institution's gates. He walked vigorously, like a man out for his morning constitution. He was accompanied by Ivan, who was now once again Abdoul, the Turkish interpreter. When they came to the stairs at the entrance they took the steps two at a time, Doc whistling a little tune as he went. Ivan opened the door and they entered just as though they were familiar with the surroundings and belonged there. Doc appeared for all the world like a man on a mission, and, of course he was. In his hand, he carried a sheaf of papers that he hoped would look good enough to gain him admittance to see not Mr. Van Der Hoosin, but Madame Zia.

He had discovered from the questioning of Cooter that her first name was Mirriam, so he revised his strategy. He was now a physician engaged by the Turkish Embassy to examine this woman for consideration for deportation proceedings. He had not a clue as to what he was doing, but he reasoned that neither would his colleague, Dr. Poston.

The receptionist at the desk was dressed in a white nurse's uniform, but Doc doubted she was a registered nurse. With all the dignity and professional mannerism he could muster, which was considerable, he said, "Yes, I am Doctor John Brady and I am here to see the director of this hospital, Doctor Poston. I am here on a matter of some importance and I would appreciate expediency as we have a train to catch to return to Washington D.C. in just a few hours. Government business, you know."

"Gov'ment bizziness, ya' say? Well, let me see if he's in."

She picked up the phone and hearing no dial tone said, "Aw, fudge. The phone ain't workin.' I guess I'll have to go upstairs and see if he's in. He expectin' y'all?"

"Yes indeed. He should have by now received the documents sent to him from the Washington D.C. office. Yes, he is expecting us."

To Doc and Ivan it seemed like an interminable long time before Miss Dum Dum returned, but as she came shuffling down the stairs she said, "OK, you guys can follow me. He'll see you. He says he never got no papers, but that ain't unusual. The mail is slower out here than any-place else in the country, I betcha.'"

Doc and Ivan followed her up the stairs. Ivan said, "View very nice from here. My view anyhow." She giggled and said, "Oh, you are a devil, you are." She knew he meant to compliment her on her good-looking ass wiggling out there ahead of him. Ivan sighed dramatically and said, "Too bad we in hurry. Maybe like to take you out to see sights in this town, eh? Well next time, OK?"

Doc rolled his eyes.

The chick was hooked. No worries. She would do most anything for this big handsome Turk. She was a plain and homely sort but Ivan had made her feel pretty by admiring her rear end. He had made an impor-tant ally. Both men knew they needed all of the allies they could get, as they were in a very precarious position. In the lion's den, so to speak.

Miss Dum Dum delivered them to a rather nicely appointed office, where behind a very impressive desk sat a fat, balding and untidy man of about fifty five years. His suit was rumpled and long out of style. His tie was a bright yellow, or had been before the numerous messes of gravy stains and spilled soup had attacked it. His shirt was a sort of gray and probably had once been white. When he rose and extended his hand to Doc, his half-hearted smile revealed a mouth full of rotten teeth. Doc took the proffered hand and found it to be sweaty and limp, like shaking a dead fish. Doc instantly disliked everything about this person. He recognized him and all of this place for what it was.

"What kin'I do fer' you Doctor Bradley?" he asked.

"Brady, not Bradley. I am here on business for the U.S. government and the Turkish Embassy. We understand that you have a Turkish lady by the name of Mirriam Zia as a guest here. The U.S. government has begun proceedings to deport her on the grounds that she has become a public charge at state expense. Now we do not oppose the deportation proceedings, but we are taking steps to see that the information we have is accurate. In fact, I have been sent to interview her for that purpose. I do hope that this does not cause too much trouble, but I am mandated to carry out the government's conditions. If I am unsuccessful in my mission the Feds will have to be sent down here in force and the government gets very testy when this happens. Those fellows are really a serious nuisance when they converge upon a place. They are the only law enforcement agency that gets to make arrest and ask question after wards. Very nasty people. Why I remember one time…"

Dr. Poston stopped him. "I want no trouble with those guys. I've heard about them. You say that some papers were sent here to me from Washington D.C. I never got 'em. Not yet, anyway. Damn mail service. Slow as molasses in January. We pay good taxes for those government services and they just fuck the public around like we ain't paying their salaries."

Doc agreed and then he said, "I must catch a train back to Washington this afternoon. Could we see Miss Zia now, please?"

"Yeh, sure. I don't know where she is. We had a runaway brought back last night and the old bat insisted on taking care of her. I paid out a reward to get her back. Little bitch. Ungrateful for all we done for her here. I'll see if someone can find the Madame for you. Probably in some dark corner cutting some guy's balls off. She is a mean one, her."

This was far more than Doc or Ivan could have hoped for. If Madame Zia was, indeed, Turkish, Ivan could be Abdoul and explain why they were really there in his native tongue without anyone else knowing what was being said.

After a short wait an attendant came through the door gripping the arm of a very defiant dark skinned woman. "I not go back to that hell place. You can not make it so. No belong here neither. I should go free. I do nothing wrong." She turned and spit on her attendant, who reacted by slapping her. Ivan figured it was time for him to take over. In English he said, "No need for to hit lady." He then gave the attendant his very best menacing look. In Turkish he said, "Be calm. We not here for any purpose that means you harm. We are here to get little Angel back. She is little one they bring in last night. Listen and hear me when I tell you what we must do." Madame Zia began to cry. "Oh praise be to Allah. You have finally come to save me. To take me from this place of Hell. Thanks be to Allah. Allah is great. Allah is good."

Ivan said "hooboy" under his breath. She was speaking Turkish, Doc was unaware of this new development and Ivan could not tell him, so he said to Madame Zia, "Yes, we will take you, too, but first, the little one. Where is she?"

To say that Madame Zia was beautiful would be an understatement. She was stunning. Dark skin, as smooth as any skin in the world. Her wealth of black hair was in total disarray. It looked uncombed for days, maybe even months. The center part was not very straight and it stood out in a giant halo of tangles and rats. Her insanity was obvious to both Doc and Ivan. Her black eyes were rimmed with kohl. The pupils seemed to be as pinpoints and Doc wondered what drugs she was getting. Her mouth was painted a bright scarlet and she wore a silver ring in one nostril. Her garments were rags. Tattered and dirty, but she wore them with a certain panache. She was barefoot and her ankles were encircled with copper wires as bracelets. When Ivan's true mission began to sink in she began her act. As Ivan talked and she listened to his every word, she stood in front of him and began to dance. She pulled her skirt down to below her belly button and swayed her hips. Ivan said, "Careful, my lovely, or I will be unable to tell you all that you must know. I will be as jelly in a vessel."

"Not all of you will be as jelly, I do not think."

"No, but I am honor bound to carry out a task and you must help me. Later I will hold you accountable for this passion you are arousing in my cock. I promise you."

"And you will take me with you, Oh Great Man of Honor. You promise to take me!" It was not a request. It was a demand and Ivan promised. He did not know how he would handle Madame Zia with all of the ramifications attached, but he had promised and he would have to do it.

Madame Zia agreed to meet him and Skookum outside the front door at twelve midnight. She said it would be impossible to bring Angel as a guard had been posted to watch her in a locked room. She agreed that she would leave a way into the building so the men could get in when it was time to implement Jack's plan.

When Ivan had finished his interview with the Madame, he relayed to Doc and to Poston what had supposedly transpired.

"OK, she say she will go back to Turkey if she can have some new clothes and some new ankle things of silver. And, yes she being the Mirriam Zia we looking for. I tell her yes, we get her new stuff and she say OK will go back. She want to tell you all she kill that man because he a rapist and a bad man to women. She say he deserve to die."

"Well," said Poston, "did she also tell you that she cut his nuts off and sewed them in his mouth while he was still alive and before she cut his throat? She nailed his hands and feet to the floor while he was unconscious and did she also tell you that he was the sheriff of Carroll County where it happened. Up there in Eureka Springs is where it all got done.

Bloody bitch. I am a bit curious as to why she is being set free after being convicted of such a crime. Government wisdom, I guess."

"Yes. I do not question the government," said Doc rather curtly. He needed to get out of there before the fucking asshole got any more curious. He knew damn well that she would never be set free. Little did he know of Ivan's promise to "The Bloody Bitch."

Doc said to Dr. Poston, "It was such a nice day we elected to walk the short distance from town. Lovely stroll, nice country here in this pastoral setting. We will be on our way. Such walks are a treat to me as I live in the city. Talley Ho, and nice to have made your acquaintance."

Ivan said, "See you another day, sir." They then walked down the road as briskly as they could without running. When they came to the truck they kept on walking, ignoring it just in case someone was watching from the building they had just left.

The truck caught up with them around a bend in the road.

By now Ivan had apprised Doc of the plan. Well, all except the promise to Madame Zia. As soon as all of the men were together they stopped and made their final plan. But neither Doc, nor none of the others were aware of Ivan's promise to Madame Zia. He knew that it had been a foolish promise, but it seemed to him that he had little, if any, choice. If he had refused her demand, he knew that she would refuse to help them and she was the only inside contact they had, now. Besides, she knew where Angel was being held. Ivan just figured that he would handle the situation when it happened. But he was worried. He knew this lady was a killer and she would surely kill again. He did not wish to turn her loose on the public, and he could not take her back with him to the circus and expose all of his friends to her and her deadly ways. She would likely kill Hiram. Star would definitely not like her, and Papa Primo would know her for what she was and put Sicilian curses on her. He even feared for his own safety as he had promised to fulfill that other stupid promise to make love to her later. On the other hand, she would be a hit on the Carnival Section as an exotic belly dancer. Wild hair and all she would be a solid attraction. But was she and all of her baggage worth it? Ivan thought not but it was his dilemma for the time being so he said nothing to the others for fear they would abort the operation. When night fell and it was time to meet Madame Zia at the appointed time and place, Jack, Skookum, Tico and Ivan were there. True to her word, so was she. She had propped the big door open with a rock. All three men slipped into the building and the Madame led them through a maze of halls and corridors to a damp, cool basement. Jack whispered to the others that they must pay attention and remember the route so when they would get ready to leave they would not get lost. When they arrived at the locked door where little Angel was kept, the others had to hold Tico back from storming the door with his bare fists. Madame led them into a room with a large window that was ground level. She said, "You, Big Man, take the glass out of that window. We not be able to sneak little one out without being seen. This part of place is under a balcony where all of the guards and attendant are sleeping. Mostly they not sleep. Mostly up, drinking, looking out window, smoke, play cards. But if Jack can make much confusion maybe everyone run to where trouble will be and we can go out here. Maybe."

Ivan busied himself with removing the glass by scraping away the old dried putty. He did not wish to let the glass fall and break with a shattering sound so Skookum was helping him. Meanwhile, Jack went back to the truck and drove it as silently as possible up to the front door. He opened the back doors of the truck and let the two tigers out, bringing them in through the front door. Once inside, he and the two beasties walked down the corridor to the second set of stars, where he screamed as loud as he could. "Tigers! The tigers are loose! Help me!! They will eat us alive! Help!" Instantly, he heard a dozen doors being opened and he led Kuki and Jambo up the stairs to a hall full of startled and half-asleep patients and attendants. The whooping, keening, screaming and yelling was so loud that not one soul could possibly remain awake in that building. He began to run; knowing the two cats would follow him and make it look like he was being chased by them. As he traveled further into the hallways more people came to see what the trouble was. They soon discovered that the tiger story was real. Pandemonium prevailed. The screaming, keening and shouting increased. The poor tigers were so frightened and confused that they were disoriented. If one were standing in front of the asylum at that time he would have believed he had been transported back to medieval times to bedlam itself.

Many of the patients were not only screaming without knowing why, they were drawn up into fetal positions rocking back and forth. Jack thought to himself that it would take days to restore order. When the men and Madame Zia in the basement heard the commotion, they knew it was now or never. Ivan and Charlie, Tico and Skookum stormed the door where Angel was locked in. They did not need to break it down, as it was unlocked and the attendant gone. Angel lay in one corner on a thin dirty pallet crying in fear. When she looked up and saw Ivan and her Tico she put up her arms to Tico, but Ivan said, "No time for kiss and mush now. Gotta' go." He scooped little Angel up in his arms and stepped through the window from which he had just removed the glass. All of the others followed. He forgot about Madame Zia. She followed as well. They all ran for the truck. So did the Madame. By now, Jack had collected the tiger cubs and was putting them into the truck's rear doors while everyone was climbing into the side door. So did The Madame. When Doc saw her entering the truck, he cried out, "No. Not you. No, we can not take you. You must not go with us. My god, Ivan, what's the deal here?!?"

Ivan hung his head and mumbled, "I promise her. She earn this. Not have her, not find Angel."

Doc said, "Do you realize what you are doing? She is a killer. She must not go with us."

At this, The Madame began to cry. Her crying became louder and louder until it was a screaming ulaluval crescendo of an old Arab sound made by the women of a tribe in the Arabian deserts.

Finally, Doc said, "Shut the fuck up. OK. You can go. You can go. Let's get the hell out of here, now. Just shut up. God Damn woman, you can go."

The Madame smiled slyly and said, "Yes, I know I can go. Want to hear more?"

Jack stopped beside Cooter's old car and when he opened the door the smell of smell's hit him full in the face. "Judas Priest. Which one of you guys shit his pants?"

He jerked Cooter out of the car first. When he untied the gag around his mouth, ol' Cooter bellered, "It was Gator. I been havin' to be in here with that stink all night. It been bad."

"God I'm hungry and I need a beer, really bad."

Jack said, "Well, fellahs, I guess you're free to go on your way. Thanks for the help. But I am not touching your friend there with the shitty pants. I guess it's up to you, Cooter, to change his diaper." He left Gator still trussed and draped over the back of the front seat with his rear end very near Cooter's face.

Amid the laughter of the crew, Cooter climbed into his old car and after a few coughs and sputters it started up. The last our friends saw of the two 'miscreants' was a cloud of dust and a hearty, "God damn, you, Gator."

Only Tico was sorry to see them go, but only because he had wanted to maim them in some gross manner. He was disappointed.

Jack drove as fast as he dared until he got to the Oklahoma border, where he knew he would not be pursued.

They arrived at the very final minute just as the last of the circus trucks were leaving to go to the town where the next engagement was. Papa Primo and his boys had done an admirable job of getting the show on the road without Mr. B. Angelo and his son had packed and hooked up Skookum's little hot dog cart and Sylvia, Jack's wife had supervised the loading of the animal cages. Star had finished packing up the office trailer and dear Mary Lou had made tons of tuna and baloney and deviled egg sandwiches, very welcome, since no one had eaten since the night before hamburgers. Angel had already got Tico's little trailer ready before her ordeal so he was all set.

Everyone was so glad to see Angel and they all wanted to know how it was accomplished, but the men just said, "Later."

Tico, had been cradling his little *Angelica* in his arms in the back of Jack's tiger transport truck all the way back. When Ivan lifted him down he said, "Ah. As Phillipe says: All is well that ends well, eh, *Mon Cherie*?"

Chapter Fifteen:
Maude Leaves

Madame Zia was an instant hit on the Carnival Section. True to his word, Doc bought her some new clothes, which, to him, looked very much like the old ones, but at least they were clean. He even bought her some silver bracelets for her wrists and ankles. Star gave her some silver earrings. She seldom wore shoes, but painted her toenails scarlet and washed her feet three or four times a day. Doc still viewed her escape and presence in the circus with great trepidation. He knew she was dangerous and unpredictable, but no matter how many times he warned the men in the troop to stay away from her, they ignored his advice and lusted after her like she was a bitch dog in heat. The Madame loved it and fucked them all, just like a bitch dog in heat. The men loved her. The women tolerated her. Madame Zia was always "on stage." Bold, sexy, even brazen, she never failed to make an impression, no matter where she walked.

Ivan stayed away and never fulfilled his promise to her to sample her delights. Mr. B, Skookum and Charlie enjoyed her as often as their work schedules allowed. Doc never indulged. But many of the local roustabouts who were hired to work in the towns where the circus played did. Early and often. Mirriam, as she was now called, was a nymphomaniac, and although Mr. B knew she could be trouble, he was unable to resist her beauty and skillful antics in the hay, or wherever she could find a place to lay down…or stand up, or kneel down. It was not long before Mirriam was independently wealthy. Well, at least she had plenty of money, which she carried in a leather bag tied around her waist. She also carried a wicked bone handled knife held in place around her thigh by a wide piece of elastic. "Quick draw," she said.

Also, she was a main attraction at the Carnival. She would appear outside during the hype to attract customers in full purda, covered from head to toe in a pale pink Burqua. However, sometime during the 'speil' she would manage to show one of her nipples. Just a peek, but it drove the rubes wild. The announcer would look at her and say, "Now you just stop that. Save it for the show." The show packed them in at twenty-five cents apiece. Mr. B was happy with her as a performer and a damn welcome diversion from the rigors of running the outfit.

But Doc waited for the other shoe to drop, and he knew it would.

Bill Bailey had a lot of other matters to attend to though, especially his poor grief stricken wife, Maude. Sex with her was non-existent. Stopped months ago. He did feel guilty about Mirriam and the others he often slipped into town to visit to relieve his sexual urges, but he was a man and damn, what did she expect? But if she ever knew she said not a word.

Maude was beside herself with grief over the death of her only child, Becky. Time did not heal her, even slightly. If anything her grief grew worse. She'd lost interest in the circus, and wanted to go home. She quit eating, slept only fitfully, and her depression was so overwhelming that her physical health was deteriorating.

"I do not know what I can do to help you, Maude," said Billy. "I have loved you as much as any man can love any woman. I know that somehow you blame me for our little girl's death, but I'm not to blame. But if that is what it takes to heal you, go ahead and blame me."

Maude just cried as Billy went on.

"Try to understand, honey, that I am suffering the same grief as you are. She was my little star and my world. Tell me, Maude, what can I do to help you? I will do whatever is in my power. At least talk to me. You haven't said a hundred words to me since it happened."

by Loma A. Phegley

Billy's voice wavered, but Maude turned away. "I know it wasn't your fault, Billy, but that doesn't make it any easier to bear. I am destroyed, finished. Not your love nor the caring of our friends can repair me. I know that I am making your life as miserable as mine. And I've decided to go back home. I wrote to my sister and she's willing to take me in and try to help. Please don't try to make me stay. Don't make it harder for me. It's over. I can never be a wife to you ever again. I want to say I love you, but all my feelings have been numbed. I don't love or care about anything. I am sorry, Billy. So sorry." And Maude cried some more.

Billy consoled her the best he could, but he didn't believe it was over. He thought the trip might do her good. Might help to snap her out of her depression and bring his wife's tender nature back to her, where she could open her heart to him once more.

"I'll wait for you," is what he whispered in her ear as she cried and he held her close. Billy left the trailer and walked out into the sunshine.

"I don't know, Charlie," he told the ringmaster. "She wants to go back to Atlanta. That's where she's from and her sisters and their families are still there. I really have no choice but to let her go."

Mr. B snorted. "Hell, I can't keep her here. I will sure be handicapped without her. She and Tico take care of the business. I suppose Tico can handle it. He's pretty sharp, and a very capable bookkeeper. He could take over the bookings and scheduling. I am pretty sure the others will help out, too."

Charlie was nodding with his chin in his hand.

Mr. B thought for a minute, then said, "You know, I've always heard you can't keep a woman if she wants to go, and I'm going to let her go with my best wishes."

Charlie was very sympathetic. He liked Maude Bailey, and felt a real pain at her loss. He said, "Maude ain't been right since it, ya know, since little Becky was, well, you know. She's just grieving her life away here. But it won't be much different for her if she goes back home, will it?"

"She'll have the comfort of kinfolk," said Mr. B, before adding, "I know she blames me for Becky's death. Says I should never have let her sleep in the big tent without having us close by, but who would have thought?"

He continued. "She talks a lot about suicide. I can't seem to help her. She leaves next Tuesday on the Atchison, Topeka and Santa Fe."

Charlie said she was a mighty fine lady and he hated to see her go; and Mr. B spoke about how kind everyone had been to them in their time of grief. Both said they'd miss her, but Mr. B, near tears, wondered out loud why she didn't understand that he was suffering the same grief as she was. Charlie tried to comfort him with words of praise.

"Well looky here Mr. B. You got some good friends here at the circus. Everyone looks up to you. They say you are such a virtuous man, that nothing so bad should have happened to you. There are those who speak of you as though you're a saint. Nobody hereabouts' knows of you doin' nuthin' bad or wrong. Uh, well, that is except maybe Mirriam. But, hey, I look at it this way. It's just your way of helping out that poor unfortunate girl. We all do what we can for her. Ya' know with her needs and all," said Charlie, looking down to hide his smile.

Mr. B laughed a short, bitter laugh. "Oh, I'm no saint, Charlie. I do try to do the best I can for all. I try to be honest, virtuous, reverent, kind and charitable like I was taught in the Boy Scouts. The Scouts taught me how to live a clean life."

"Yeah," said Charlie. "Eagle Scout, weren't you?"

"Yes, I was at that. Joined when I was fourteen, after my little sister died, and my mother retreated into madness. Seems like the past is kind of repeating itself. The Scouts was the only thing that saved me, seeing how my Dad was always drunk or gone, especially after my sister's death. But I made it, although it hasn't been easy. Now I'm back where I started, but such is life, Charlie, my friend, such is life."

by Loma A. Phegley

Charlie offered any help or solace that was his to give, and Mr. B graciously accepted, thanking him and all the performers for being there for him and his wife.

Everyone in the circus crew genuinely liked Maude. Some of them called her Mrs. B, but most of the folks just called her Maude. They made every effort to cheer her up with jokes and stories, but it just did not help. There were times when the poor woman was almost catatonic. Mostly she was just uncommunicative. She went about her work at the circus and often Tico had to redo it or take over and do it himself. The whole crew helped her as best they could, but it was sometimes overwhelming. Mary Lou, Star, Sylvia, and the Caesar girls took over the burden of not only Maude's work, but their own as well.

Mary Lou was always cooking up some gourmet dish to make her work a bit easier. She also sewed fancy pillows and dresser scarves and handkerchiefs for her, as little surprise gifts, but Mary Lou knew that it was not going to cheer up any woman that had lost her baby girl. Mary Lou's heart was so kind and loving it made her feel better, anyway.

It was a sad parting when Maude left. Both she and Mr. B did a lot of crying as they said goodbye. Not one of her friends believed that she would last very long in Atlanta. They thought she'd be back in no time, once the grief had subsided a little with time and the comfort of family.

For Mr. B, it was almost a relief to see her go. She had been so silent and unresponsive in all matters and he felt so alone and depressed in his own home. Since there had been no sex and he didn't even try to approach her for it. It was natural that he seek it elsewhere. Mirriam was not really a comfort, but just a release. Charlie was the only one who knew about Mirriam and him. Occasionally he would go into town and find a warm and willing body. But not a soul knew about that. Nothing serious, he would say. Just someone to make him feel less alone for a few minutes.

Like most of the other men in camp, he sometimes thought about Starshine's palpable sexuality. He called her a "helluva woman," but his thoughts of having her were far-fetched, and he knew Star chose her own men. She made that abundantly clear whenever she talked about men, saying she did her own selecting. But, he thought about her lustfully anyway. Every man in camp had thought of her that way at one time or another, and many used her as a fantasy in their private solo sex acts.

Star's intuitive powers and her gift of keen observation were acutely aware of Billy Bailey's thoughts about her.

Star also knew that Maude Bailey would never return to her husband. She had read the cards and consulted the Crystal Skull and saw nothing but darkness and sadness. She believed that Maude would soon die, but she told no one except Angel. The only reason she told Angel was because Angel had told her of the same fear that she had for the poor sad woman. Sometimes Star thought that Little Angel also had the sight. She did seem to know things long before any of the others knew. Probably a gift born of her affliction.

Star and Angel were right. The healing that Mr. B and the other circus performers hoped would happen for Maude once she got home was not to be. After just two months, Maude Damon Foster Bailey walked out into a raging flood thinking she'd seen a glimpse of her dead daughter, and drowned. She'd been talking about seeing the child in the rain for a couple of days, and while Maude's death seemed like an accident, there was plenty of speculation that it was quite deliberate. She was a tortured soul.

Mr. B and Charlie "One Shoe" went to Atlanta and buried the sad remains of Billy Bailey's wife, and the only consolation was talk that the mother of little Rebecca Jane Bailey was finally at peace. She had finally joined the child in the hereafter.

Mr. B grieved for several months, but finally eased out of it and even took a permanent lover, forsaking the lovely Mirriam. Mirriam didn't care a wit. She had more men than she could take care of anyway. To everyone's surprise, his fantasy became reality, and his lover became the sleek and sensuous Starshine Moonstone who had chosen him.

At first, nobody believed it, least of all Mr. B, but there was no telling who or why Star made her choices. The two were in no way compatible, which some speculated kept Star free of too deep an involvement. She aimed to remain emotionally free at all costs.

Mr. B was cool, laid back, morally straight, and to those who knew him well, practically asexual. Star, on the other hand, exuded sexuality. All the performers knew she still took an occasional man into her bed, but not wishing to hurt Mr. B, not a soul talked to him about it except Star herself. Mr. B would not talk about Star to the other performers, and the subject was dropped immediately if it ever did come up.

"It's none of nobody's business," was what Mary Lou had to say. "And besides, nobody knows nobody. No, not really." She was thinking of her father, a well-respected member of the community by day, and a depraved violator of his own child at night.

She was right. No one really does know the secret inner workings and private perverted desires of even the people with whom they associate on a daily basis.

Chapter Sixteen:

Secrets

Doctor Brady loved the times when he could seclude himself and read his newspapers. His favorite place was in the feed tent where he would drag two bales of hay around to form a desk of sorts on which to lay the paper and another bale to serve as an "office chair." It was there in the quiet of the afternoon where he would study all the papers from around the country. He loved the New York and Chicago papers, but he also had to read what was available to him in some of the small towns. He was well-schooled on the price of hogs and eggs and local gossip and church news in these little burgs. And was often amused at the writing style. It would never pass muster as literary masterpieces, but it got the message out well enough. Some of the papers were days and even weeks old by the time he got them or had a chance to read them. There was one issue discussed from place to place that troubled him. He saved up each issue that mentioned this item and one day he hailed Mr. B in the feed tent.

"Say, Bill. I would rather like to discuss something with you, if you have a moment."

"Sure thing, Doc. I'm trying to count these bales to see if we have enough hay to last until Friday. What's up?" Doc handed Mr. B several copies of newsprint and said, "Uhmmmm…I do not know exactly how to broach this subject, but I have been reading about a number of child murders occurring around the country and I must tell you, they bring me some concern. To be sure, the whole thing could be nothing more than a whole string of coincidences, but I do believe it merits some scrutiny."

by Loma A. Phegley

He handed Mr. B the papers and continued to speak. "If you will peruse these tabloids, at your leisure, you will see some of the cases to which I refer. If you will recall, some of these killings happened in most all of the towns where this circus has performed. Now, as I say, could be coincidence, but it warrants some serious consideration. It surely does, sir."

Mr. B, still counting bales was not really paying much attention. He said, "Damn. Lost track again. Go ahead, Doc, I'm listening," but he was not. He was distracted. Doc went on to explain the conclusion to which one could arrive, but continued to remind Mr. B that it was only conjecture on his part.

When he had finished Doc got the feeling that Mr. B had heard very little of what he had said.

Mr. B, still distracted and still counting bales, said, "Yeh, I'll read these when I have the time. I can see the implication but it is just speculation and no one gets accused by the law for speculation, let alone arrested or convicted. Besides, what the hell can we do…two hundred and forty one…I can't think of anyone here at the circus who would be capable of such acts."

Doc Brady said, "Well, there is Hiram."

"Aw, Hiram is just a harmless old windbag. I doubt he would have the brains to plan any crime more complicated than stealing booze or beating his poor wife." At that he stuffed the papers Doc had given him in behind a bale of hay and declared that it was time to call Tony Azavedo and order more hay. He took leave of Doc as he said, "I will think on it Doc. Hey Tico, call Tony and order about three more tons of alfalfa. See ya' Doc."

Doc could understand that Mr. B did not want any scandal to touch the circus. It was the livelihood of several dozen people and Mr. B's sole investment in life. Doc picked up the papers that Mr. B had stashed and went on his way shaking his head and thinking to himself, 'My, my. You would think a man who had lost his own child to a killer would display

· 111 ·

more interest in this matter' Doc decided to just keep his mouth shut about this, but to keep it in mind.

Strolling back to his little trailer he encountered his good friend Tilly.

"Well, good afternoon, my dear. Where are you off to this fine day looking so ravishingly lovely?"

"Aw, Doc. You silver-tongued devil, you. I'm going over to Angel's to do some sewing and measuring. Come along, old darlin,' I want to talk to you."

Everybody in the circus called Mary Lou "Tilly." At first, the new name worked for her because "Tilly" was really "Tilly the Fat Lady" and Mary Lou could divorce herself from her performing personality by using the name. The pseudo-anonymity lessened her stage fright, and gave her a kind of mask she used to release some of her inhibitions at getting out in front of a crowd.

She loved the part of her performer self that sang, but the part of her that was "Tilly the Fat Lady" still reminded her of the words her father had said.

"No man is ever gonna' want such a fat pig for a wife," echoed in her ears. She had proven him wrong, but her weight was starting to get in the way of things she wanted to do.

Mary Lou dreamed of traveling, but she couldn't fit in a single seat in the bus, unless it was the very last one that stretched across the entire back of the vehicle. When the circus moved she had to ride in the back of one of the trucks, Charlie always made it as comfortable as he could, but she sure would have loved to ride in a car. Gee, maybe even her own car. She was too embarrassed to move all the way down through all those people to get to the back of the bus, and getting out of the seat was a challenge. The one time she had tried it, she needed three men to extricate her from the bus seat. And there was also no way she could ride in a small private airplane. Phillipe had told her about weight limits when she'd inquired once.

Her back ached, her thighs were chafed from rubbing together, and she had to use the trick seal, Sweetie's, galvanized water tank to bathe in. Mr. B and Charlie would clean and fill the seal's water tank for her every Saturday morning. Her husband was no help. Instead of assisting her, he merely made fun of her, and she was, mostly on her own.

Mary Lou also dreamed of purchasing a store-bought dress. Even though she was a spectacular seamstress and could whip out a costume in no time, she still wanted the pleasure of picking something off of a department store rack, and wearing it home.

By now, Mary Lou weighed in at 417 pounds. Her breathing was labored, her feet and ankles swollen, and her ability to get up and walk was impaired on bad days. She cried and ate, and ate and cried about it.

One dreary day, Mary Lou was crying in her trailer when one of the trapeze artists came to pick up her repaired costume. She caught Mary Lou wiping her eyes and asked what was wrong. The Fat Lady confessed. She didn't want to be fat anymore. The trapeze artist had a possible solution, and told Mary Lou that the doctor who traveled with the circus had pills to take away the appetite. The doctor had gotten these pills for several of the performers, and she reckoned the pills might help. Mary Lou held out little hope that he could help her, but it was worth a try.

So by the time she encountered Doc on this day, she was ready to ask him about doing something about her weight.

"Doctor John Brady. How come you haven't got a sign out front of your place?" she asked. "Ain't you a doctor no more?"

"Why, my dear, I am a doctor. I just don't have a regular practice that's all. Besides, I like it here at the circus," said Doc.

"Yeah, I know. But I heard maybe you made some big shot mad and they took away yer license to be a doctor," said Mary Lou, in her somewhat blunt manner, but Doc didn't seem to mind.

"You are partly right, Tilly. I did indeed make someone mad. And he was a big shot. In fact, several big shots. Can you keep a secret?" he asked her.

"You betcha' I can keep a secret. I'm real good at that. Cross my heart and hope to die," she said, leaning forward to hear.

"OK," began Doc. "About five years ago, I had a practice, and a very good one at that. Made lots of money. Had a wife and two kids, nice home, and two automobiles. Well, I became very self-indulgent. Thought the world turned just for me, and then I discovered a substance that made me feel like I was king of the world!"

"Booze!" Mary Lou interjected. "Now that there's the ruination of many a good man."

"No. It was not alcohol, although I did drink my share of that too. No. It was something else, something far more insidious. Cocaine. It took over my life and made me into a kind of a man I never was. Made me an uncaring monster. I lived for cocaine. It was easy for me to come by, since all I needed was a prescription. But hell, I was a doctor so I could get as much of it as I wanted. Found me a girlfriend who liked the stuff too. My nurse at the office. First thing you know, I wasn't going home for days at a time. She and I would lay up in a hotel room at the beach and just put that stuff up our noses until we didn't even know where we were. I could always afford the best nose candy too, and since it was so pure, we didn't need as much. We also called it 'Booger Sugar' or 'Hot Snot.' Well, it was hot and it was sweet to be sure. But we needed more and more as the days went on."

"Wow!" Mary Lou took a deep breath and the doctor went on with his story.

"A little girl came into my office one day. She had appendicitis. I sent her over to the hospital and when I got there, I operated. Never should have, I was so high on cocaine. Hadn't slept for three days. Well, the little girl died. Tragic. It was a routine operation, but her daddy was the police chief. He did some investigating, and found out about the cocaine from my girlfriend. Poor girl. Scared the hell out of her. Well, they put me in jail, but I still had a few friends, and one of them was the District Attorney. He helped me some, but the folks in town wanted my scalp. I didn't blame them. I was as guilty as sin. I did one year in jail for manslaughter, my wife left me for another man, and the state took away my license for life. I heard my wife went to Connecticut, and I haven't seen my kids since. Her father is a doctor, and she got a divorce and married another doctor. And there you have it," he said.

"I heard of that cocaine stuff. 'Course I don't know what it's like. I don't even drink. My daddy drank and I couldn't stomach the smell of booze. Makes me sick. Food. Now that's something I can hardly get enough of. And that's why I'm here today. I heard you have some pills that might help."

Doc said he just might be able to help, but first he needed to take some blood tests to find out if Mary Lou had a thyroid condition. He wanted to make sure her condition was not a medical one before prescribing diet pills, and he knew something of her abused childhood. He'd seen a couple of other cases of women who blew up into sizable bodies after being abused as a child. Seemed like some kind of protective armor to Doc, but a thyroid condition had to be treated if that was part of the problem.

Doc had a friend in town that was willing to give him test results, which wasn't illegal. Those tests revealed that Mary Lou did indeed have a thyroid condition and Doc Brady told her about it when she came back to see him the next week.

"It's pretty complicated and hard to treat," he told her, "but it can be done. Problem is, it takes the total commitment of the patient. It's almost impossible for most people to curb their appetite and change their eating habits and it takes a great deal of will power."

"Doc, are you saying that if I can commit to…. Look, can you help me get skinny with some medication?" she asked.

"Whoa, sweetie," he tried to backtrack a little. "In a way I guess I am saying that. But I would have to prescribe a medication called Thyroxin. You would have to take it every day for the rest of your life. From the experience I've had with it, it'll make you jittery and nervous. But along with that, no more candy. And you'd have to cut down on bread, potatoes, butter, gravy and bacon. Then we may be able to get it under control. But that's a tough order, since those are all the things we like to eat."

"Well, I hear cocaine is so powerful, not many folks have much luck kickin' the habit," said Mary Lou.

"True, very true. It was tough. Nearly killed myself for craving it so much," said the Doc.

"If you can quit takin' that evil stuff, I can cut way down on all the fattening foods. I know I can. Let's do it. I'm willin.' You just don't know, Doc, what I gone through bein' fat like this," she said.

"Perhaps I don't, but I can imagine, Tilly. I can just imagine. And you say you're in danger of losing your ability to walk. That should be a motivator. But since I have lost my license to practice, I can't prescribe medication either."

Mary Lou's hopes were dashed, but she pursued it anyway.

"So if I go into a drugstore and hand the druggist a prescription, will he call someone to see if you been throwed out of the doctoring business?" she asked.

"I doubt it. But if the state should get hold of that prescription, they'd know I was practicing again and they could put me in jail."

Big tears welled up in Mary Lou's eyes. "Oh, I thought for a minute I was gonna' be saved," she said, sniffling.

"Tell you what. I still have a friend who is a doctor in Redding. I could send your medical profile up there to him, and he could prescribe the medicine and make it refillable for an indefinite period of time. What do you say about that?"

The Doc gave her renewed hope.

by Loma A. Phegley

"Oh Doc! If you would do that and I could get started, I promise, cross my heart, I promise to do whatever you tell me to do. I will, I will. Oh please!" she begged.

"OK, I'm going to give you this little book. It's a calorie counter. See here how it lists the portions and the calories? From now on, you are forbidden to eat more than 2,000 calories a day. You'll have to write down everything you eat. We'll adjust that to 1,000 after you loose a little," instructed the doctor.

"Huh?" Mary Lou was puzzled. "What the hell is a calorie? Have I ever ate one of them before? I probably won't like 'em."

Doc laughed. "Yes, you have. Lots of them. Let me explain further," he said as he went on to explain caloric measurement in terms he thought Mary Lou would understand.

When he was done, Mary Lou added one caveat. "I don't want nobody to know about this. Hiram would just torment me about it. He'd be real mad if I got skinny 'cause I couldn't be no fat lady no more. And I'd lose my job, though maybe I could hold on to the singin' part. But that would make ol' Hiram kill crazy, ya know?"

The Doc agreed to keep the secret. "Right. Mum's the word then. Now we hold each other's secrets. A deal?"

"It's a deal. And one other thing Doc. Would you mind calling me Mary Lou? That's my real name. I wanna' change my life and be who I'm supposed to be. Not Tilly the Fat Lady, but Mary Lou, the skinny one."

"You bet. I shall. I never liked the name Tilly anyway. I am not sure you will ever be really skinny, but let's give 'er a whirl, old girl," he said.

"Hokay Doc. I'm with you on that, so amen."

The tide began to turn for Mary Lou once the prescription was finally in her hands, and a few days later Doc saw her and asked her how the diet was coming along.

"Well, I don't rightly know. See, I ain't got anywheres to go to get on a scale since none of them will weigh over three hundred pounds. But I do know my underpants don't fit so tight. It's only been a few days but you said at first it would only be water I would lose. I don't seem to get too discouraged about it. I feel less hungry. All this fat didn't get here overnight and I doubt it'll go away very fast. I did take them water pills you gave me and man, I pissed buckets the first two days. I take my thyroid medicine regular and try to keep busy. So far, so good," she reported.

Doc had an idea of how to keep track of her progress. "We could go down to the feed store and weigh you on the scales where they weigh the hay and grain. Tell you what. I'll borrow Mr. B's car and we can go over there. Does that suit you?"

"That's fine. I just wish there weren't so many fantastic chefs in the circus camp. Tico's always cookin' up something and passing it around, and so is Papa Primo."

With Hiram passed out, no one had any questions about Mary Lou going to town with Doc, and when they arrived at the feed store, they were greeted by a lady every bit as fat as Mary Lou. She told them it would be no problem for them to use the scales since she did it herself now and then. She went with them to show them how to interpret the giant mechanical scale and Doc took a little notebook from his pocket to write down some figures. When he had finished weighing Mary Lou, he wrote down four hundred seven pounds. She had already lost ten pounds in the two weeks of the diet, though neither of them knew it. As Mary Lou was getting situated on the scale the Doc used the opportunity to tell the fat merchant lady that her own weight might be caused by a medical condition. She made an appointment to see him the next week.

"Now my dear, from now on, every time we come to a town that has a feed store, we will weigh you and mark it down in this journal. Time will fly by and first thing you know, you'll be wearing hand me downs from the trapeze crews."

by Loma A. Phegley

They both laughed heartily at the joke, and on the way back to the circus grounds, Doc stopped at a tavern. Mary Lou was a bit worried that he might get drunk, but he ordered a ginger ale for each of them.

Then he told Mary Lou, "You have inspired me to quit drinking. You were right. If I could kick the cocaine habit, by golly, I can kick the booze. And you can kick the calories. I'm proud of you for undertaking such a task."

"I'm proud of you too Doc," echoed Mary Lou.

"Mary Lou, you know, I keep thinking about something Tico said the other day."

"What's that?" she asked.

"Life is like a river. It can surround you, but you gotta' keep swimming," he said.

The two of them sat at the bar, pushed the bowl of nuts away, took a sip of ginger ale and contemplated how life was like a river.

Chapter Seventeen:

Star And Beelee

Starshine Moonstone had been with the circus about two years when she decided to take Mr. B as her lover on a regular basis. She knew she could never be faithful to him but she didn't care.

"He no like?" she thought to herself. "Too bad. A girl gotta' live. One man not enough for one woman."

Mr. B was a long way from being a desirable lover. He was not a handsome or a sexy man. Just a common, accountant type, guy, about five-feet-nine inches tall, just a little on the stout side, and he wore dumpy, rumpled suits. But Star knew that although she was only twenty-six, life was tough when a girl was on her own. She knew too, that Mr. B was a man of means and brought in a steady and substantial income. Certainly no small consideration for a girl in those days and times. The Great Depression was not quite over yet. Star had been lucky all through it. Thanks to her talents, wit and ability she never went hungry or without a warm place to sleep. She was a dancer, a singer, a fortuneteller and even a whore when times and circumstances called for it.

Star was not really a gold digger. She'd been making her own money since she was an adolescent and she learned well about making money from her gypsy mentors. She did not steal nor cheat any man, but she knew that if she became Mr. B's lover, it would be a two way street. He would get a fair barter for their union, and it would not be as if she were a whore. At least, Star didn't think so. Just business. Love had nothing to do with it.

by Loma A. Phegley

The gypsy's intuition and psychic ability also drew her to Mr. B. It felt to her as if he held some secret, and the feeling around this secret was dark and mysterious. Star felt it was related in some way to his sexuality, and she wondered if he would ever reveal it to her. Anyway, no big deal. Most men thought they had a deep, dark secret when it came to sex, but usually it turned out to be some inconsequential thing like a desire to have a pair of women at once. And if there was one subject in this world that Starshine Moonstone was an expert on, it was men. She didn't question her instincts about her lovers too closely, because she knew that when it came to her private life, the psychic senses step aside to allow the person to go through whatever they're supposed to go through. The readings she gave to people visiting her on the Carnival side were accurate precisely because they were strangers. At first she had been jealous of Mirriam, but as time went on she realized that this lady was a nut. No competition for the intrepid Star.

Elaborate preparations were made for Star to get ready to take on her new lover. It was a veritable ritual of preparation. She gazed a long time into the crystal skull, while thinking about the man she was about to take on as her next lover. Slowly, she felt compelled to be different than she had ever been with any other man. Ivan had told her that Muslim women shaved all the hair off their bodies, and she found that intriguing. A thought flashed through her mind that Mr. B would like something different like that.

A new Star? Something different. This was a seduction, not business. "Ah yes, Star know what to do," she thought. So with a straight razor, she shaved her thick, black bush. The hair on her pussy was so thick and lush, the part in her cunt could hardly be seen. She lay on the bed and shaved herself with the razor without a single nick. She liked how it felt so smooth. She shaved under her arms, and liked that too, so she shaved her legs. It was a very daring move in these times, for a girl to shave her body, and Star was very daring. Good girls did not do such things. But

Star reasoned and said, "So what? I not good girl. If I like, they be my legs, my armpits and my pussy!"

When she finished, she stood before the mirror and smiled.

"Just like a little girl child, now, is Starshine," she said out loud, laughing to herself. "Maybe mens think I am virgin." But she reconsidered. "No, I not think so."

She waited until nightfall when it was time to slip over to Mr. B's trailer with her plans to fuck him until he was so exhausted he could scarcely move. Star knew just how to do that since practice had made her perfect.

Through the window of her little trailer, she could see Mr. B's office trailer. This night, she watched until she saw the light go out and then she knew that he had gone on over to his place. She had bathed, loosened her abundant hair from it's long braid, applied an exotic and magical scent to areas inside her wrists, behind her ears, under her breasts, and on the small of her back, as well as along the sides of her arms. Putting on a long diaphanous gown of a ruby red Bombay silk that swept the floor and opened down the front, she was ready for what she had no doubt would happen.

Her knock on his door was hardly a brush of touch, but Mr. B heard it. He was not surprised to see Starshine at his door. Circus performers often came to him with problems after the office was closed. But he had no idea what her real purpose in coming to him was. She had never, by word or action, given a hint of wanting to have a sexual liaison with him. When she stepped into the door, she let her gown fall to the floor and stood naked before him. His eyes flew open wide with astonishment.

"Why Star," he said. "How, how, how…. oh God! How gorgeous you are. What a set of knockers. Are you here for what I hope you are here for? If so, come right in."

And she did.

This time she did not repeat her usual routine. This was different, she kept telling herself. She walked to the bed with her slow, sensuous stroll, turned and faced him, cupping her hands under each big, perfectly formed breast. She planted her feet apart so he could see her slick, and by now, very wet cunt.

"For you. It is for you," she said. "I have come to make love to you. For to fuck you. Has been long time, huh?"

"Yes," he said weakly, lying of course. "Has been long time."

He stared at her shaved pussy and said, "I like that. Oooh. I like that, yeah."

Star slid her hands down her belly and parted her slit with two fingers so he could see the pink wetness of her "garden of delights" as she called it. She laid back on the bed with one foot still on the floor. He knelt down and at first softly applied his tongue to her prominent clitoris, flicking, sucking, and licking it, and finally taking as much of it into his mouth as he could.

She cried out, "Yes, yes, for me. Do for me! Is what I like for me."

He rose from the floor and mounted her, driving his erect cock deep inside her.

"And now for me. For me!" he mimicked. "This is for me, and for you. You like this, Sweet Star? You like this?"

But she was too lost in the moment to answer with anything but a strangled cry as her body stiffened and she came. Once he felt the rhythmic, strangling pulsation of her climax, he followed in a split second with his own.

He lay there on her for a long time. Finally, he said, "I never knew. You have never said a word or given any idea that this was what you wanted. I have often thought of you in my bed, but I didn't follow up on my thoughts with action."

"Good you did not," she said. "I choose the mens I want to fuck, I do not let them choose me. I would like to be your woman. Be here with you."

"Well, Star. I don't know. I know you like to sleep around with other men."

He thought for a moment, "but that excites me. I like to think of you being fucked by other men. Would you still do that?"

"Sure. Star always be Star. Never to change. That does not mean that I do not like you. Tell you what. When I fuck other man, I come to tell you all about. I tell you how big, how he do it, what I do. You like. Is OK?"

"Fine with me, baby. I'll like that just fine," he said as he cupped his hand over her *mons venus*. "I like this. Man, oh man. I do like this. If I had known you shaved it, I would probably have made a move to get in there sooner."

"I do for you. Just tonight. I do for you. You like? I do for always. Keep it like you like."

But she knew damn well that she had not done it just for him, although he was part of it. But she had a wish to be different. To be Star.

She lay back on the pillow and said, "Mr. B sound so formal. I not like that. I call you Billie. Better. I like that more." She pronounced it "Beelee."

He laughed and said, "Fine. Whatever you want."

The sexual liaison was underway between Billie Bailey and Starshine Moonstone and it would be a long while before the other performers knew anything about it. But when they found out, it was a shock and a subject of gossip for months.

Chapter Eighteen:
Tico's Dream Comes True

The long tiresome trip between Topeka and Denver had always been one Tico slept through as much as he could. It was boring until they reached the mountains of Colorado. But this time he was wide awake, sitting in the big truck with his little Angel between him and the driver, Charlie "One Shoe." Every once in awhile, Angelica would pat his leg. *Like you might pat a dog's head*, Tico thought, but he felt comforted by it because he knew she was trying to reassure him.

Tico knew that from now on, all of his life; his nightmares would be of losing his Angel. He knew he would hold the brief time she had been taken by the two hillbilly kidnappers as a constant nightmare from which he could never escape. No terror or any other bad thing that could ever happen to him could equal the agony he had suffered when he thought she was gone for good. He had known that if he had never gotten her back and there was no hope of doing so that he would have killed himself.

He tried to sleep but every time he closed his eyes the specter of her being in the hands of any but his own would cause him to come awake with a start. He thought that as a dwarf that he had trained himself to accept any loss, any disappointment, any grief. But he knew now that he was vulnerable to all of it. He compared himself to Adam and Eve when they were thrown from God's Garden. What a shock they must have suffered when they discovered they would now know all of the tragedy and trials of life as a real human. He picked up Angel's left hand and compared it to one of his own. He almost laughed out loud at the contrast.

Hers was perfectly formed. Graceful fingers no bigger than a carpenter's pencil. His own hand was almost square. His fingers were so short they appeared to have no joints. He could scarcely make a fist. Tico had trouble holding a cigar between his stubby digits, and a ring was practically out of the question since it would never stay on, he thought.

He looked at her sleeping. Her hair was clean and combed and she wore a new dress Mary Lou had finished just before they hit the road. It was a light green, and it brought a glow to her face. She looked so fine, as her hair shone in the sunlight when it touched her through the windshield.

Tico's arms were so short he had difficulty combing his hair. He seldom went to a restaurant because he could not reach the stool at the counter, and when he sat at a table, the height of it swallowed him up, and he could not reach the food. But when he did go, it was always with Ivan. Without a word, Ivan would lift his little friend up on the stool at the counter or silently get a couple of phone books and place underneath him.

Tico's legs were twisted and one was shorter than the other. He never spoke of it, but he suffered a tremendous amount of pain in his bones. Why should he complain? It just was. It was the price he had to pay to be alive.

As the troupe prepared to leave the circus that morning, Angel had taken the comb from his hand, and as one would do for a small child, combed his beautiful head of shining black hair, pressing the waves in with her fingers. It was just right, just like his mother had done it when he was a boy. When she finished, she had kissed him on the top of his head, and then on his cheek. He thought about that now, as they traveled along, and wondered if it had been preordained that they were meant to care for one another. For a moment, he let himself consider a future with Angel for the first time.

Tico contemplated the considerable sum of money, a fortune, from the perfect diamonds he had sold for his father when he first arrived in

New York. His father had left the money in a bank account in case his son should need it. He told Tico to put it in both names, and he would let him know what to do with it sometime in the future.

Tico's father, Emiliano De La Porto was a very wise man. He did not like the political climate in Europe. He hated Mussolini and he feared Hitler. Franco was Fascist Pig. Hitler and Franco were openly anti-Semitic. All three of these men had gained such power that their presence upon the political scene in Europe had grown, in his opinion, dangerous, especially for Jews. He knew that he must leave his home and take his family to a better place, at least for awhile.

Emiliano was one of the few Spanish Jews that had traveled the world. He had been to Paris, South Africa, and Burma. China, Russia, Ceylon, Indo China, Siam, India, Turkey, Persia, Arabia, Morocco, Afghanistan, Italy, England and America...all were places where Emiliano could claim to have friends and connections.

His first choice for relocating his family was America. He could see calling it home but he knew that immigration and customs laws were such that he and his family could never get permission to go there in time, and it would have been out of the question to take his large and valuable collection of gems. So he chose Argentina where he had a brother. Emiliano's brother Sebastiono, had seen the war clouds darkening even sooner than Emiliano had. He had lived in Italy where he was alarmed at the actions and antics of Benito "Il Duce" Mussolini. He tried to warn every one he knew. Some of them heeded his words and those who did not were to perish just because they were Jews. Sebastiano had moved there several years before and the De La Porto family was relocated in the beautiful Argentine countryside near Buenos Aires.

When the family had sailed for South America they had managed to hide many of the gemstones by sewing them into clothing and hiding them in tins of tobacco. Of course, much of the inventory had been smuggled into the country by trusted couriers and employees. Many of the stones were secretly sold and the American dollars hidden in Swiss banks and into the most secure banks in the world, in the U. S., Mexico, Canada and Argentina. The bulk of his fortune was safely out of Spain.

Tico had had no reason to even think of the money in the account until now. He reasoned that his wise father had left the money there as a precaution against unsettled times. But Tico wanted to use a small sum to take his *Angelica* to the home of his Mamma and Papa if she would go, and an even larger sum to purchase a wedding ring for his *Angelica*. He knew it would not be a problem with his father.

"What if she says...?" he thought, but then stopped himself. "No. I will meet that when it comes."

Argentina was one country Tico had never visited and he knew nothing of the place except where it was on the map. His father and mother and two sisters, Constancia and Carmella had gone to the city of Rio de Janeiro for their children's schooling and the jewelry business. Emiliano had suffered only the loss of his rancho and the house in Seville by fleeing Spain. He was to recover the property at a later time after the war, but never returned to face his old archenemy, Francisco Franco, by now Dictator of his beloved country. King Juan Carlos would wait many years to resume his place in European history.

He reasoned that it would be easier to deal with the leaders of Argentina than with Franco, anyway.

With business interests in South Africa, Egypt, Formosa, Burma, Russia and Japan, he had a well-informed worldview. He was not fool enough to believe that he would suffer no losses from those investments should a war descend upon the world. So he divested himself of many of his holdings in Burma, South East Asia and India, re-investing it in steel, petroleum, arms, coal, and iron in the U.S., Mexico and in South America. If a war was inevitable, Emiliano De La Porto would make even more money as a result.

He anticipated a war of great magnitude since he was so well informed, and he knew the real state of affairs across the European and

Asian continents. He knew that very few of the issues that had brought about the First World War had been resolved. There was still the Ottoman Empire that had not been dealt with in a satisfactory solution.

President Wilson was a blind fool, drunk with the recent victory in winning the "War to End All Wars." He was so out of touch with the real situation in Europe and Asia Minor that he had actually set the stage for the war that would soon be upon them all. His brother, Sebastiano, had been a member of several British and American Jewish organizations and had been privy to secret U. S. State Department information, so his decision to leave Europe for Argentina had been one based upon facts in evidence.

On top of that, Emiliano also knew Benito Mussolini and despised him and his brutish party they called "The Fascist Party." Emiliano knew this man as a former editor who's only claim to fame was that he made the trains run on time. He knew that this Italian thug's policies could but end in disaster for all of Italy, when "*Il Duce*" as he called himself, threatened to seize Rome with his army of "Black Shirts" and threw up his hands in disgust when he attacked Ethiopia. While *Il Duce* was not particularly anti-Semitic; he was a Fascist bully and Emiliano did not like him personally. When *Il Duce* allied himself with history's arch demon, Adolph Hitler, Emiliano knew it was time to leave Europe.

By the time Emiliano decided to take his family out of Europe, commerce with many countries had become nearly impossible. Hitler's influence had made many businessmen reluctant to deal with Jews on any level. It had become too dangerous. His greatest concern was for his friends and some family members that had scoffed at his fears and stayed behind.

Tico's mind was also on his immediate family. He was thinking of them as Angel slept and the big truck filled with circus gear rolled on, hauling his small trailer behind it. He longed to see his sweet mother and father. His two sisters were grown up and had families of their own, and he wondered how his nieces and nephews would treat him now that they were of an age to understand that he was deformed. But Tico smiled at the thought, knowing the children had been introduced to Emiliano's fierce anger and disapproval. He knew they would treat him with the utmost respect if their grandfather was anywhere in the vicinity when they were introduced.

Tico remembered his father's wrath as being an awesome force, to say the very least. But today he remembered it with some fondness.

Charlie "One Shoe" brought the big truck to a stop in front of a small art gallery in Campio, Colorado, in the late afternoon. It was near the highway. Angel woke with a start and wore a look of puzzlement on her face.

Tico said, "Hey *amigo! Que paso?*"

"I know the lady who runs this place. Come on. I want you to meet her," Charlie told Tico and Angel.

Once inside the shop, they were warmly greeted by a very handsome lady that Charlie introduced as Sheila Hellums. She seemed genuinely fond of Charlie, who explained that Sheila and his late wife had been sisters.

Sheila was a beautiful woman, with a regal face and exquisite features. Her hair was very blonde, and cropped close to her head. She wore a bright red artist's smock and no shoes. She had an easy laugh, a ready smile, and put Tico at ease immediately.

Charlie had brought Angel's sketchpad in with them and he produced it to show Sheila the sketches Angel had done.

Sheila regarded it closely, and smiled at the girl, nodding in approval.

"This is not her best work, I'm sure," she said.

"She drew this with an old pencil, a pulp writing tablet of the cheapest kind and yet this is very, very good. It shows some training."

She slipped inside her studio for a minute, then turned to Angel and offered her a good sketchpad along with several excellent art pencils.

Angel's eyes were shining and she smiled broadly, as she stood touching the paper delicately, and stroking the many pencils. She was delighted and she handed the supplies back as Sheila, realizing the girl was deaf, spoke to her face saying, "this is my gift to you."

"She can't talk," explained Charlie, "or hear."

Sheila nodded. "I surmised as much," she said, and wrote a note to Angelica.

Where did you get your art instruction? she asked on the tablet.

Angel wrote back, *From a man who used to live in my building. He was called Pietre Van Der Hoosen. He was very kind to me.*

Angel noted the surprised look on Sheila's face as she read the words.

"My God! I thought he was dead! He killed his wife and his model all in the same day. Nobody ever knew why and he wasn't talking. Last I heard, they put him in the booby hatch. He was one of the finest artists of his time," she said, and Angelica managed to catch almost everything she had said.

"Van Der Hoosen was very famous, but very nuts. I heard he used to walk in Central Park at two or three in the morning naked as a jaybird. Bathed in the fountain there. He was a friend of that arrogant old bastard Picasso. They were a pair!" she said.

Tico shot a knowing glance at Angel and asked her silently if it was OK if he told Sheila how she came to be with them. She said it was fine by shaking her head yes, but just the same she wrote on the pad of paper, *I am not slow or crazy, but I do not hear or speak.*

When Tico was finished telling her the story, Sheila wondered out loud if Angel would consider staying on with her.

"I could sell her work with no difficulty. I could give her a very decent home," she said, and Tico reluctantly wrote her words down, although Angel had caught most of the conversation already.

Tico felt his heart sink. His head was swimming and there was a lump in his throat that held back tears.

"Ah, the moment of truth," he thought. "Like the bullfighter, this is the ultimate test. Better now than later." And he put her words and her offer down on the pad verbatim. Charlie intervened as Tico was writing and said, "Hey little buddy, are you sure? I thought you and her were, well, you know."

"Yes, at least I want to believe that we are," said Tico with his head down so Angel could not see his lips, "but it be her choice." Tears welled up in Tico's eyes and he kept his head down. Charlie understood what was happening perfectly.

"OK, Tico. Your call, my friend," he said.

Tico took the pencil, looked deep into the eyes of his Angelica, then began to write.

My dear Angel, I love you, but this lady has offered you a home and career doing art. What you want to do?

Angel's eyes filled with tears and she shook her head no several times. Then she took the pencil back and tried to write through her watery vision, as she brushed the tears aside in order to see. Sheila brought her a tissue and she wiped the wetness from her cheeks. But the tears did not stop.

She wrote, *No, no! I stay with you! You say you love me? I love you too. Please do not throw me away. Please. I am yours forever. My Mama and my Papa did not want me. Nobody ever wanted me before. Please, I want to stay with you. Oh, Tico, my beloved, do not throw me away.*

Angel fell to her knees, sobbing on the floor and Tico put his arms around her and cradled her face against him. Instinctively, he began to sing the old Spanish lullaby his mother had sung to him.

Sheila understood at once what was going on, and she picked up the pad of paper that had fallen to the floor, and read it.

Tico sang to Angel because she could "hear" the singing through the vibrations of his body close to hers. And Tico knew this would be a comfort to her as it would be to a child who could hear. Angel knew he was singing just for her, and she soon stopped crying. Touched by the emotional scene, Sheila's lovely cheeks were wet with tears too, but she made an attempt at humor anyway by saying, "Sorry I asked."

Charlie hugged her and bent down, pulling little Angel to her feet.

by Loma A. Phegley

He cleared his throat and said, "Well, we best be on our way then." Then turning to Tico, he asked, "Does that answer your question?"

Tico looked at Angel's face so she could read his words. "We go. You and me. We go forever." And Angel knew exactly what he had said.

Tico thanked Sheila for the art supplies of pastels, charcoal, watercolors and brushes, as well as pencils and sketchpads.

"I pay you for art stuff," said Tico.

"My word," exclaimed Sheila. "Never. It is a gift from one artist to another. It is my pleasure, to be sure."

Charlie kissed his sister-in-law goodbye and promised to visit when he could stay longer. They took their leave with Tico digesting the news that this love had been declared permanent by Angel. He was beginning to swell with happiness, but the news was only just sinking in, and he was still comforting his *Angelica* after her abandonment scare.

Back on the road, his good fortune sunk in and he was happier than he had ever been. He smiled, held Angel's hand, and gazed at her lovingly whenever he could steal a glance without Charlie catching him too much. Angel's emotional upset soon subsided and she took out one of her smaller sketchpads and a newly sharpened pencil.

She drew a caricature of Charlie "One Shoe" capturing his florid face and heavy eyebrows perfectly. His pudgy double chin and bulbous nose did not escape her artist's eye, though she softened them a little since Charlie's kindness added to his attractiveness in her eyes. The bald head and oversized ears were there too, but she made him look downright handsome. All the characteristics of Charlie were there in the picture, but somehow he looked good. There was even the one shoe on his foot, while the other one was bare. She showed the drawing to the two men. Tico smiled and Charlie let out a hearty laugh.

"Say, if she can make old Charlie look this good, she could make a fortune doing these drawings on the Carnival Section at any circus in the land!" said Charlie.

"No. Not my Angel," replied Tico, "we got other plans."

Then Tico used rudimentary sign language to tell Angel to do a sketch of him. She agreed by nodding and smiling, but turned his face away as she drew, and blocked her drawing whenever he tried to look at it before she was done.

When she finished, she handed it to Tico with a funny little seated bow as the truck rolled along. Tico took her gesture with a comical flourish of his own.

The small man looked hard and long at the likeness and the look on his face went from jester to serious and wistful. There was no mistake the likeness was him, but she had drawn him as she saw him, and not as he saw himself. She accentuated his long, dark eyelashes and perfectly shaped eyebrows. She added his beautiful, neatly trimmed and coifed hair, but his pockmarked face was smooth and his nose was not quite so large. It was him alright, but she had drawn the picture with the love she had in her heart for him. Angel saw only good in him. She drew him as her rescuing angel, with a naked cherub's perfect body, a halo above his head, and a set of feathered wings.

For the rest of the trip, Tico slept some and so did Angel. When she was awake, Angel drew designs, flowers, small animals, trees, houses and fashions. The men were entertained by her drawings and it made the time pass more easily. Both Charlie and Tico came to understand the genius of this little girl's talent. The new pencils and paper made a great difference, and the supplies seemed to make her very happy.

Tico took the pencil and asked her if she liked jewelry. He asked if she would like to design a ring, one with a big diamond in it. Angel enjoyed drawing the jewelry and Tico thought the designs were some of the most exquisite he'd ever seen. But he encouraged her to make the stones a bit bigger since her first creations had very small stones.

Tico wrote to her on the pad of paper, *Draw me a ring with a diamond as big as Charlie's nose. No. Only joke. As big as...let me see. Si. Si. A raisin. A big Spanish raisin.*

Angel complied with the fantasy. She had never owned a ring, not even one made of cheap, colored glass. But she indulged her lover's fancy and drew exquisite creations of different rings with different colored stones she could not even imagine owning.

Then he asked her to pick her favorite. She studied them for awhile then made her selection. Tico studied the design and saw that it was a workable creation. At the next truck stop where the trio took a break, he tore the pages of jewelry designs out of her book carefully so she would not miss them, folded them up, and stashed them behind the seat.

The circus crew finally arrived in Denver where everyone, including Charlie, set to work on a make shift camp that would serve them at least overnight. They fed and watered and walked the animals, and readied for more advertising in town. Tico helped Ivan and the crew, leaving Angel to arrange things in the little trailer.

As soon as the work became less hectic and night began to fall, he sought out Mr. B and found him in the office trailer going over schedules.

"Come in, Tico my boy. Come in. How did you and little Angel fare on the trip?" he asked.

"*Con mucho gusto, amigo.* Very well, thank you. Mr. B, I tell you now. Soon, I go to my father in South America. I take Angel if she go. Now, must know if we go to San Francisco soon. Yes?"

"Yes, indeed," said Mr. B. "After this engagement, we are scheduled to go to a small city near San Francisco called Walnut Creek. Why do you ask?"

"Well, I to do business there," he said. "Old friend to my father's, Señor Belknap, has big jewelry business there and I going to make a ring for my *Angelica*."

From the inside of his jacket, Tico took the small chamois skin bag. He emptied the contents on the desk in front of his friend. Mr. B was stunned.

"You have been carrying these around with you? How foolish, man!" he said, "men have been killed for far less than that."

"So it not happen. I bring many gems from Spain to America. I bring many stones here for my father to deliver to New York diamond dealers. But these are my own collection. Some I buy, some were my Grandmother's and some I just...hmmm, how you say? Acquire?"

The stones that Tico had spilled out on Mr. B's desk were obviously without peer to anything Mr. B had ever seen. One was an emerald of at least twenty-two carats. Another was an exquisite ruby, bright in color and big as a peach pit. It was carved into the turbaned head of an Indian Sultan. The features were so tiny and delicate that Mr. B was amazed at such perfection. Tico said, "This one is known as '*El Sultano.*' Is very famous rock in my country. Is...oh...maybe ten carat. Some beauty, eh?"

"My God, Tico. Some beauty is right. I have never seen the like. I know very little of gems, but it sure seems like a priceless bauble to me."

"You betcha is some bubble. Now, stone I will have ring made from for my *Angelica* not here. Will buy from Bellknap, maybe. Here is emerald. I have ring made for my dear friend Mary Lou, and here is ruby."

"I can't get over that ruby. It' as big as a..."

"Seed of peach, no?" Tico completed his question with a chuckle, and images of fine jewelry and elegant designs danced in his head, along with a vision of his *Angelica's* eyes shining when she would receive the magnificent ring along with his proposal of marriage.

He packed the jewels back in the bag, with admonishments from Mr. B to be careful and tell no one of the gems in his little trailer. He nearly floated the few feet to his own place and to his beloved little *Angelica* for another night of pure love and unparalleled lovemaking.

The crew was exhausted from a summer of engagements across the country, from Kansas City to Denver, the Great Salt Lake to Reno, Sacramento, and now Walnut Creek. The Contra Costa County Fair was next on the agenda, but the gear and the animals were all settled in and the fair didn't start for five more days giving the crew a few days to relax and tend to other affairs.

The Primos went off to San Francisco to visit old Dago friends and look for a home big enough to house all of the family, even Phillipe. They all knew it was time to retire before someone of them was injured, as they worked without nets. Papa had saved all of the money he had gotten over the years from selling his wine. It rested comfortably in Mr. Gianinni's Bank of America in San Francisco. It was the only bank he trusted, and trusted it only because it had been founded by an Italian immigrant. With high hopes, the entire clan set off in a big enclosed truck loaned to them by Mr. B. They'd fixed it up to accommodate the whole family somewhat comfortably for the short trip to San Francisco. The Primo's made important decisions like buying a house as a group, but Papa Primo was the deciding patriarch and they all knew it.

Chapter Nineteen:
Angel's Diamond Ring

Tico and Angel also made the trip to San Francisco. Angel was dressed in a gorgeous new pink gabardine suit from Hart, Shaeffner & Marks. Tico had had his very expensive custom tailored black pin striped threads from Spain cleaned and pressed. He was smelling of the pungent odor of Burma Shave and the Brilliantine Angel had slicked through his thick black hair. He also sported not only a new gray Homburg, but a short black Malacca walking stick, as well. The couple looked elegant. Their first stop was to the Hotel Saint Francis, highly recommended by Doc Brady, where they secured rooms and dropped off their luggage. From the hotel they took a taxi to the exclusive jewelry store of Tico's father's friend, Mr. Harvey Bellknap.

They entered the store, Tico firmly gripping his Angel by the hand, and after a few minutes wait were approached by a typical flashy type salesman, who strutted up to the couple displaying a rather supercilious manner and said haughtily, "Yes, may I help you?" Tico knew the game. He had seen it played by some of the employees at his father's shop, so Tico decided to play.

Tico took a moment to ignore him and then said, in a manner even more supercilious than this salesman could ever approach. "Yes. I am here to see the owner of this establishment. Will you please to tell him that Teodoro De La Porto is here to sees him?"

The salesman answered as one might when explaining to a child why he couldn't have a cookie, "I am sorry, but Mr. Bellknap is otherwise occupied and has asked not to be disturbed."

"Ah," said Tico in mock resignation, "I see. I look for ring for wedding for my lovely lady, here."

The salesman, without a word, turned to the glass topped counter and slid the door open, withdrawing a small, delicate diamond from a tray of rings that all looked about the same. He handed it to Tico but Tico did not take it. Instead, gesturing, he said, "Put it on the counter, there." The salesman laid the ring on a black velvet cloth on top of the counter and was somewhat surprised when Tico fished in his vest pocket and withdrew his own loupe. Fitting it to his eye in a most professional way, he looked briefly at the ring. He laid it back down on the counter and without removing his loupe, changed his view from the ring to the salesman. He stared contemptuously at him for a moment without saying a word. The salesman shifted nervously from one foot to the other. Quietly and evenly with more than a bit if malice, Tico said, "How dare to try to cheat the son of Emiliano De La Porto! This so cheap. Next class down be glass. This crap!"

He slapped his little Malacca walking stick on the glass top case. It made a smart crack just loud enough to make the guy jump a bit. With great authority and dignity, Tico said, "You! You to bring me Mr. Bellknap. Do not tell me he is busy. He will sees me. I am Teodoro De La Porto of Seville, Spain. I am the son of Emiliano De La Porto. Ah, I sees you know the name."

Tico was in his element, demanding respect from the disrespectful that only money and power could achieve. The salesman, who certainly did indeed know the name, was deflated and intimidated. He said, "Yes sir. One moment, sir." He then rushed to the back of the store returning with the owner, Mr. Harvey Bellknap.

Mr. Bellknap, recognizing Tico immediately, greeted him with genuine enthusiasm. "So good to see you again, Teodoro. Not since the trade show in Paris. You were but a lad then, about twelve, eh? And how is your eminent father?"

"My father be well, sir. Kind for you to ask. He sends greetings and best wishes for you continued health and prosperity. Yes, I was but twelve years old when we last met. My third trade show. Ah, yes, Paris. Is good you remember." He turned to Angel and said, "With great pride and even greater humility, I present to you my soon to be wife, *Angelica*. It has been my great good fortune to have find such a wonder in this world. She is a gift from Heaven."

Tico had practiced and practiced this little speech over and over. He tried to make sure his English was proper and his accent not quite so pronounced. He wanted everything even remotely connected to his Angel to be perfect.

It was a speech he would make many times in the next few weeks. He glowed with pride each time he would make this little speech of introduction of his "Angelica." These were the most sincere and heartfelt words he would ever speak. By now the salesman had vanished. Bellknap escorted Tico and Angel into his opulent office. He closed the door and seated them in high-backed velvet chairs. Knowing Tico's limitations, he placed a small footstool close to the chair for Tico's use in sitting in the chair.

"And now, treasured son of my treasured friend, what brings you to me?"

Both Bellknap and Tico laughed at the formality of the words. Tico began by producing his chamois bag of gems, laying it on the desk but not opening it. "First let us talk of stone for the wedding ring for my bride." Through it all, Angel sat bright eyed and attentive trying to catch all the words by lip reading. If Bellknap sensed that anything was amiss in her demeanor, he said not a word. He had no wish to embarrass either of them.

Tico continued, "I do not have a stone worthy of such a ring in my humble collection. Do you..." Before Tico could finish his sentence, Bellknap cried out, "I have it! Yes I have it. It is a magnificent stone I have just acquired from a dealer in South Africa. It is a De Beers rock. It has been cut and polished by the finest cutter in the De Beers stable of cutters. It is flawless and is a canary stone of three carats."

He rose from his chair and said, "Come. I will show you."

He led them to a carved teakwood door that he unlocked which led into a steel-door vault. He admitted them to the vault and from the rows and rows of black velvet trays he selected a red velvet pouch. Carrying it to the viewing tray, he slipped it onto the tray with an exaggerated flourish.

Tico had seen many wonderful stones in his life, but the minute he saw this one he knew it was the one to place in the setting that Angel had designed that day in the truck while traveling through the countryside. But true to the De La Porto tradition of shrewd dealing, he placed his loupe in his eye and pretended to critique the gem. He did not even acknowledge its desirability. Instead he sighed and said "Yes, is good rock, But maybe too rich for me. I am but a poor…"

Mr. Bellknap gave out a hearty laugh. He knew this game, too, and had played it with Tico's father many times. He knew the extent of the De La Porto family wealth and knew well that Tico could afford this stone. He also knew Tico coveted it. A dealer just senses these things. He also knew that Tico would spare no expense when it came to a wedding ring for his *Angelica*. But the bartering process must be respected.

Bellknap knew the price he would ask and the price he would take. Tico knew that he would not need to pay the first price quoted. With all this in mind, the three of them returned to Bellknap's desk to practice "the art of the deal."

When the deal was finally struck, Bellknap complained that he had been cheated and Tico was bemoaning the fact that the sale had robbed all of the future children of this union of food and clothing and even shelter. It had been great sport and both men had enjoyed it immensely. Bellknap called the salesman in to bring them coffee and brandy. It gave Tico some satisfaction to see the salesman have to serve those he had so arrogantly treated previously.

While they were having coffee, Tico opened the chamois bag.

One magnificent stone at a time came out of Tico's well-worn chamois skin bag. The first one was the ruby. Bellknap placed it on the black velvet cloth and pulled out his loupe to have a closer look.

The jeweler peered a long time at the stone and realized that the glowing stone was carved into the head of a Sultan. The figure sported a turban and a wicked smile that reminded him of a genie just liberated from his bottle. It was of the highest quality and exquisitely designed.

Bellknap had never seen anything like it before, but he knew the stone by reputation. He let out a long, low whistle of amazement and admiration for the intricate work. "Burma. Yes, the famous 'El Sultano' I have heard of it but never seen it, there are no words to describe such a treasure."

"Yes," said Tico. "Burma. Was my *Abuela's*…uh, you know…you say Grandmother. I was her favorite *Nieto*." Tico chuckled. "Only one, too. My *Abuelo* find it in India. Nobody know who the carver was. Some say it is magic. Only to be give to one you love. He give to my *Abuela* when he marry."

"This is worth more than you would make in a lifetime of working at the circus. What are you going to do with it?" he asked.

"I think a nice *lavaliere* for my Angel," he said with a smile. "She like, yes, she like. To hang here below lovely throat." And Tico pointed to a place on his chest where he thought it might hang on his *Angelica*. "Maybe with some gold. Yes, gold cage around it. Yes, I think so." He turned to Angel, and taking the ever-present pad from his pocket, he wrote: *Angelica, my beloved. This is stone was give to Mia Abuela by Mia Abuelo. Now I give to you. You to design nice cage of gold for to surround it. OK?*

Angel took the pencil and without hesitation drew a lovely, delicate gold wire cage to surround the huge stone and a small loop to hold it to the chain. When Tico handed the drawing to Bellknap he was more than impressed.

by Loma A. Phegley

"My, my. What a sense of design and such talent. You wouldn't consider going to work for me, now, would you?"

Tico answered for her. "Maybe you notice. She not talk. Not hear either. But I tell you I have other plans for us. We go to my father and my sainted mamma in Argentina soon. To be marry there. My mamma like that, I think."

"Yes, I think you are right. Knowing your mother as I do, I am sure she would be ecstatic to see her only son married in the family home. You have never been there, but I can tell you that this home in Argentina is every bit as elegant as the family home in Spain. Your mother is just old fashioned enough that such a wedding will be a social event that the guests will talk about for years to come."

Tico laughed, "Yes, my beautiful and sainted mother be very traditional. I am sure she has dreamed me to marry, but never to think it really happen. When she hear that her only son; her little baby boy to take bride, well…" His voice trailed off in an unfinished sentence. "And," he continued, "wait until she see my *Angelica*. She be vision from heaven send to me by God himself. Of this I sure!" To hide his tears Tico began to sort through the rest of his cache of gems that he had carried with him in his little chamois skin bag all the way from Spain and all over the country here in America. He selected some nice one-carat diamonds from the pile of stones.

"These for studs. You know for ears. My friends…yes, are men, but I think they wear one in right ear each. Look good. Let us see. Yes. One for Primo, one for Ivan, what you say? And this one." He selected an enormous rock from the pile and said, "Ring, set in gold and platinum. Here is design my Angel do. Is for Mr. B. Ring for Mr. B. He like, no? OK, these for big gold hoop ear things for Star. *Angelica* have design, and this, this big emerald is for ring for my dear sweet friend, Mary Lou. She need something very special. She very special. Oh. I most to forget. Here is stone to make stick pin for ol' Charlie 'One Shoe.' I not to think he wear ear stud." Tico handed Bellknap the designs Angel had made for Star's "ear things" and Mary Lou's ring, as well as the ring for Mr. B.

"Well, Teodoro, these are all workable designs, I suppose the De La Porto family will utilize the talents of your wife. She is destined to become famous for her style and design, of that I am sure."

"Now all of my good friends have some small tokens and remember Tico."

"Ah, my good friend, I am sure you will be remembered even without these tributes."

"Well, OK. How long to come back to get stuff you make up?" queried Tico.

"Hmmm. Let us see. What about a month? I shall put my people to work on this as soon as you leave here. How does that sound?"

After saying their good byes and deciding when to return, Tico and Angel left the shop to return to their rooms at the hotel. Tico was tired and his bad leg hurt. He took out his ever-present pad and wrote to Angel. *Tonight we eat dinner in room. Here. We have some nice lobster, maybe a Caesar salad, fresh asparagus…and for desert…hmmm. Let me see…* He raised the pencil, thinking. Angel took the pencil and wrote *Tico, my beloved!* Tico laughed and wrote, *Well, we shall see. We shall see.* And they both collapsed on the bed laughing.

After dinner and "desert," Tico lay awake, thinking. Yes, he thought, *it is just like my mamma say. 'Life like river, It will surround you but ya' gotta 'keep swimming.' Well, if like this, I keep swimming forever.'*

The next morning, Tico awoke first and laid gazing at his "Sleeping Beauty." Finally, he laid his hand on Angel's breast and said, "Up, my sweet and lovely. Time to go soon." He and Angel took a taxi all the way to Walnut Creek where the circus had it's next engagement. Tico explained to Angel. "Hell, I rich man. Is better live rich, so we live rich."

Chapter Twenty:
The End Of An Era

When Tico returned to Contra Costa County Fair Grounds, he decided it was a good time to discuss his plans with Mr. B, so he went to the office trailer. Mr. B said, "Ah, just the man I want to see. Come in, come in." He asked Tico to go over the books with him in detail, and perform a preliminary assessment of the worth of the circus. They combed through the numbers and the bookkeeping, with Mr. B congratulating Tico on a great job in taking over the business side of the circus that his late wife had abandoned. Mr. B was grateful for his good business head and his help over the few years they'd been together.

Soon the two men lapsed into a reverie of memories about the circus.

They spoke of Phillipe and his daring ace adventures in the sky, and of the baby elephant Arnold, who had shat all over Mr. B's new convertible. Of the insurance money that had paid off, and how the whole circus had fooled the insurance company. Tico ribbed Mr. B about getting a car with a hard top next.

They talked of Hiram and Mary Lou, and how Tico hoped his good friend would someday escape from such a man, about her kind heart, and the clothing she'd made for *Angelica* so beautifully.

They talked about Starshine a little, and although it was a subject Mr. B was usually mute about, he let Tico know that he knew that the crew knew the two were lovers. Tico finally got around to telling Mr. B about his plans to marry Angel and go to Argentina to join his family. "I have write to my mamma about my Angel and I not hear back yet. But my mamma be so happy to hear her little baby boy to marry. I know she never think to happen in a million years."

Mr. B said, "Good for you, Tico. Good. And now I have some news I wish to share with you. I had good reason to have you peruse the books just now. I want you to be the first to know. I'm selling the circus. I'll have enough money to retire, and I want to pass this outfit along to someone who can afford to invest in some new equipment, tents, trucks and the like. It came down to either investing a considerable sum in new gear, or letting her go while she still has some value," he told Tico.

"I wanted to get your opinion," he added.

"Hmmmm. Is good time to sell," said Tico, and he went on to explain some things about the depreciation of some of the equipment and what kind of money would be needed to upgrade it. The two also discussed the aging performers, and how long they expected to be around, which wasn't long.

Tico was still surprised by what seemed like Mr. B's sudden decision though, and concerned about the performers who would lose their jobs, but Mr. B reassured him.

"I will make arrangements with the new owners that all employees may remain if they wish, or I won't sell to them. I have someone who's interested, and they've assured me that they will agree to this. But I would appreciate it if you do not speak of this to the others yet. Since you do the books here, you will be privy to all of the facts of the sale. In fact, I'd like you to assist in the negotiations of the transaction," he added.

"Yes, sure. You know Tico help. Anytime. Just call. OK, I go now to cook *comida* for my lady. Maybe tonight I cook rice and..."

"Hey," said Mr. B, "don't talk about eating. I have been so damned busy all day I never got to eat. I'm already so hungry I could eat the ass out of a rag doll!"

Tico laughed.

"Bon aperitif, amigo. Bon aperitif."

Walking back across the grounds, Tico encountered Hiram with a group of roustabouts around him. Hiram was talking in his usual drunken and slurred voice, loud enough to be heard in the next county.

"Why, hell," he was saying, "that little piece of fluff is sure enough a cute one. No bigger'n a minute. Can't see what she sees in that ugly little Jew bastard. I betcha' his dick ain't no bigger'n a peanut. Can't keep a gal like her less'n ya got a big prick. Them little ones like them big 'uns. Just wait 'til she gets a taste of what Ol' Hiram's got here for her."

Hiram covered his genitalia with one of his freckled hands and shook it in a lewd gesture.

"She'll throw rocks at that dwarf. When he's toe to toe with her, his nose is in it, and when he's nose to nose with her, his toes is in it!"

Hiram roared at his own cleverness, but no one else did. He sensed something was wrong, and turned around to see Tico standing behind him.

He tried to let Tico in on the joke by saying, "ain't that so, Tico?"

Tico said nothing. He just glared at the vulgar cretin, walked over to Charlie's truck, reached through the open door, and pulled a lead pipe from off the floorboard. Then he walked back over to Hiram and stood behind him.

Tico took the pipe firmly in hand and hit Hiram with a forceful blow across the right ankle. Hiram took a second to register what had happened, then screamed in pain and fell to the ground. Tico raised the pipe again and hit the downed man another whack on his left ankle before Hiram had a chance to fully register what had happened the first time.

By now, Hiram was in so much pain he was writhing in the dirt, still screaming.

"You little Jew fucker! You ugly little bastard. I'll kill you for this. I'll have you throwed in jail. I'll have the cops onto ya!"

The roustabouts cleared the way for Tico to continue. No one was inclined to come to Hiram's rescue, most believing he deserved what he got. There was a code about respecting other men's lady folk, and Hiram had violated that big time.

Tico remained calm.

"No, you do not do anything like any of that stuff. You big bag of wind. Coward. I ever hear you say one more word about my Angel, I kill you. I cut off you balls and make you eat 'em. Then I kill you! You understand? *Comprende*? You hear good?"

Tico raised the pipe again and brought it down on one of Hiram's hands. Hiram had not had the sense to get out of his way, and he couldn't move anyway with both ankles fractured. In a New York second his hand swelled up to the size of a hand of bananas. There was a bit more screaming until Tico raised the pipe again. The anger was the force behind his blows and it made him strong, but Hiram put up his good hand to indicate he'd had enough.

"Yeah, yeah. I hear. I hear," he said with a pleading tone.

By now, the roustabouts had melted into the rows between the trailers and tents.

Ivan and Primo had heard the screaming and had come out to see what was going on. Ivan knelt beside the now writhing Hiram, who gasped in a half scream and a half moan, "Stop him Ivan. Help! Get this dwarf off'n me!"

Hiram thought Ivan had come to rescue him as the tall Turk knelt down, but Ivan said, "Turks have old time way for guys like you. Next time I cut open you belly and pull you guts out. Let you crawl in dirt and drag 'em all over. Then I cut tendon in back of foot. No let any peoples help you. Let you flop in dust. That what you want? Ivan will do. Now hear Tico and Ivan."

"You goddamn dirty A-rab. I thought you came over here to help me," said Hiram near tears.

"You think wrong," said Ivan, and he got up and walked over to stand by Tico.

Primo spat in the dirt close to Hiram's face and when Hiram looked at him, Primo drew the menacing, crooked arthritic finger across his neck in a throat-slitting gesture.

Ivan did help some. He dragged the helpless Hiram to his trailer door and said, "One thing I forget. You never, not never, hit you wife again. Never touch her mean like. You do again, you be very sorry guy, I tell you."

Ivan's soft spot for Mary Lou was showing.

"I tell you, too. When you to walk again, you leave. Go far away. No to ever see you face what look like asshole never again!!!"

Under his breath, as Ivan turned to talk to someone else, and not loud enough to be heard, Hiram said, "who the fuck does he think he is, talking about my wife?"

Mary Lou heard the commotion when it reached her trailer door, and came out to see the sorry shape her husband was in.

"Who caught up with you and beat yer ass this time?" she asked him.

Hiram whimpered. "Tico. That dirty little Jew son of a bitchin' fucker! I'll get his ass. Yes sir. I will. I woulda' kilt him 'cept someone stopped me."

And then he passed out from the liquor and the pain of three fractured limbs.

Ivan was still standing there.

"Ivan, drag this sorry asshole to the feed tent and get Mr. B. Let him fix this stinking drunk up. I ain't touching him again," said his wife.

"With pleasure," said Ivan, and he smiled as he turned away, dragging the carcass of Hiram.

Hauling him by the back of his shirt collar, Ivan drug him all the way to the feed tent and called Mr. B, who came and bound Hiram's ankles. He did it because Hiram was part of his show, but he didn't blame Tico. He understood that Hiram had gone too far.

Hiram, meanwhile, was not able to walk for nearly three weeks. For all that time he cussed Tico out and threatened to kill or maim him. But by now everyone else was in agreement with Mr. B, Ivan and Primo. Most of the crew just laughed at him for getting disabled by a dwarf only half his size.

When the pain got too intense, and Hiram's withdrawal from booze nearly drove the troupe crazy listening to him whine and babble nonsense in his high pitched annoying voice. Starshine would bring him a bottle of the potato vodka Primo had tried to make and failed. It was the nastiest tasting shit on the face of the planet, but Hiram got drunk on it nonetheless. He was the worst kind of drunk, and would drink anything that even remotely smelled like booze. Hiram never even knew it tasted so bad after the first gulp, and he drank himself into oblivion and passed out, giving the others some peace.

Of course, Hiram thought that Star was bringing him the bottle because she was in love with him, a mistaken idea and she was damn quick about disabusing him of such an impossible notion.

She handed him his bottle of hooch one day, and he reached out to touch her rear end. She whirled around and yelled, "You ugly, stinking, diseased, drunken piece of alligator shit! Never touch this person again. You try it, I turn you into frog! No. Is insult to frog. I turn you into cockroach. Then I call you wife and say, 'hey you nice girl, come over here and step on this cockroach for me!' Then I call everybody to come see old ugly, stink, squashed into pile of cockroach guts for good laugh!"

Hiram was not sure she could or would conjure up such a spell, but he took no chances.

"OK, you fucking gypsy whore. Didn't want to touch your stupid ass anyway!"

Star let out a scream like a locomotive whistle.

"Aaaiiieeeaaah! You are now a cockroach! Watch this spell!" And she began to dance around the helpless drunk, pouring the potent potato brew in a circle around him where he sat on the ground. She chanted in Romany all the while.

"Now you just quit that!" yelled Hiram. "I need that booze for the pain. The pain! Mr. Beeee! Make her stop and give me my medicine!"

Laughing, Mr. B took the bottle from Star and handed it to Hiram, who gulped it down so greedily, he emptied the rest of it into his thirsty gut.

As he was passing out, Star leaned close to his ear and whispered to him.

"You wait. In night time, you be big ugly cockroach."

Then she dropped a lighted match into the circle of booze she had poured around him. The nasty stuff ignited the circle in the dirt surrounding Hiram.

"You in hell now," she said, as she walked away.

Hiram was not a cockroach in the morning, but the hairs on his arms were singed. The fire hadn't lasted long but it had scared him. Hiram's hangover the next day was so powerful, he might as well have been in hell. And the remainder of his days would not improve much as the circus began its run in Walnut Creek in the final days of its existence, where Hiram's days were also numbered. He'd made too many enemies who were just waiting for him to do himself in with the drink. The crew envisioned an unpleasant end for the man who had tortured the good woman they called "Tilly," and they waited and watched.

Chapter Twenty-One:
"Tico My Beloved"

The air smelled warm as an early summer breeze wafted through town, and the circus crew was busy getting another performance ready for the evening's entertainment. A certain nostalgia hung in the air and there was a pregnant feeling in the air now that the circus was completing its run at the end of this season.

Plans for some of the long timers like the Primos were in place, contributing to the feeling. The flying trapeze artists were all ready to settle down in San Francisco, and move on to their future lives. While much of the crew was transient, some of the other old timers were beginning to plan their retirements and the atmosphere was both electric and heavy with the possibility of impending changes.

The other shoe dropped, just as Doc predicted it would. Skookum announced that he and Mirriam were leaving together to go to Chicago. Doc was dismayed, as he was pretty certain that Skookum would one-day wake up dead. Mirriam was a killer. She liked killing. Although she fucked every man with a dick that was willing, she really hated men. Doc knew this and tried to tell the besotted Skookum that he was in danger, but Skookum just laughed. "Naw, Doc. She likes to play around, but she loves me and I know better than to cheat on her. Then she might kill me. But what the hell. She is some woman and I will be OK. Don't worry about me. I'm a big boy."

Angelica had become an integral part of the life of Tico and of the circus having lived with them for several months. This lovely day found her where she could often be found, in Mary Lou's trailer, pinning up

by Loma A. Phegley

the hem of a new dress she had designed for the portly woman, who was less and less portly these days.

Angel had designed and Mary Lou had sewn several new dresses, since nothing she owned fit anymore. Mary Lou had stuck to her diet, and the thyroid pills had been extremely helpful in getting her weight under control.

The new dress designs hit at mid knee, which was much shorter in length than she normally wore. As the weight melted away, Mary Lou had gained confidence and with it, had raised her hemline. She was so proud of the pounds she'd dropped, and knew she looked normal, now, for the first time since childhood. The slinky dress Angel was hemming showed her still ample bosom daringly and the hem at mid knee was pretty brassy for this day and time. But Mary Lou was a new person. With her weight down to a little less than two hundred pounds, she felt as slim as a movie star. It had been at a bit more than four hundred and seven pounds when she had begun her weight loss program.

Interrupting their pinning and measuring, there was a knock on the door, and the two women welcomed Doc Brady in to have a cup of coffee. Doc loved his caffeine.

"Hand me them pins, Doc," said Mary Lou. "She gotta' pin the hem up so it'll be straight and I'm makin' it a little bit shorter than my old stuff. Do you like this material?"

"Very pretty, Mary Lou. You look stunning in that frock," he said. "Now, let's see…" he continued, taking the little book from his pocket he'd been recording her weight loss in, and flipping through pages.

"Hmmmm. To date you have lost exactly two hundred and twelve pounds. This has got to be some kind of a record! Man, oh man! Am I ever proud of you!"

"Yeah, and now I can weigh myself on those bathroom scales ya' got for me. I'm proud of me too," she said, beaming.

Angel had drawn some wonderful designs for Mary Lou's new figure, that showed off her ample bosom and even a little leg. They were

· 153 ·

sparkly and sequined and the former fat lady was now singing up a storm in the show, instead of appearing as a sideshow freak. The crowds loved her, and she loved singing. Her music pulled the whole show together, and gave the performers a chance to change clothes and acts. Her voice was amazing and she could have been on stage just about anywhere. But she was comfortable with the circus. Although she saw very little of Hiram, she knew he was still her husband and she would have to deal with getting rid of him for good, and very soon.

Mary Lou had also begun to notice it when men took a liking to her. They opened doors, took her arm to help her cross the street, and did all kinds of chivalrous thing that they'd never done before when she was fatter. And there were some funny changes too that she was noticing. Some of the women held their men closer to them when she was around, and some were a little jealous now that she was both slimmer and a star performer. Losing weight also alienated some of her former women friends, and caused some of her former men friends to be more flirtatious. But her best friends remained unchanged.

Mary Lou, standing on a chair while Angel pinned the hem, looked down and tugged on the dress to get the deaf girl's attention.

"When are you and Tico getting married?" she formed her lips around the words deliberately so Angel could read them.

Angel laughed, shrugged her shoulders, and picked up the pad and pencil they'd been using to communicate.

He hasn't formally asked me yet! But we have talked about it a little. My Tico wants to wait until we get to his father's house in Argentina. He wants us to have a big formal wedding, but I think he wants it more than I do.

She continued to write, while Doc and Mary Lou talked about the weight loss and the medication. Mary Lou also took care of some hand stitching on another dress while she chatted with Doc.

Angel wrote: *I want to say something to you and to Mary Lou. You have been my friends since I came here and I want to set your minds at ease about me and Tico. I am afraid you might think I will do something to* hurt him just because of what he is. Maybe to the world, Tico is not hand-some. Not the man many girls dream about marrying. But I never had a dream to marry anyone. I do not see Tico with the same eyes others see him. I see him as the person he would have been if he had not been born a dwarf.

My Tico is not ugly to me. I lived all of my life in a place where there were really ugly people. Tico has a beautiful soul, and I see that clearly when I look at him.

In my life, no one really wanted me, although some used me because I had no one to protect me from all the bad people who made me do things I did not want to do. I could not help myself. I was but a child and weak. My parents or my grandmother, whoever that woman was, took me, their little child, to a place where it was sometimes like the depths of hell.

How could they do this to a little baby that was given to them to love and care for? A baby is a gift, not a possession. I endured much, and did not deserve to suffer so much.

But there were people there who cared for me and taught me. Professor Brockhurst was an English teacher at the University of Arkansas. He washed his hands a hundred times a day until they were bloody. He talked to himself non-stop, and he killed his wife after he found her in bed with another man. He told me he was sorry that he had done such a wicked thing, but he taught me to read and write on the days when he knew what was going on. He found me books like "Ulysse"s and "Jason and the Golden Fleece." He recited poetry and Shakespeare, and even though I couldn't hear him, I felt it when he spoke strongly and saw his emotion in the read-ing.

Mr. Aramis taught me math on an abacus. I am very good at it. The abacus is only part of it. I have a knack for design and for geometry, too.

Mr. Van Der Hoosen taught me to draw and to paint, and Madame Zia taught me to dance.

I can write several languages a little, and my best language, after English, is Spanish.

So in some ways, I have been fortunate. But I have never been so lucky as when my Tico found me and told me he loved me. I will always love this fine man. He is not ugly to me. He is my savior, my guardian and my family. He will take me home to be part of his family, and I will be worthy of him and make him proud of me. I will try to help him heal his wounds and he will help me heal mine. I will kiss his crooked body and make it better. I will rub his aching legs and comb his hair and he will cook for me and love me.

Mr. Aramis told me, 'hope springs eternal in the human breast.' I believe that since my hope for a better life never dimmed. It is what I have lived with all my life, and I suspect that Tico has too.

With that, Angel put the pencil down, and shared her note with Doc and Mary Lou. They read, simultaneously nodding their heads and gave her a big hug when they'd finished.

Then she turned to Doc with a serious look on her face, and took the pencil and pad back to ask him a question that had been on her mind.

Doc, if we have children, will they be alright? I worry, but I have said nothing to Tico.

Katerine, now called Angel, laid the pencil down and flexed her tiny fingers. It had been a long note.

Doc Brady picked up the paper, read the question, took the pen and responded.

Well, my dear. You are wise beyond your years. Adversity will turn us either for or against life. Looks like you and Tico will make it. And not to worry, your children have as good a chance of being normal as anybody else's.

It was obvious that Doc Brady was touched by the courage of a girl so young. He too was strengthened by her outlook. After all, hadn't she said 'hope springs eternal?' Maybe there was hope for him as well. Maybe even for Mary Lou. She was certainly doing well on her diet, and Doc took a certain amount of personal pride in her monumental weight loss. He was her partner in the deed. And he had accomplished something personal along with her.

by Loma A. Phegley

Doc had not touched a drop of alcohol since Mary Lou started her diet. They'd made a pact, and both of them had kept their word. Doc had even applied for a job at Fort Miley Veteran's Hospital in San Francisco. He knew he could not be a doctor, so he had applied for a job in the research department, and was awaiting a reply from them. He had also written to his son and daughter, and gotten a very kind and encouraging letter from the girl. His daughter had even said that the boy intended to write as well.

To himself he thought, "I am surrounded by so much courage here in this unlikely setting, and I guess I am part of it. Hope does, indeed, spring eternal. It shall sustain me. I shall forever hope."

To Angel and Mary Lou he said, "Well, it is time for my din-din. I believe I would like lobster thermador, a bit of Brie cheese…"

Mary Lou held up her hand to stop him from saying any more.

"Dream on, Doc, but not out loud. Tonight it will be a big green salad at my house and a bowl of soup. Maybe I'll splurge on croutons. Gourmet stuff, but you are welcome. And hey! Jell-O for desert, and tonight it's strawberry!"

"Gourmet Jell-O. Ah, yes. Should I dress for dinner at your place Mary Lou?" he asked.

"Well, you can come nekked if ya want. I sure won't be shocked," Mary Lou laughed heartily.

"Good. Then see you about five-ish, eh, what 'ol girl?" And Doc was out the door.

"Pip, pip, old boy. Five-ish it is."

Mary Lou was still laughing when Angel gently stuck a pin into her behind.

She looked down to see that Angel was also laughing.

Life was good for Mary Lou these days. She had lost most of the weight she had set out to. Hiram was drunk most of the time, so she didn't have to deal with him much, and she was relieved when he passed out each day before noon.

In fact, Mary Lou had secretly formed a close alliance with Ivan. She visited him after Hiram passed out, and they became close friends. He was sympathetic and understanding, and he obviously cared a great deal for her. He had begun to touch her in little ways, like putting his arm around her and kissing her on the cheek. His touch made her tummy do little flips.

She also modeled some of her new clothes for him, and he kidded her about how perfect she was, but added that he thought she had always been perfect, and encouraged her to love herself, recognize her talents and not lose much more weight. He loved her abundance and felt she was just right and always had been. She knew it was time to dump Hiram. Long overdue, in fact. She and Ivan were even tentatively talking about making future plans together and waiting for the right time to implement them.

Mary Lou was also successful in something besides whoring, and that was singing, which was another dream come true. She came off stage every night feeling on top of the world, and Ivan always seemed to be nearby to give her a wink and a nod, and to call her "Little Blossom." Hiram was absent as often as he was there performing. Mr. B was constantly on Hiram for not showing up, but he was wise enough to have a stand-by clown to do the work.

It would not be long before Mary Lou's life changed again for the better. The little girl whose daddy made a whore and a fat lady out of her, and who said no man would ever want her, was now married, pleasingly plump, an amazing songstress, beautifully outfitted, and quite attractive. Mary Lou, the woman all the performers said had a heart as big as all outdoors, could scarcely believe life could get any better, but just around the corner, several nice surprises would catapult her into an even sweeter life.

Chapter Twenty-Two:
The Negotiations

Travis Young and Bob Parsons, the two representatives from Ringling Brothers who had been sent to negotiate the purchase of Billy Bailey's circus, were seated in Mr. B's small office trailer. It was nine o'clock in the morning, and the men had stayed the night at a local motel to make their morning meeting on time.

Travis Young was a man of average height, with mousy brown hair, a thin moustache that drooped at the ends pulling his face downward, and a rounded felt hat that made him look a little comical. He was a serious negotiator, with several successes behind him that gave him an air of arrogance. He put his hat on the table and gave his coat to Mr. B when he entered the trailer, sat down, and brought out a pile of papers that carried some of the details of the Ringling Brother's offer.

Bob Parsons had black hair that ran in a 2-inch strip around the lower part of his head. He was only in his late thirties, and prematurely bald, which made him a little insecure and apologetic. Parsons played the mild-mannered side-kick to Young, gaining the trust of the seller so as to rescue the deal if the negotiations got out of hand. But there was a glint in his eye that reminded Mr. B of a used car salesman. His suave manner was just a little too fake and unbelievable, and one of his front teeth had a bit of gold on it that threw a beam across the room if it was hit with sunlight.

Naturally, Mr. B had brought Tico, whom he introduced as Teodoro De La Porto, but after the introduction, both men more or less ignored the dwarf and focused solely on Mr. B during the negotiations. Tico was already seated, and Mr. B had seen to it that he had a couple of books underneath him, so he would be able to reach the table with greater ease and be on a level with the Ringling people. Mr. B knew the value of eye contact and he also knew that Tico was ready to do battle, so to speak. This should be a show of it's own, he thought. Both men had nodded slightly at Tico when they entered the trailer, but did not know whether or not they were supposed to shake those tiny hands, so they hurriedly moved on to removing their coats and hats. Still, they felt somewhat badly about his condition, and thought they were offering Tico a lifeline when Travis Young said, "Say, Bill, what are you going to do with the dwarf here? We can always use an extra clown or two in the show."

The expression on Tico's face was fierce and angry. Although less than four feet tall, he sat very straight in his chair in an effort to appear taller, and if looks could have killed, those two men would have been stone cold corpses.

Mr. B replied, "In the first place, Mr. De La Porto is not a performer. He is my accountant. Just for your edification, he holds a master's degree in mathematics from the University of Seville, speaks seven languages, and has taught Greek, Latin, French, Mathematics, Astronomy, and Science to children and adults. If you wish to speak with him, please do so directly. Be advised, also, that his skill as a contract negotiator is legendary. It will be your privilege to deal with him as my representative."

Tico gave Mr. B a stiff, but courtly nod and his eyes shot darts at the two guests.

Tico talked of himself in the third person.

"This dwarf speak English not well, but adequately. However, I understand very, very well."

He smiled a broad, toothy, somewhat menacing smile and continued.

"I take it that you not aware Attila the Hun was dwarf? *Es verdad*. It is truth. Management and philosophy of this man much admired by all who know and understand it."

Tico allowed a pregnant pause for effect.

"And so now we proceed gentlemen. Beware the tiger, yes?"

His eyes were mere slits and his smile downright evil.

The negotiations were lengthy and involved, and Tico drove a very hard bargain, especially in light of the giant *faux pas* the two visitors had made when they arrived. But not 10 minutes into their dealings, the two Ringling men had gained a profound respect for Teodoro De La Porto.

Tico understood almost immediately that Ringling Brothers wanted the deal badly, and he knew exactly why they wanted it. He had an excellent grasp of the market, and of supply and demand, and Ringling Brothers wanted to expand its operation and needed an established troop to pull it off on the timeline they'd projected. Americans, who had little money to spend, spent it on affordable entertainment, and this operation was definitely well run, had plenty of talent, and the gate would be very satisfying with a minimum amount of equipment upgrade.

By the time all three men had signed on the dotted line, Mr. Bill Bailey was a very well off man. Tico had not only secured his asking price, but some royalties as well. The bonus was totally unexpected by Mr. B, but not by Tico, who had known exactly the outcome before the negotiations had even begun.

"Wow!" said Travis. "I feel like I have just been in a shell game. I am not too sure my bosses will be pleased with the deal I just made for them, but it will be in the high range of what I was allowed to offer."

Then he looked Tico squarely in the eye, and in a most contrite and respectful manner bowed his head slightly.

"Correction, Señor. It is the very top dollar you were authorized to offer, yes?" asked Tico.

Travis smiled and replied, "How astute. Señor De La Porto, I wish to offer my profound apologies to you. I did not mean to offend you by devaluing your worth as a professional. I am a graduate of New York

University and I certainly know respect and good manners. But I have let myself become an insensitive clod in my dealings with the rough crowd that makes up most circus crews. Some of my teachers at the school where I took my business courses could take lessons from you and be much better off for it. Forgive me, sir."

With a quiet dignity that was Teodoro De La Porto, the businessman, Tico inclined his head ever so slightly, waved his hand in a gesture of dismissal, and said, "*No hay de que*. It is forgotten. Not even a memory."

At that, Mr. B drew a box of very fine Cuban cigars from his desk drawer. He offered the box around, and each man took one. Then from a fancy crystal decanter, he poured each one of the four men a three finger shot of some of Papa Primo's most desirable whiskey. Travis, Mr. B, and Tico rolled the cigar around in their fingers, clipped the end with the cutter, drew the fine tobacco stick along the bottom of their noses, and lit the ends. Then they turned to the liquor, rolled it around in the glass, and smelled its bouquet with a show of appreciation. But Parsons went straight for the drink, and laid the cigar down to deal with it later.

"My God!" exclaimed Parsons. "This is nectar from the Gods! I have never had such a fine drink of whiskey. Where did you come by this gift of the God Bacchus? My father would assassinate the president for such a drink!"

Mr. B laughed heartily, and told Parsons that the whisky was the courtesy of a master vintner he knew.

"I too have never tasted such a liquor. Not before, and not since. I fear, however, that the supply is not only limited, but the method of creation is a closely guarded secret. I assure you, if I had the recipe I would sell it and be a millionaire tomorrow. But alas, I expect the creation will die with its creator. However, he may have a few bottles to sell you. I will ask, and pass along his answer to you by letter if you would like."

"May I offer a toast to the art of the deal?" asked Tico, as he raised his glass. "It is a time honored toast in my country." In Spanish, he said,

"Here's to the fucking you just took. Good luck with the turkey you have just purchased."

Travis began to laugh so hard he almost snorted his whisky through his nose.

But instead he said, "When I told you I went to University I did not tell you I also took language courses, Spanish being the one I studied most. So here is my toast to you. 'May you all die with a full belly and a hard dick.'" He delivered it in a perfect Castilian Spanish. Tico did not share the joke with Parsons or with Mr. B, but both men had a hearty laugh over it.

Travis went on to say, "And a toast to the booze. May it last forever." Mr. B was feeling a very lightheaded from all that drink and very little food, so he stood up to signal an end to the deal, and the other men followed his example. Tico asked Travis if he was interested in considering the purchase of some fine jewels before he left, and Travis said he was. Parsons was also interested in at least seeing some beautiful stones, so Tico pulled out his ever-present chamois skin bag. He ended up selling Travis a huge ruby and a few smaller diamonds and Tico was several hundred dollars richer. He'd made a fair deal with them, selling the ruby and two of the stones he still had left. But if the deal was weighted, it was weighted in Tico's favor. He had purchased the gems for very little and sold them for an excellent profit. Whenever he could add a zero or two on to the purchase price, Tico thought it was a good deal. It was not that he needed the money. He was a dealer and when he was practicing the art of the deal, he was ruthless. He had learned the art of the deal from the many experts with whom his father traded, many of them Chinese, Swiss and hard-nosed Jews. These people were traders of the highest order. His father was the best of them all.

By day's end, Mr. B was drunk and rich, the two men from Ringling Brothers were quite drunk, and Tico was also richer and knee-walking drunk.

Tico rolled down the stairs of the office trailer and passed out right there. That is where Ivan found him. Ivan took him home and put him into his bed, telling Angel that she had nothing to be alarmed about. "He just drunk, little one. He make good deal for circus. He very pride. Deserve to be drunk." Poor Tico slept until late the next morning. He couldn't go to work all day and part of the next day was given over to sleeping and taking headache powders.

Chapter Twenty-Three:
Tico And The Angel Fly Away

Time seemed to creep along for Tico until the day he and Angel would go back to San Francisco to get the rings and the other jewelry from Mr. Bellknap. Tico knew it would be a few months before the Barnum people took over the circus. He knew it would soon be time to go back to the city and pick up the finished jewelry from Harvey Bellknap.

They played several towns in and around the Central Valley. It seemed to him that they all looked alike. He was restless to get going toward his new home in Argentina. He had heard from his mother and sent pictures of his *Angelica*. His family, who it turned out had despaired of ever seeing their son again, was overjoyed at the prospect of not only having him home again, but of his impending marriage. It was an accomplishment the whole family had thought was never to be for their beloved son, so afflicted with dwarfism.

By now, Tico had had all of his money transferred to the Bank of America in California, and was personally a very wealthy young man, although he remained with the circus until it would be time to leave. When the time came to go see Mr. Bellknap, they were in Oakland, just across the bay from San Francisco, Tico hired a taxi to take them there at the appointed time when Bellknap had said the jewelry would be ready. Angel had only ridden the ferry twice on their last trip over. Still, she was so excited she stood on the deck the whole time, drawing pictures of the city skyline, the people, the ferry, the taxi and the driver. She drew children and the bay looking toward Alcatraz, the ships and even the clouds. While she played about the ferryboat, Tico napped. He dreamed that he was sitting at a sidewalk cafe in Paris. His *Angelica* was beside him. He was drinking Turkish coffee and washing it down with Kircsh. He was smoking little Italian cigars that looked like dog turds and tasted like *manuro de El Toro*. His legs were straight and he looked just like his handsome father. When he woke, he looked around and realizing where he was he said to himself, "*Ah, yes. Nice dream, But only one dream at a time, Tico. Only one dream at a time.*"

Tico had booked two rooms at the Saint Francis again. They went immediately to the hotel. From the rooms, Tico telephoned Mr. Bellknap.

As always, the jeweler was delighted to hear from Tico.

"I shall be right over. The jewelry is finished. I believe you will be pleased.

And because I will be carrying so many gems, I will be bringing my son. He is a detective with the city. I do hope you have no objections," said Bellknap.

Tico assured him that the arrangement was fine.

Within the hour, Mr. Bellknap and his son, Harvey Jr., arrived at the Saint Francis, and knocked on the suite of rooms where Tico and Angel were staying.

As soon as introductions were made, young Harvey produced a leather briefcase. Upon opening it, the dazzling display of gold, platinum, rubies, emeralds and diamonds nearly blinded them all. Angel's eyes flew open in amazement. Mr. Bellknap rather formally presented the diamond wedding ring to Tico.

The finished product of the sketch that Angel had made when she designed the setting was revealed for the first time. It was hard to imagine that any setting would do such a magnificent stone justice, but Angel's design set it off brilliantly. Tico took the ring from Bellknap with a slight bow, and turned to Angel. He took her tiny hand in his, and placed the ring on the third finger of her left hand. As was expected, she began to cry tears of joy. Tico patted her hand and spoke to her in Spanish.

"*Hoy, si hoy. Tuesta es mi esposa. Yo te amo. Si, yo te amo mucho. Si, mucho. mucho, mi pajarita.*"

Little Angel, once a child of no hope for love or happiness, shed tears of joy and love and gratitude. She grasped Tico's hand in hers and the tears flowed onto them as she held those dear hands to her lips and kissed them over and over again.

Mr. Bellknap was somewhat embarrassed at this impromptu display of affection. How could he have known what this moment meant to these two little ones? He could only imagine what finding love meant for the dwarf. But to the two lovers, it was nothing short of a miracle. It was the moment they both realized their impossible dreams had come true, and it felt like being reborn into a whole new world.

Mr. Bellknap and his son shifted from one foot to another and stole glances at each another, waiting for the outpouring of adoration to come to an end so the business of trading could once again resume. He interrupted their magic moment after an appropriate interlude.

"Ahem. I take it she is pleased…somewhat," he said.

"A-ha," said Tico, "appears maybe she like this ring…somewhat."

With that, the two men laughed, and resumed their business dealings.

"Here is the emerald ring for Mary Lou, here is the ruby lavaliere for your ladylove, here are the golden hoop earrings for Starshine, and now the diamond ear studs and the stick pin for Charlie. Also, allow me to present the gold ring with the diamond for your friend, Bill Bailey," he said, laying all the jewelry out for display.

Tico took the golden chain with the ruby pendant from the velvet case and dropped it over Angel's head. It rested in all its majesty between her tiny breasts and was a perfect compliment to the pink gabardine suit. The ruby glowed with a mystical ambiance.

"The ruby is happy," said Tico. "My grandmother said good ruby will change with the mood of who is wear it, and with the weather and also with the times."

"Well, I assure you that is true," replied the jeweler. "I have seen many rubies and this one is a gem of the very finest quality. Did you not say that this one belonged to your grandmother as well?"

"*Si*. It came from Burma, and India I think. Maybe from the time of crusades. When my grandfather die, she tell me ruby did not give off the light of its former self. And then when she die, I see for myself. This is true. Ruby was dark and cloudy, until now."

"Ah," continued Tico, "you have done me a great service. Never shall I forget this kindness. You are fine man. I happy to know you. Maybe when I am with my father in Argentina, we do more business, you and I, eh?"

"Absolutely, amigo, absolutely," said Bellknap, and as he handed over the bill he added. "By the way, is this Angel's first trip out of the country?"

Tico told him it was and Bellknap offered the name and number of an excellent photographer where she could get her passport pictures.

The offer sent Tico's mind into a whirl. He had never considered passports. He did not even have one. When he and Ivan had arrived in America, they had just walked off the boat and were never stopped by immigration. Angel had no birth certificate. *Oh, God, what now*, he thought. He nearly panicked, but he covered up his distress and decided Mr. B would know what to do.

Tico went to his own leather briefcase and withdrew a stack of American hundred dollar bills. He laid it on the table. Harvey Jr. picked it up, but did not count it, then placed it in his father's case and locked it without much more than a nod. He took his leave, but his father stayed.

Angel served Angel Food cake and coffee that they had ordered from room service earlier, while Tico and Bellknap chatted like old friends.

by Loma A. Phegley

But soon Bellknap also had to get back to business. The two seemed
sorry to say goodbye, but the conscientious jeweler was distracted from
being away from the office for the afternoon, and Tico also had a lot on
his mind. With promises of keeping in touch and future business deals,
Bellknap left the Saint Francis.

Angel saw and felt her fiancé's worry over the passport, and assured
him it would be alright, but when the two arrived back at the circus
grounds, Tico went straight to Mr. B's office. He burst in excitedly,
speaking high-speed Spanish. Mr. B and Ivan were talking when he
interrupted them and Tico completely forgot his manners in the concern of the moment.

Ivan said, "I think he want to talk about a passport, Mr. B. We not
have any. Neither one of us. We just walk off the ship in New York and
go to Florida."

Tico tried to calm down.

"That not be all! My Angel. She not have a passport, not have a birth
certificate either. What I do Mr. B? What now?"

Mr. B thought for a moment.

"That is a problem, Tico. We'll figure out something here," he
soothed.

Ivan had an idea.

"Hey Tico, you remember Captain Papadopoulas? Runs big fish boat
out of San Diego?"

"Sure," said Tico, "good Greek. I remember."

"OK. He in port right now. San Diego. I know. He send me hashish
last week. He go from here to Chile. Town call Valparaiso. Then he go
around *Tierra Del Fuego* to some port in Argentina. I forget where. He
take you and Angel. No need no fucking passports. Only one problem.
He gotta' leave tomorrow night. No way you can make it by time he go."

But Mr. B was thinking too.

"The hell there isn't! Phillipe! Phillipe can fly them there."

Ivan exploded.

"That crazy Frenchman no fly my family. He get drunk kill them all."

"Aw, come on, Ivan. He hasn't killed anyone yet. Except for that poodle a year or so back. We'll see that he's sober when he leaves. Who cares how drunk he gets after he lets Tico and Angel off in San Diego."

Ivan still did not like the plan, but he finally agreed.

"If he kill everyone dead, he better no come back here again. I break his fucking head and maybe his neck too."

Mr. B reminded Ivan that if he crashed the plane and killed everyone dead, Phillipe's head and neck would already be in pretty bad shape. Nevertheless, Ivan made sure he was the one to propose the plan to Phillipe so he could impart the rules and the threats on his life should anything go wrong. Tico told Ivan what he would be willing to pay for the flight, and Ivan left to go make the deal with the Frenchman.

Meanwhile, Tico and Angel went to pack what few things they would be taking. Angel put the two pinafores, and the pink dress that Mary Lou had made for her into a wedding dress box she had scrounged from behind a J.C. Penney store. Into a borrowed suitcase she packed her two new suits, underwear and shoes, along with the silver fox stole Tico had bought for her in the city. Tico's new suit, his underwear, shoes and even the little walking stick fit tightly into the case.

Angel's vision was to make the pink dress her wedding gown. It was a vision of lace and tulle and organdy that made her look like a doll dressed in cotton candy. Tico has called her a fairy princess when she put it on the first time.

Phillipe was sober when Ivan approached him, and that was a small miracle, although it was still somewhat early in the day. Ivan warned him of dire consequences should anything happen to his little friend and his little friend's lady love. When Phillipe found out what kind of fee Tico was offering him for the trip, he reassured Ivan that he would carry the two to San Diego safe and sound. Ivan told Phillipe he would hold the money until the pilot was back safely with the full report.

by Loma A. Phegley

Five hundred dollars was plenty of motivation to keep Phillipe sober for two days.

The parting between Ivan and Tico was emotional. Both men tried their level best not to cry, but they were fast friends, and Ivan had been Tico's protector in this new and sometimes unwelcoming land. Ivan decided to ride along to the airport in Oakland to see them off, and Mr. B drove the four of them that very night.

"OK, you big ugly Turk. You come see Tico and Angel, you hear Tico? You come!" warned Tico at the airport.

"Sure," assured Ivan. "I come see you little shit. I come. I promise."

And they both shed a tear.

"Yes, Tico miss to see big ugly Turk face every day. You were good friend to Tico. When you go back Mr. B have som'ting for you so remember Tico. He tell you som'ting for Mary Lou and Star, too. You see."

The journey back to the circus was almost silent. Both Ivan and Mr. B were lost in their own thoughts. Ivan thinking about how he would miss Tico, and how his little friend had at long last found love. Ivan blessed the union and wished them many healthy children. He was happy his friend had found such a beautiful lady to be his wife.

Ivan also reflected on his new love, his relationship with his "Little Blossom" He felt lucky to have found such a woman. It sure seemed like she loved him, too. Hooboy.

Mr. B was also lost in thought, remembering all of the things that the circus had meant to him, and about Star and the anticipation of retiring in Sarasota. He wasn't sure he could be idle. Time will tell. A more immediate problem was bothering him. The upcoming transfer of the circus. There would be inventory to take, money transfers; whew, he thought, what a job. And the problem with the two tigers, Barbarossa and Sinbad, who were un-trainable and not suited for a zoo. Everyone knew by now how dangerous they were and no one would buy them. He reckoned he may have to just shoot them himself. He was reluctant to do so, but he knew he might have to, and if he did, they'd make a fine pair of rugs.

Phillipe returned from his trip three days later, and reported directly to Ivan that Angel and Tico had made it to Captain Papadapoulous' ship safely and on time. Ivan handed over the money. Phillipe then proceeded to the Primo trailers where he was met by his father-in-law and his tearful wife, both wanting to know why the trip took so long.

"Ah, yes," he explained, "the good captain had some very important legal papers that had to be delivered with great haste to a city called Reno. And me, being the soul of accommodation, delivered them for him."

"Reno, I know it well," said Papa Primo, suspiciously. "I trust you enjoyed yourself in that big, little city?"

"No, of course not, papa," lied Phillipe. "I had no time for pleasure as I was delivering papers. Yes, taking care of business. Why the good Captain even paid me for my services."

He withdrew one hundred dollars of the five hundred Ivan had just given him and handed it to his wife. "You see, Mon Cherie, all is well that ends well."

But Papa Primo knew, and behind his daughter's back he drew the imaginary knife across his throat with the old, arthritic finger.

Chapter Twenty-Four:

Lust Is The Enemy Of Reason

Captain Ernest P. Bumpo came through the door of the Los Angeles City Police Station at precisely 7:30 a.m., just as he had for the past twelve years he had worked there. He passed under the sign that had been placed there years before by the former Police Chief.

It was meant as a warning to all the cops who read it but none of them ever read it. It was the warning that Nietzsche has penned for just such people as cops.

Those who fight monsters must be careful that in the process they do not become monsters themselves. When you look long into the abyss, it also looks back at you.

Not only did they not read it, it was doubtful they would have even understood it.

Bumpo was a man of great presence, tall, well put-together, fit and a fine man to look at, even as he growled at his secretary.

"When Lieutenant Delaney comes in, send him into my office. Tell him not to fu...uh, mess around, and to get his ass in here pronto."

"Sure Captain, I surely will," cooed Honey Sweringer, a tight blonde that had been on the job for three whole months. She was already in love with the Captain, Lieutenant Clyde Delaney, and a couple of the other cops as well.

Honey was a cutie, but the Captain hardly noticed. It was doubtful he would know her if he met her outside the station house, since he barely made eye contact with her at all. He had no clue that she dressed each morning with him in mind. Her hair was coifed as she thought he would like it, and the neckline of her dresses just low enough to show a little cleavage tastefully. Her skirts were also hemmed just high enough to show a bit of thigh, and she bought heels as high as she could find at the local J.C. Penney store.

When Honey walked through the office, she wiggled her fine little ass until all the cops had powerful visions of raping and ravaging her right there on the spot. Honey was well schooled in how to jiggle her tits and delighted in the reaction of all the guys. But the one she was really interested in didn't seem to give a fuck.

"Fuck." She liked that word ever since she had heard her brother say it to one of his buddies. She had asked what it meant and her brother told her in no uncertain terms. At the age of fifteen, she had been shocked, but the word had a certain ring to it, and now it was the shock value of it that she enjoyed the most. She thought about the reaction she would get if she said, "Fuck you, Captain," or how about "I don't give a fuck, Cap, so go fuck yourself."

But Honey knew she would never say that because she would lose her job and she loved working at L.A.P.D. headquarters. She even liked the smell of the Captain's cigars. She did allow her language to relax in the presence of certain other cops on the force, including Delaney.

"Good morning, Lieutenant Delaney," Honey said in her childish voice when he arrived at work that morning. "The Captain said for you to get your ass into his office, pronto."

The Lieutenant looked at her with a smirk that hid his smile. He laughed, asked her what she was working on as he leaned over her desk, trying to look down her blouse without being caught.

Delaney proceeded to the Captain's office and pulled the door closed as he went in.

"Cap, your secretary is some little chick. She told me you wanted me to get my ass in here pronto," he said.

"And that is exactly what I said," replied the Captain. "I want you to look at this phone bill here. Most of these long distance calls are the ones you have made all over the United States of America about that killer you claim has done all those children. Now, I don't hold with your theory that one man is traveling around the country killing little girls. Too far fetched. Nothing like that has ever happened before and it has not happened now either. I gave you a lot of leeway in this case because you are normally a pretty bright man when it comes to police work, but you are way off base on this one. I can't go with you any further. The phone expense is just the straw that broke the camel's back. You understand, Delaney?"

Delaney just grinned and took a red and green pack of Lucky Strike smokes from his shirt pocket. He took his time about drawing one out and lighting it. When he spoke he did so with an air of gravity. "Cap, I'm almost there. I'm going up to Northern California to a circus this weekend to see a guy about this case..." he began to speak but the captain interrupted.

"You are not going at the expense of the department, I will tell you that!" he said, his voice rising a bit, and his eyes widening in anger as he chewed on the stub of his morning cigar.

"OK, OK, Cap. I'll pay for it myself."

Delaney tried to calm him down.

"I love the circus anyway. My new car needs some miles put on it, and maybe I'll take Honey with me. Strictly business, Cap. Strictly business."

"Honey? Why she's just a kid! You are old enough to be her..."

"Brother, Cap? Her brother? Little Miss Honey is no kid. She's a grown up woman. She's 20 years old, and ripe as a summer peach. I don't suppose you even noticed her sweet ass and even sweeter little titties. Oh, she's old enough. But that is not what I have in mind. I just don't want to go alone. However, I do intend to fuck your little Honey, and if I do, is that a problem?"

The Captain did not answer Delaney, but it was obvious he did not like the idea of the Lieutenant taking Honey on a weekend trip. Of course, he also realized there was damn little, if anything, he could do about it. And there was no policy about dating within the department. Hell, many a cop had found his wife at a secretary's desk in other precincts.

Delaney knew the case inside and out, and he wanted the Captain to understand something before he took the trip to Walnut Creek.

"Captain, I know you think my theories are all wrong, but I want to remind you of some of the facts of the case so when I catch this bastard, everyone will know who did it," he said.

The two men sat opposite each other across the Captain's desk as he listened reluctantly.

"Here about two years ago, we had a little girl killed out in West Hollywood. She was about six years old, if I remember right."

The Captain nodded, said he remembered the case, and that it was bad, very bad.

Delaney agreed with him, saying, "Yes, very bad. I can't get the looks of that little girl out of my mind. She was raped and strangled. There should be a national center to report all of these kinds of crimes so that if we have one happen we could call the center and find out the killer's M.O. and the details and geography of the crimes.

"Without such a crime center, I had to make that many long distance calls. First, I called all of the Attorney General's offices in each of the forty-eight states to find out if they had any such murders in their states in the past five years. Then, if they said they had, I called the Sheriff in each county where the crimes occurred. Those calls gave me dates, an M.O. and locations where the crimes were committed.

"Come look here, Captain," continued Delaney as he led the Captain to a wall in the coffee room, where the detective had placed push pins in a map of the U.S. that was pinned to the wall. The pins were colored according to the year the crime was committed. There were eleven pins in all, which seemed to travel along the southern half of the nation and California.

The Captain's imagination was piqued, and he listened more intently.

"Go on," the Captain said.

"I talked to a Sheriff in Butte County who said he didn't know anything about murders. The only child's death he could recall had been a little girl of about six, who had wandered from her bed and drowned in the Feather River. He said the child had belonged to a circus that was in town at the time. Billy Bailey's Circus."

The two had returned to the Captain's office, and he interrupted Delaney's story of the child serial killer to bark orders at Honey about bringing them some coffee.

"Hey girl, bring us some coffee. Mine black, Delaney wants two sugars. Come on. Get a move on, Honey," he said, then turned his attention back to Delaney.

"Anyway, the mention of the circus triggered something. In another of my inquiries, it seemed like the circus came up, like it was in town when it happened or something. As I recall, that was also Bill Bailey's outfit, and I want to find out more."

He wrapped up his last few words as Honey jiggled into the room with two cups of coffee on a small tray.

Honey's ass wiggled from side to side, and she made sure to hold the coffee tray up at the same level as her boobs. The Captain stared intently. It was the first time he had really looked at Honey closely. He continued his conversation with Delaney as she bent down slightly, spreading her tight skirt across a rounded bottom.

"I see what you mean…yup, I surely do," he said to Delaney as they thanked her for the coffee and she swung her hips out of the room.

Delaney tried to resume his revelations about the case, but they both had to take a moment to reflect on Honey's feminine pulchritude, and their physical reactions to it. The Captain was still thinking about Honey's ass, and how he could have missed such a fine specimen, when he realized he was at work and Delaney was trying to tell him some-thing important.

"So I was saying," Delaney tried again, "the circus was mentioned a couple of times as being in town. That's how one person remembered when the killings occurred, because they'd gone to the circus that week-end. The Butte County child, who allegedly drowned, also has a circus connection. Her Dad owns the outfit, and I can't count on the inves-tigative efforts being accurate either. The Sheriff there has a very poor reputation as a drunkard and an incompetent. He doesn't care much for out-of-towners either, so I'm sure the investigation was sloppy to say the least.

"If this child was indeed murdered, that will mean there could be a connection to the circus, and more investigative work is needed. I'm gonna' talk to this Bill Bailey and get a schedule of where the circus has been performing this year; compare that to where the little girls have been murdered and see if there is a connection. I'm sure he'll cooperate. After all, his own child could have been a victim. Any father would want to help track down a child killer, even if his child really did drown acci-dentally."

"OK," said the Captain. "You go ahead on up there. But the depart-ment cannot justify the expense. You're on your own."

"Fine. I'll go ask Honey if she wants to ride along," he said. As a part-ing shot, he added, "I'm sure she can handle whatever comes up."

The Captain, alone in his office, reflected a few moments on his libido that had come alive slightly as he gazed at Honey and her coffee cups, and also on his own sex life. He was married to the Police Commissioner's daughter, Patricia. Decidedly a matter of ambition, Captain Bumpo now wondered where his youthful lust had gone.

Patricia was a cold, sexless bitch that gave his cock a chill. Through the years, the Captain had trained himself not to think about sex...probably the reason he did not notice Honey. But he was definitely noticing her now, and the icicles on his cock were beginning to thaw.

by Loma A. Phegley

When Delaney mentioned taking Honey up the coast with him, it started the good Captain thinking…contemplating Miss Honey Swerringer's attributes above and beyond her secretarial abilities. For the first time he let himself imagine how that dear little thing would feel in his arms. He thought about her ass and her tits until he had a full-blown erection. Forget the part about in his arms, he really wanted to just fuck her…and now. He threw his cigar stub away and yelled, "Hey, Honey. Come here a minute."

Miss Honey hurried in and was met by a man ready for a good fuck, anyway he had to get it. The first thing he said was, "I want to fuck you. Come over here and lay down on my desk. Come on spread them legs. I have very little time. This is a busy office and we have a lot of work to do."

Honey was so astounded and confused by such a romantic approach she did not say no. Instead, she hiked up her skirt, pulled off her panties, and spread herself across the desk the Captain had cleared with a sweep of his hand. She had wanted him for three months and now she had him.

The Captain pushed her down on the desk, grabbed her legs behind the knees and pulled her toward the fly of his pants. He unzipped them, pulled out his erect cock, and guided it into her. He did just what he said he wanted to do. He fucked her good, and little Honey Swerringer liked it. In fact, she loved it. No man had ever taken her quite like that.

It took him about eight pumps to finish his mission. He stood at the edge of the desk shuddering with the climax for a few seconds. "Take the rest of the day off," he said, then feeling a little guilty at taking advantage of his authority, he reached into his pocket for money.

"Here," he said, giving her a $20, "get yourself something nice. And by the way Honey, that was damn good. We will have to do that again some time. Are you going with Delaney this weekend?"

"Yes," she said taking the money and stuffing it down her brassiere, "unless you don't want me to."

"Sure, go ahead. He's a good enough guy. Enjoy yourself."

When she had gone, the Captain laughed to himself. "At least I beat old Delaney to that. All he will have are my leftovers!"

The warm weather continued and it was balmy all the rest of the week and into the weekend. Delaney had his new Dodge washed and waxed, bought himself a new pair of slacks with a matching sport coat, and picked up a fifth of gin at the liquor store in preparation for the weekend trip.

He thought Honey might be a virgin, and a couple of shots of gin would loosen her up and put her in the mood.

"I'll probably have to teach her the finer points of the art of fucking," he thought. At 8 a.m. on a summery Saturday, Lieutenant Delaney stopped in front of Honey's apartment building. She was ready, and came out the door before he had a chance to get out of his car. He watched as she came down the walkway, bouncing her boobs and twisting her sweet little ass from side to side.

She was dressed for the weekend, and a lot less conservatively than she dressed for the office. She wore a red polka dot halter-top dress, no bra, and white high heeled sandals. Delaney got out and went to the other side of the car, opened the door for her and put his hand on her arm to help her into the seat.

She gently removed his hand from her arm, and placed it on one of her bouncing boobies. She looked him boldly in the eye and asked, "This is going to be a fun trip, isn't it, Lieutenant?"

"You bet, Honey. In fact, I have some fun things planned for us to do that will take our minds off of the job I'm going up there to work on," he said as he massaged the nipple until it became erect.

She let her eyes drift to his crotch. They both obviously had the same thing in mind. He was definitely aroused, and the trip had not even started.

Delaney closed her door and went around to get in on the driver's side. Honey moved over closer to him and put her hand on the inside of his thigh.

Damn, he thought to himself, *we are certainly going to have to make a stop long before we get to our destination. This little gal needs a good fucking, for sure. No need for me to be selfish and withhold it from her. Poor little thing.*

The trip from Los Angeles to Santa Rosa was about six hundred miles one way. Delaney knew if they were to get back in time for work on Monday morning, he was going to have to wheel his new Dodge at a good seventy miles per hour and keep on it. Not much time to give dear little Honey what she so obviously needed and wanted and what he lusted after. But his intent was to make a monumental effort to get the work done, and still stay on schedule.

A little over a hundred miles into the trip, the blue Pacific and the city of Santa Barbara came into brilliant view, and the Lieutenant was unable to endure the things Honey was doing to him. She would stroke his leg up as far as his pants fly, toy with his belt buckle, at his stomach, and squeeze his balls, then let her skirt ride up so he could see her pink panties. The strap on her dress was so loose he could see her nipples.

Honey knew exactly what she was doing to him, and she savored having him out of control. She felt very much in control, but she loved to fuck too.

Delaney pulled off the freeway onto a stretch of beach that was busy on this summertime Saturday. But he knew of a secluded spot the California Highway Patrol sometimes parked, where their cruisers were obscured by several scrub oaks and other trees.

He turned the key off, and Honey looked up into his eyes. He pressed his hand on her breast and kissed her deeply, moving his hand quickly down her waist to her skirt hem. They were both focused on having each other.

Delaney's hands moved as slowly as he could manage up her skirt. He felt the pink panties he had continually seen during their drive, and hooked his index finger under the elastic that surrounded her thighs. Honey helped him pull off her little pink panties, then she pulled him over to the passenger side and straddled his lap.

The red polka dot halter dress was easily pulled down to her waist and her delectable tits bounced in the breeze as the Lieutenant tried to suck one and then the other.

Honey was the kind of gal that was meant to be fucked every hour, on the hour. Delaney had his weapon out, and it stuck straight up out of his trouser fly. Honey put one leg over his lap, and slid it inside her as he groaned. She knew just what to do, as she moved her sweet ass up and down, sliding on his stiffened cock, fastening her lips near his ear and moaning.

"Oh baby, it's so big. I'm gonna' come," she whispered to him close to his ear, and goose bumps sprouted on his arms and back.

And come she did. Delaney felt the first throb of her cunt and was right behind her. They exploded in orgasm, first her then him, as she rubbed her clit against his pelvis bone.

After they held each other for a few moments and the quaking subsided, Delaney said, "Well, so much for teaching you how to fuck, baby!"

"Oh, I been doing this ever since I was fifteen. I love it. Now, we gotta' stop at the next service station so I can clean up," she said.

"Sure," said Delaney, "me too. I want you to know that I plan on doing that again when we stop for the night."

"Of course," said Honey, "probably several times. Wait 'til I tell Captain Bumpo that you have a bigger cock than he does."

"Captain Bumpo?" exclaimed Delaney. "You mean you been boffin' him too?" Delaney was shocked. Really shocked.

"Why not?" she said. "He wanted to right after you left his office yesterday. He just got the urge and we did it right on his desk!"

"Hmmm," he said. But he thought to himself, *this is going to be a weekend to remember. If the Captain is fucking this gal, we don't have to be back to work by Monday morning. He won't dare fire her as long as he knows I know he's doing it. And I don't give a rat's ass if he fires me or not.*

Delaney stopped at a service station and while Honey went in to clean herself up, he did the same. But he finished first and went to the pay phone to put in a call to his boss.

"Bumpo? That you?" he said above the traffic noise. "I've run into a snag here. It's gonna take longer than I thought. We won't be back until, oh, maybe Wednesday. I'm sure that you can do without Honey for a couple of days, now can't you?"

"No, damn it," said the Captain. "I cannot get along without my secretary until Wednesday. I want you two back here at eight a.m. Monday morning and no excuses. You hear, Clyde?"

"Well, I can understand that Cap, but you see, I've taken a fancy to Miss Honey's attributes, like her ability to screw me to death. And by the way, she says I've got a bigger cock than you do. So, since I don't think the present Mrs. Bumpo would…"

"OK Delaney, Wednesday it is. I'll manage without her. Sure. Fine piece of ass, ain't she?" he said. He was understandably pissed off, but under the circumstances he felt he had little choice. As far as Honey was concerned, he reasoned, "Once the cake is cut, who's gonna' miss a slice?"

"See you Wednesday then," said Delaney and he hung up.

The rest of the trip was uneventful, and no more stops were mandatory, only desirable. They ate lunch at a drive-in and dinner at a nice steak house along the road. Delaney chose a decent motel in Ukiah to stay the night and he and Honey had a great time of it. With two beds in the room, they tried out each one, along with the shower and the bathtub.

Little Honey taught Delaney the finer points of the art of fucking, until sheer exhaustion took over and he dropped off to sleep. Both of them were still totally exhausted when they checked out the next morning.

From the desk clerk, Delaney got directions to the Santa Rosa Fairgrounds where Bill Bailey's circus was performing. The two strolled the grounds, eating popcorn and cotton candy. Honey had her fortune told by a gypsy named Starshine, who told her she had a great future in her job. But to herself Star thought Honey would have a great future in anything she undertook because she would sleep her way to the top. Honey encouraged Delaney to have a reading too.

When he entered Star's tent, she said, "You are cop, yes?"

"Yes, I am cop, how did you know?"

"Star know everything," she said.

"Well then maybe you know who killed the little Bailey girl?" he asked her.

Star did not show any change of emotion.

"How you know child was killed? They say she drowned."

"But you know better, don't you Starshine? You know all, see all. Says so right here on your tent."

"You are right. Star see all and maybe not always know all. That baby...someone kill her. She not drowned. Sheriff, drunk, stupid. Not care. I can not see man who did it. He is always...out here."

She gestured as though the killer was out of her sight.

"Was man. That I am sure. This mans, he kill before many times. That I am sure. But I not to see him. Maybe kill more since that. Not know. I tell you all this for free. No charge. Sometimes, I feel this man close to me. Can't see him though. Very evil feeling. Star try very hard, but I think he here with us...sometimes is stronger than other times."

"How about her father?" asked Delaney.

Star thought he was asking whether it could have been her father, when all Delaney had meant to ask was where the father was. Star, mindful of her relationship with Bill Bailey, closed up. Delaney registered that, along with a little flicker of uncertainty.

"Star through, you go now, "she said and waved her hand in a dismissive gesture.

Delaney got up and left the little tent. He had much to think on. He left Honey playing some of the games along the Carnival and went in search of the owner of the circus, William S. Bailey.

He found the office trailer and knocked on the door.

"Come in. It's open," was the reply from inside.

Delaney was greeted by a man of about 40 years old, not too tall, nothing outstanding. Pretty common looking he thought.

"Yes sir, may I be of service to you? I am Bill Bailey and I own this establishment," he said grinning, and holding his hand out to be shaken.

Delaney took the proffered hand and said, "Sir, I am Clyde Delaney of the Los Angeles Police Department. I am here on official business and I surely hope that you *can* be of service."

"Sit down, Mr. Delaney, sit down. I will do what I can. What is the question?"

"I am investigating the deaths...murders...of young children that have happened over the last few years. I do not wish to distress you, but it is my understanding that your own child was killed a few years back. What can you tell me about it?" he asked.

Mr. B held up his hand as though to protect himself from the words. After a moment he answered.

"That was a very tragic time. You may or may not know that my wife, Maude, finally committed suicide because of the loss of our child. She never could get over it. I could hardly get over it myself, but I have so many people depending on me, like a family, I held it together and I have gotten past it and made a life of sorts. You use the words 'murder' and 'killed,' but the Sheriff where it happened said 'accident.' That is very astute of you. Mr. Delaney, my little girl did not wander from her bed and drown in the river. All of us here knew she did not, but we had to accept the verdict and move on," he said.

Mr. B took out a cigar and stuck it in his mouth, but did not light it.

"There is some suspicion and I must admit that it is my own suspicion, that the killer is connected to the circus," said Delaney.

"What makes you think that?" asked Bailey.

"Well, this is only a guess, no evidence to back it up, but everywhere I go for answers, the name of the circus comes up. Now, I will admit, that only the death of your child occurred while the circus was in the same town at the same time. The others have been weeks or months before the circus came to town. Do you send an advance man out to put up posters or scout the sites?"

Mr. B was not anxious to involve the company in any kind of legal problem, so he thought very carefully before he answered.

"Yes, but it is not always the same person. Sometimes it is Hiram Lockstep, our clown. He is up the coast right now doing just that…putting up some posters."

That was a lie. At that very moment, Hiram lay drunk in his trailer. He was passed out and likely to be that way all day. Mr. B did not care if Hiram got arrested for murder, but he didn't want it to happen while he was on the grounds. He was trying to save the whole company a hell of a lot of trouble so he was as vague as he could be while trying not to appear evasive. And Hiram had been too drunk to do the pre-publicity gig for quite some time.

"Here is my card, Mr. Bailey. I would like you to go through your records and write down when you sent someone out of town on circus business, who it was, where he went, what day he left and what day he came back. Do you think you could do that? It could mean bringing the killer of your child to justice. You could just mail the information to me in Los Angeles."

Delaney handed him a business card with his left hand, and extended his right one in a gesture that said he was finished with the interview.

"Why sure, I can do that, Mr. Delaney. It will take a few days as my bookkeeper has all that information. I will have him get right on it come Monday morning."

Another small lie, as the bookkeeper was in Argentina by this time. But Mr. B was anxious to protect the circus, so he excused himself for lying. Mr. B shook the detective's hand and bade Delaney farewell. Delaney backed out of the trailer, and was anxious to find Honey and get back to the motel.

"That will be just fine. I will be awaiting your correspondences then. Thank you for your cooperation," he said, as he took his leave.

He found Honey soon enough, talking to a big bald headed guy who was the circus' strong man. Typical that he would find her with some hunk.

"Come along, Honey. I have concluded my business here," he said as he took her arm and dragged her to the car. Honey was amused by his slight jealousy.

"Too bad you came up just when you did. That guy looked like a man with a big dick. I was about ready to fuck him. I just never get enough," simpered Honey.

But Delaney just chuckled.

I hope the good Captain lives happily ever after with this one. He deserves her. Meanwhile, I deserve her, he thought to himself.

"Right now, you are going to fuck old Clyde Delaney. Get your ass in the car, baby. My dick is stiff and it keeps looking at you," he proclaimed.

They went straight back to the motel and spent the next few days in bed, except to eat and sleep and shower. And because of Delaney's stiff dick, that was the extent of his investigation.

Before he knew it, it was Tuesday and they were headed back to L.A.

Maybe if he had stuck around and talked to some of the others, found Hiram, talked more to Mr. B…maybe Ivan or Mary Lou. Or perhaps Star had more to say. But he did not. His good intentions and his good police work were never realized. Delaney let lust get in the way of his investigative work.

Instead, he took Honey to Santa Cruz and rented a room on the beach, so he could hear the surf and watch the waves while he and she enjoyed each other's company in every position he, and she, could think of or invent. Lust is the enemy of reason.

Chapter Twenty-Five:

Ivan And Mary Lou

Mary Lou was no longer Tilly, the Fat Lady, she was Mary Lou the beautiful vocalist whose music made the transition between acts at the circus pass quickly so that the performers could change costumes and set up the next act. She had lost more than two hundred pounds by now, and was down to pleasingly plump. She was a tall five-foot-ten, so two hundred pounds did not set badly on her. She sometimes chuckled to herself, "Well, at least I don't have more chins than a Chinese phone book no more," she would say.

For the first time, she felt good about herself and her work since she had kicked old Hiram out of her trailer and her life. He slept, or really passed out, in the feed tent anyway. Angel had done a painting of her that she scarcely believed was her own self because it was so lovely. At first she chalked it up to Angel seeing her through the eyes of love, but then she began to notice that she really looked like that when she stared in the mirror. She mounted it over her bed and said goodnight to the new Mary Lou each night and good morning when she awoke. The painting was precious to her on many levels.

Like Tico says, she thought, *life is like a river, but you've got to keep swimming.* She felt content, and if this was life, she was willing to keep swimming for the rest of hers...without Hiram.

Mary Lou knew that just by giving Ivan the proper sign, he would come running. They had developed an enduring friendship and a mutual support system enjoying each other's company over coffee or tea. She had decided she wanted more from him, and she knew the only thing in the way of her happiness now was her abusive husband.

There was a light knock on her door that she knew was Ivan, and she also knew that this was the moment when their relationship would change. Hiram had not returned to work for several days. Nobody really knew where he was, least of all, Hiram, and Mary Lou's mind was made up about leaving him and taking up with the love of her life. Ivan had wanted her for a long time, but he knew she had to decide for herself what direction to go.

Mary Lou was freshly bathed, had a splash of toilet water behind her ears and on her wrists, along with a dusting of lilac talcum powder, and her hair was tied back with a red ribbon. She looked good and smelled good too. There were flowers on the kitchen table, and clean sheets on the bed. She was ready to change her life, but still she was nervous about turning this wonderful friendship into a more intimate relationship.

Although she'd been a practicing whore for years, she had not been that person in a long, long time, and this was different. This was romance. This was love.

When Ivan came in her nose told her that, he too, was freshly bathed. His head was closely shaved and polished to a shine with a bit of olive oil. Even his shoes were shined. He must have known the time was near to consummate their love. She felt a little thrill go through her, and it seemed to center itself right there between her legs.

It had been months since Hiram had wanted to make love, or whatever it was he did. It sure didn't feel like love, but more like whoring or worse. She hardly felt involved in the act at all when Hiram mounted her and satisfied himself, so she had avoided it whenever possible, which wasn't very hard since her husband was too drunk most of the time, nowadays.

Ivan could not wait any longer, and he knew that Hiram was out of town. But he wanted her to know his intentions were honorable. He came through the door with a smile on his face and a red rose in his hand.

"I want you for long time, my Little Blossom. I want you forever. I love you and hope I marry to you some day. So what you say, Little Blossom?" Ivan asked her, after he kissed her hello on the cheek. Tender love talk was new to Ivan, so it may have seemed a bit flowery and mushy, but his words were true to the way he felt and he was anxious to make Mary Lou know it. He had rehearsed his little speech for days. He had modeled it after some of the words spoken in some of the bad movies he had seen.

"I say yes, Ivan. I love you too. You're a gem, and I want to be with you," was her answer. It sounded like it came out of the same bad movie, but to Mary Lou it was a truth and she had no other way to say it.

He kissed her deeply then, and they stood there entwined for a moment, smiling into each other's faces.

He put his arms around her still ample waist and kissed her on the neck, on her face, on her chest. She let the fastener on her dress slip and it fell beneath her breasts. Ivan glued his mouth to her nipple and sucked greedily.

His hand wandered down to her crotch, where he cupped it over her *mons venus*, letting one finger part her plump folds so he could manipulate her clitoris.

She sighed a long ragged breath. "Oh, God, so…good. Ohhh!"

Ivan backed her up to the bed and laid her down on it. She spread her thick thighs and he began to kiss her belly murmuring sweet compliments to her.

"You are so beautiful. I love you big belly, you big legs, you big titties. I love you little…"

He thrust two of his sizable fingers into her.

"Your little…here ah, it like little blossom. Yes. Like flower," he said softly.

Mary Lou breathed in hard at the ecstasy.

"What kinda' blossom, baby? What kind?" she said breathing out.

"Maybe a rose. A rose not open yet. A bud. Yes. Yes. Like a rose. A little rose like grows on a mountain in my homeland."

He moved his kisses down and with his fingers, he parted her and at the same time kissed her in a way she had never before been kissed. He felt her body stiffen as her climax mounted. She dug her heels into the bed and raised her heavy bottom up to meet his eager caresses.

When he felt the first contraction of her coming he mounted her and with no further gentleness he drove deep into her. As she came, she screamed out, "Oh, I'm...coming. Oh, God! I love you!" and then Ivan The Terrible began a wild, unrestrained bucking, groaning, panting and gasping. And then he came too, letting out a roar that everyone in camp probably heard.

"Oh you big hot assed wonderful doll!" he cried. "What a fuck!"

Not the most tender, romantic words one might wish to hear at such a time of consummating, but it suited Ivan and Mary Lou just fine. His words were music to stir the gods, as far as Mary Lou was concerned.

As much as her marriage vows had meant to her in the past, Mary Lou felt no guilt. In fact, she felt vindicated, happy, and relieved. She also felt free. She had made her decision.

Ivan made her feel beautiful, loved and wanted, as though she belonged to the world, no longer an outcast. She had had but a taste of all that she had missed out on over the years and it had only taken a short time, the briefest of brief interludes. Nothing could dispel all of the residual pain she had in her tender heart, but while evil had instilled it in her central being, only love could lessen its damage. It showed this poor bruised little girl the path she must take towards fulfillment of a life that had so far been denied her.

The two lovers lay there, not saying what was on their minds or in their hearts. Ivan had not let go of her, and still held her in his arms close to him. He began to stroke and caress her with the most tender of touches. She'd never been touched that way, with loving caresses.

He cupped his hands around her breasts and toyed with her nipples. He squeezed the flesh of her belly and gripped her bottom with his strong hands.

"Ah, you are true like a blossom. You better than hashish, better than dates and honey with almonds, better than a dish of *cous cous.*"

"Ivan, we better get up from here before you talk yourself into doing it again...and it sure looks like you can," she said.

"Too late little Blossom," he said, and rolled over top of her. "Ivan already do it again, and maybe again, and ahgghh. You fine piece of ass, my little Blossom."

When they had finished their second bout of love making, Ivan groaned.

"Sonamunbitch. My dick feel like it run over by big truck. I feel like this forever. I never want to do that again!" he said.

Mary Lou had her doubts.

"Betcha' you will. I betcha' by tonight you gonna' be back around here sniffin' like an ol' hound dog and saying 'please, Little Blossom, please. Just one more time.'"

Mary Lou was laughing and teasing him.

"You've got a big peter want to be took care of pretty often, I bet," she said.

"Ah yes, you so right. Maybe one more time, but not now. Later."

Mary Lou adopted a more serious tone as she got dressed.

"Ivan," she said, "You know I can't stay with Hiram no more, especially after this. I make enough money sewing and singing around here, but Hiram is right. I lost so much of my fat I ain't really a fat lady no more. I quit that part of this job several pounds ago. I still got plenty of it left I know, but not enough to be a circus fat lady. So now that we're officially engaged, will you move in here or what?"

Ivan thought for a minute. He hadn't yet considered the logistics of his proposal, only that he wanted her now and forever.

"Tell you what," he said. "Soon as Hiram come back you tell him you live over my place with me now. But that drunken Hiram have to get out of the circus, leave here. I no have him around bothering me and you. I maybe have to kill him."

Mary Lou didn't seem to worry about Hiram's potential death threat, and for that matter, Ivan's, but she was concerned. Concerned about Mr. B's circus clown.

"But that would put Mr. B in a bind. He wouldn't have no clown. Oh, he's got Bertram and Lenny and Skinny, but they ain't as good as Hiram. Or at least as good as Hiram used to be before he was drunk all the time."

"Mr. B gonna' fire Hiram. He don't do it so far on account of you. Hiram always drunk, sometimes don't show up. Or show up drunk and be stupid. He on way out anyway," said Ivan.

"OK," said Mary Lou. "As soon as Hiram comes back I'll tell him I'm leavin.' I been plannin' to anyways."

"Hokay, my little Blossom, it's me and you. Hokay?"

And with a contented giggle, she replied, "Hokay!"

Chapter Twenty-Six:
Let The Punishment Fit The Crime

Hiram was back. He came into the little trailer yelling, "Hey, you ol' fat whore, where the hell are you?"

"If you wasn't so drunk you could see where I am and I ain't so fat and I ain't a whore," replied Mary Lou.

"Hey bitch, just who the hell ya' think yer a talkin' to? Nobody talks to Hiram Lockstep thataway," he said as he staggered in and plopped down on a chair.

"Besides, I brung ya a present. Here."

He thrust a whole box of Hershey Milk Chocolate bars at her.

"Eat these afore ya fall away to nothin'," he said.

But Mary Lou declined.

"I don't want 'em. I don't eat that kinda' stuff no more," she said, shoving the box back at Hiram.

He looked puzzled.

"Ya don't? Well you jest eat them there candies or I betcha' I shove 'em down yer' fuckin' throat," he said.

"You're a moron," said Mary Lou, "and I guess this is as good a time as any to tell you I ain't stayin' here no more. I'm leavin' your sorry ass."

"Like hell you are!" roared Hiram. "Besides, if'n you skiddo outa here you ain't takin' none of my stuff with ya. Everything here belongs to me, lock, stock and barrel. You take jist one thing, and I will likely kill yer ass."

Mary Lou started to laugh. She was no longer afraid of Hiram's threats. And everyone knew not one thing in that trailer had been purchased with any of Hiram's money. Hiram felt he'd lost his control of

Mary Lou and in a fit of anger and frustration, he threw the entire box of chocolate bars at her and hit her in the face.

"You worthless ol' bitch. You eat them there candies or I'll kill yer fat ass, you…pig," he yelled.

But Mary Lou did not even respond. She knew to answer him would be like farting in the wind. He wouldn't even hear her. The veins stood out on his scrawny, wrinkled, wattled neck, and his face was crimson. He had begun to spray the room with his spittle.

"You done lost over 200 pounds already. You're gonna' get fired. Who ever heard of a skinny fat lady? We need the money you make, and I ain't gonna support no lazy, skinny old whore. No sireebob. Not Hiram Lockstep. You gonna' tote yer' weight or you're outta here."

"I'm already outta' here," she muttered under her breath. She knew it would do no good to defend herself. She had hidden away some of the money she made singing for the circus, as Hiram just thought she did it for the love of singing. Mr. B had been willing to keep her secret, and he'd made the checks out to her directly. Hiram's salary for clowning had not been spent on paying the bills, anyway. But she had saved some of hers without him knowing, Hiram's money had gone to fancy clothes, bars, women, and booze. But because of his drunkenness, he had not earned much for some time. Since she paid for their trailer, of course, she'd had to spend only the sewing money on their monthly bills.

"And another thing. You think ol' Hiram don't know you been fuckin' that big Turk? Jest wait till I see him. I'm gonna' tell him he owes me for your services. Yep! Four dollars for every time he tapped ya.' That's fair, ain't it? If'n my old lady is gonna' be whorin,' then I oughta get paid fer it."

"I don't reckon you're gonna' say much of anything to Ivan. He just might break ye' silly, drunkin' neck," she said.

Hiram snorted.

"Huh? Why that big Turk ain't nothin' but a coward. He ain't gonna' come up against a man like me. Why I've kilt more people accidentally than them soldiers kilt in the war on purpose. Think I'm scared of him? Not likely."

He began to strut around the room muttering to himself.

"Anyhow, I got me a young gal I been fuckin' and we thinkin' about blowin' this pop stand together. Leaving your fat lazy ass here to starve. That's what will happen to you without me. I was good enough to get this here job fer' ya.' Hell. You never did 'preciate it. Jest rode my coat tails fer' all these years. Bitch! Ungrateful bitch. I oughta' jest kill you right now."

Hiram made a menacing move toward her.

"Hiram," she said, holding up her hand, "you ain't gonna' kill no one. I ain't afraid of you."

But she still had a bit of fear in the pit of her stomach that she thought she had gotten over. She knew how vicious he could be, though, when he was mad, and especially when he was drinking. She was convinced he could and would kill her, if he thought he could get away with it.

"That's what you think! I kilt before. Lotsa' times. Why I can jest hear that bone a crunchin' when I squeezes my hands around someone's neck. It takes awhile. Sometimes a whole minute," he said, pretending to be choking someone with his bare hands.

Hiram could see that he had Mary Lou's attention. Even though she had lost much of her fear of Hiram, there were times, like now, when she recalled just how violent a drunk he could be if the object of his wrath was someone a lot weaker than him. She was at least alarmed about his threats, and seeing that she was becoming terrified, he went on.

"Specially them young 'uns. Why they scream and kick until they ain't got no breath left," he said.

Mary Lou gasped in horror. Of course! It had been Hiram! All these years, it had been him! She could see it all so plain. It was Hiram in those towns that Mr. B had said that Detective Delaney had talked about. Her Hiram was a deadly killer! Worse, he was a killer of little children.

She tried to squeeze out the door past him, but he hit her a solid blow with his bony fist. Hit her right on the side of the face. She fell to the floor with a crash, and shaken, she hardly dared to breathe. She considered that this might be the end of her if she couldn't get away, but she screamed with a long shrieking noise like a train whistle at full steam. Hiram kicked her while she was down, a hard, nasty blow to her ribs.

"Shut the fuck up or I really will kill ya!" he said.

Mary Lou had developed strong lungs from singing and her screams went out across the circus grounds where several other performers heard them, including Ivan.

He was out the door and over at Mary Lou's trailer in a matter of seconds. He jerked the door open, nearly pulling it off its hinges. Hiram's face went white as the door flew open and he was confronted with the burly Turk. He hoped Ivan had not heard his bragging a few minutes earlier, because Hiram knew that the truth was, Ivan could kill him with one good left hook to the temple. Ivan was not the circus strong man for no reason.

With one hand the muscular Ivan grabbed Hiram's shirt and without a word, threw the scrawny, cowering clown out the door and into the dirt. Hiram began to whimper and cursing, all the while getting up and preparing to run for his life, and that is exactly what he did. He ran like a scared rabbit.

Ivan turned to Mary Lou, who was still on the floor. Her left cheek was bleeding, and her left eye was already starting to swell. A blood vessel in her eye had ruptured, and she looked badly damaged. Ivan knelt beside her and tenderly helped her to the bed. He ran a cloth under cold water, squeezed it out, and applied it to her face.

"You OK, Little Blossom?" he asked her, patting her face with the cool cloth.

"He hurt you? Ivan no let him hurt you no more. That is end of you living here."

Mary Lou just nodded that she was ok, but tears welled up in her eyes. She buried her face in Ivan's chest, and wept for a minute.

"OK, Little Blossom. You safe now. You not have to stay with that bum no more. You come stay with Ivan now. Ivan no make you cry. Ivan make nice to you. I promise. Ivan kiss you on every place. Make love to you and keep you safe from that asshole!" said Ivan as he kissed her other cheek and put his massive arms around her.

Mary Lou was shaken, and although she'd been through this many times, she'd never had a protector before. Tears still trickled down her cheeks.

"Oh, gee Ivan. That'll be so nice. No more beatin,' no more Hiram Lockstep. I only stayed to tell him I was goin.' But I can see that was a mistake. And no more bein' the fat lady. Tilly is dead. Mary Lou is alive and now the fiancé of Ivan. Things is better already, sweetie."

Mary Lou continued to cry. She was letting go of so much in that moment. She was burying Tilly the fat lady, and putting a lifetime of abuse behind her. The sobs sounded like a small child. Gasping in ragged breaths, coming close to hyperventilating, Ivan just held her. He knew she needed to get it out. She was lost in the tender embrace he offered her, and the tears flowed. Then she remembered what Ivan had said.

"Oh my God Ivan!" she said, stopping the tears abruptly. "Find Mr. B! Hiram told me he was a killer. He said he had killed lotsa' people. Young people. It was him! He's the one kilt all them little girls that detective told Mr. B about. It was him. I know it now. He did it! He as much as confessed! Oh God, Ivan! Oh God! We gotta' tell Mr. B. Oh, God Almighty!"

Mary Lou was wild with fear and rage. It had taken very little to convince Ivan of Hiram's guilt. He had always known he was a no good prick, and it was a short leap to make him believe that Hiram was also a killer. He knew, too, that Hiram was a craven coward, and it only made sense that he would prey on helpless kids.

Ivan suspected that Hiram would run, probably out of the country, now that he'd confessed to his crimes, and the big Turk did not want him to get away.

He grabbed Mary Lou's hand and dashed as fast as the two of them could, Ivan dragging her along on her still chubby legs toward Mr. B's trailer. They burst into the office where Mr. B and Charlie "One Shoe" were drinking Ivan's Moroccan coffee, smoking his big, fancy Turkish cigars, and discussing what to do with the two Indian tigers that could not be trained. The new owner didn't want the beasts. All conversation stopped as the door burst open.

"My God!" said Mr. B as they burst in. "What happened to your face?"

"Oh Hiram got a hold of me again," said Mary Lou. "But that's not important right now." She was out of breath.

Ivan chimed in.

"Mr. B! Hiram not to get away with this!" he said. Mr. B shook his head, thinking Ivan was talking about the damage he'd done to Mary Lou.

Mary Lou began to stutter out the story in unintelligible syllables. She was not only in a panic from the news, she still trying to catch her breath from the short run Ivan had dragged her on.

"Whoa there, little lady," said Mr. B, "slow down. I can't understand a thing you're saying." So Ivan took over, so excited, he didn't realize he was speaking Turkish.

"Holy shit, Ivan! You sound like a crazy man. Talk in English so Mr. B and me can get what you say." Mary Lou sat down on a stool and tried to catch her breath.

"Aw, Mr. B," she began, "it's Hiram. He done it. He said so. He told me he is a killer. Said he kilt plenty of people. Said he like to kill the young ones. Liked to hear their bones crack when he squeezes their throats."

She stopped in dread, remembering that one of the victims had been Mr. B's little six-year-old Becky.

"Oh, I didn't mean to…he done it, "she said. "He done it, I know he done it. We gotta' stop him before he does it again. Oh, please Mr. B. Listen to me."

Mr. B was listening. More than that, he was out of his chair and had a look of horror on his face.

"God Damn me! I should have known it was him. He was the last one I sent out to put up the posters. You're right Tilly, you are right. Oh, God!"

By now, Mr. B was pacing the small space in his office.

"That little son of a bitch. I always knew there was something evil about him," Charlie chimed in. "We gotta do something to keep him from ever doing it to more little kids. Hell, I'd like a crack at him. Squeeze his fuckin' neck 'til he can't breathe no more."

After a minute of thought, Mr. B turned to them and said, "Look here, you guys. This takes some strategy. We've got to be mum about this until we can get him to confess."

"But he already confessed to me," said Mary Lou.

"Not good enough. A wife can't testify against her husband. No. Let me think. Let me think," said Mr. B.

He took a long drag on his cigar and finally said, "OK. I got it. Listen to what we are going to do. Where is the rotten son of a bitch right now?"

"Well," Ivan began, "I guess I scare him. I threw his sorry ass out the door. Last I see he runnin' off to some place. Maybe to find more booze."

"Yes, probably went over to the feed tent to sleep. Good. He'll be there for awhile," said Mr. B.

"He was pretty drunk. He usually goes to bed and sleeps it off. He sometimes don't even remember what he done or said after he gets sober," said Mary Lou.

Charlie spoke up again.

"Huh!?! Since when has he been sober? He's always drunk. He's so full of that booze he never gets sober no more."

They all fell silent for a moment until Mr. B said, "Tilly…"

She stopped him.

"I don't want nobody to call me Tilly no more. I ain't the fat lady, I'm Mary Lou, the singer now, and the future wife of Ivan. Call me Mary Lou," she said.

"If it weren't such a somber occasion, I'd be congratulating the two of you. But we'll celebrate later. Sure, honey. Mary Lou it is. Now Mary Lou, can you keep silent with this secret and help us put this vile man out of the killing business?" he asked.

"Oh, God, Mr. B, I would cut off my tongue before I would say anything to keep him from getting caught! What do ya want me to do?"

"First, I want you to stay with Ivan. Don't even go back to your place. Then I want to tell everyone that I have sold the circus. And as a bonus to everyone, I am sending them all on a trip to San Francisco to take in the sights before we all have to part company."

Mary Lou was stunned.

"Sold the circus? What about us? Do we go with you or with the circus? What about our jobs? The Caesars? What will they do? Gee, Mr. B, what will we do?"

As usual, Mary Lou was thinking of the others.

"I have made arrangements with the new owners to let anyone who wants to stay with the circus. Some may have to change jobs, but at the same salary they're making now," he said.

Mary Lou's head was swimming.

"Oh, Christ! I got a headache from all this. I gotta take some headache powders," she reported.

"As far as the Caesars are concerned," Mr. B continued, "it is no secret that they all want to get out of the circus business. They found a big apartment building on Greenwich Street in San Francisco. Right in North Beach District, heart of the Italian section of town. Papa Primo had saved all of his vino money and had enough to buy it. So no need to worry about the Caesars. Those folks can take care of themselves.

"And as far as Tico and Angel, they're already gone on to Argentina, so we don't have them to worry about, which reminds me, I have some gifts to present to you all in Tico's behalf. I have just been so busy I have not had the time to give a little ceremonial party for that occasion."

Mary Lou spoke up. "Gosh. And all the time we thought nobody would ever marry Tico," she sighed. "I sure hope their babies comes out right. You know, not like Tico. Him and that little girl sure do deserve some happiness in this lifetime," she said. She was close to tears. "I sure do miss 'em."

"There you go again, little girl. Thinking about the others. Well, you're a good girl, honey," said Mr. B, "and don't worry. Most babies come from dwarfs are normal. We've seen that just in the ones we have known. And about you and Ivan, Mary Lou. I thought if you two want to, you can go back to Florida with me. What with a war coming on and all, there will be plenty of jobs for both of you. Whadaya say?"

Ivan thought for a moment and said, "Boy, Mr. B. This all come so fast. I gotta' talk it over with my little blossom here. If she go with me, I go!"

Mary Lou was always ready for a new adventure, so she said, "Sure sweetie! I'll go. I like Florida. Do we go through the town where I grew up? I would like to stop there and give a look."

"I don't know. What town is it?" asked Mr. B.

"It's Oliveville. It's in the Sacramento Valley. I just want to see it once. You know, after all, I did live there 'til I was thirteen, and maybe my old man is still..."

Mr. B told her that Oliveville was right on the way along Highway 99 East, and that it would be no problem to go that way. His plan was to take Route 66 on down to Arizona, and follow the southern states after that. That suited everyone just fine.

"But first, Ivan and Charlie and I have the little problem of Hiram to take care of. Everyone is going to San Francisco for a big going away party and a sightseeing trip. How about day after tomorrow while you folks are all gone, us three will take care of that murdering bastard," he said.

"You're gonna kill him, ain't ya?" she asked.

"Well," Mr. B lied, "I don't really know yet. Don't bother your pretty little head over it honey. Whatever we do it will be fair. As far as killing him goes…well, that is what a man like him deserves. Maybe we should just turn him over to the law."

Ivan wasn't so sure. He came from a place where justice was fleeting.

"Fuck the law!" said Ivan. "He need to die. That law not good. Maybe just let him go. No, he gotta die!"

"Yeah," said Charlie grimly. "As my old man used to say, 'let the punishment fit the crime.'"

"Huh," said Ivan, "no punishment bad enough to fit his crime!"

Mary Lou got up off the stool. She readied herself to leave.

"I guess you guys has got plans to make. I'll just go on over to Ivan's trailer and begin start to get it fixed up how I want it. That OK with you Ivan?"

"Sure, is OK mine Little Blossom. You just make big noise if that bum bother you. Ivan come a runnin.'"

As soon as the door was shut behind her, the three friends began to make plans for Hiram's punishment.

Charlie "One Shoe" had been with the circus from day one. He had always been a fair man, and he had always disliked Hiram. He was devoted to Mr. B. In fact, Charlie had been the one who had found Mr. B's little daughter. Her dead body was floating in the river. To have the opportunity to realize revenge upon the one who had committed such and act was a dream fulfilled. He was not a vengeful man by nature, but he had never gotten the sight of the little dead body out of his mind. He had carried her, played with her, and loved her. He had no trouble whatsoever believing it was Hiram who had killed her, and yet he said, "Well, Mr. B. I guess you're sure he done it. I sure wouldn't want to be part of doing in an innocent man."

"Charlie," said Mr. B, "I am sure of it! All the times that detective told me those other children were killed. Those are the same times Hiram was in those towns. Detective Delaney gave me a list of all those times. After he left, I checked the list against the times Hiram was where a kid was killed. You guys know that when Hiram takes off to put up posters that I usually go and visit Becky's grave if we are close enough. So I know pretty much when it was. I never said anything to that detective because I wanted to be sure. But after what Hiram told Mary Lou, I have not got a single doubt."

Ivan was adamant. "I ain't got no doubt neither. I know was him. We know, all of us, how mean he always to poor Mary Lou. He do it. What we do to him now...we do. Is OK I sure!"

"Well," said Mr. B, "I've been thinking on what that would be. We can give him a chance to live..."

"Fuck that! He no get one chance, no not one," interrupted Ivan. "Let Sinbad and Barbarossa eat him. Put him in cage. Eat all of him. No Hiram left."

Charlie grinned. "By God, Ivan, that's a fine idea. I always heard Turks were mean enemies. We could do that, Mr. B. No dead body to get rid of!" he said.

"Hiram is afraid of heights. We could make him walk the high wire and put the two tigers in that open top cage right under the wire. When he falls, he'll fall into the cage right at supper time!" said Mr. B.

"Yep, we do it. Just like that! Soon as bus leave for San Francisco. He be so drunk he not even hear bus leave."

"OK, tomorrow the guys from Ringling will be here. There are some transfers of funds and inventory and vehicle titles to sign. Should take most of the day. Then next day, that will be Thursday, I'll send the troops on their free holiday in Frisco. There won't be anyone here but you two fellows and me. Of course, Hiram will be passed out drunk, so he'll be here. That way we can take care of what has to be done," intoned Mr. B.

Mr. B pondered on the thought for a moment, and then said, "It's a done deal then."

"Yeh," said Ivan, "and so my coffee and big cigars I get from my Greek friend, how come you guys get in my stuff? You owe me big lot of bucks." Ivan wasn't mad, he was just pretending to be.

"Well hell, Ivan, you did leave that package over there at my place this morning. We're just toasting your...a...you know," said Charlie.

"Sure, with my good stuff. Good you not find my stash of good hashish. You be stone on you ass, damn good, I think."

The two culprits laughed and had another swig of good ol' Ivan's coffee and puffed away on one of the cigars, laughing and blowing smoke at Ivan as they did.

Travis Young and Bob Parson, the two representatives from Ringling Brothers arrived the next day, and spent most of it transferring titles and filling out paperwork with Mr. B. They finished up the inventory; transferred bank accounts and tied up loose ends, and with the sale complete, left with good wishes all around.

"What the hell are you going to do with those two man-eating tigers? Boy we sure don't want them. Too dangerous by far for a circus. They belong back in the jungle," asked Travis on his way out.

"I have them sold to a big game farm down in Texas," said Mr. B. "Big shot guys from the city go down there and pay big bucks to hunt wild animals. They'll get what they bargained for. Those are definitely wild animals. I know they must be killed, but better they do it than me. And this way, I got paid something for them. Not much, but it wasn't a complete loss. They are sending some men to pick them up. Should be here day after tomorrow."

And with that, the Bill Bailey circus was in the hands of the new owner, and the plans for Hiram were well underway.

No trainer had dared to even approach the cage of the two tigers. Even Ivan fed them with a long pole.

After the Ringling guys were gone, Charlie asked Mr. B where he got such a pair of animals.

"'Cootchie' Priest," said Mr. B. "He sold them to me cheap."

"Oh God, Mr. B. You should have knowed better than to deal with that old bandit. Why hell, he's crookeder than a barrel of buzzard guts. I just bet those are the same ones got loose in Kansas City last year and killed and half ate that guy before they could get them off. I still don't know why they didn't shoot the sons of bitches. I guess because he wanted to sell them to some dumb sucker…beggin' yer pardon, Mr. B." Charlie laughed after saying this.

"Well, he darn sure found one. I lost plenty on the deal," said Mr. B.

Charlie looked skyward.

"Maybe you'll get your money's worth yet. Time will tell," he said.

Chapter Twenty-Seven:
Hiram Comes To Dinner

Sure enough, as predicted, Thursday morning when the bus left with the circus revelers on it, Hiram was so drunk, he never even heard it leave, nor did he know about Mr. B's announcement that the circus had been sold. Everyone who wanted to would keep their jobs, and all were being treated to this day on the town in San Francisco by the Bill Bailey circus.

Hiram heard nothing until Ivan grabbed him by his scrawny arm and shook him awake. When Ivan threw him out of bed and he hit the ground in the feed tent where he had been sleeping, he began to sputter and yell.

"What the fuck! You ass hole. Leave me be or I'll bust your chops fer ya, you big ugly Ruski prick!"

"You bust nothing," said Ivan. "You drunken low-life killer of leettle keeds.

We gonna' show you what happen to big cowards what kills leetle ones."

Hiram took one look at Ivan and knew he was in deep, very deep, dog shit.

He noticed that Mr. B was just outside the trailer, so even someone who normally protected him somewhat was in on what looked like an impending beating.

"Whatdaya' mean? I ain't never kilt no one. Mr. B, make this here big palooka leave his fucking hands off'n me!" he pleaded.

Hiram was now afraid in earnest when Mr. B did not answer him, but said, "OK, Ivan, yank his clothes off of him," he ordered.

Ivan pulled the hung-over Hiram's clothes off easily enough, and pushed him back into a chair. Hiram shivered with the morning cold and with fear.

Mr. B spoke next.

"Here's the deal, Hiram. We know you killed all those little children. That Detective Delaney told us all about you and how you did it. Mary Lou told us what you said about killing those children too. You just bragged one too many times while you were drunk, Hiram, and we're not about to let you continue killing children," he said.

"Aw, shit," he said, "that was a big lie. See, I was in jail with some guy who told me that story about how he killed kids. Why, that's how come he was in jail. I was just a'joshin' ol' Tilly…uh, Mary Lou. See, Mr. B, you got it all wrong. I never kilt no kids, nor nobody else neither. You knowed me a long time, Mr. B. You know how I love them kids. They all love me too. Now that ya' know the truth o' the matter, let me go. You know I ain't a liar."

But Hiram saw that he was getting nowhere and by this time he was slobbering so badly, the front of his dirty shirt was wet. He was spraying spit all around him. Then he began to cry. Everyone, including Hiram, knew he lied all the time.

"Them little girls you rape and kill, they cry too. I bet they cry for they mamma's while you hurt them, you snake. They beg you I sure to stop hurting them. Beg like that Hiram. Beg on the ground, you dirt," Ivan said, unmoved by his tears.

"This is crazy! I never raped and killed no one. Ask Tilly. Ask anyone who knows me," Hiram whined. But he knew he had no one who would back him. No one liked the drunk he had become, and they especially hated him for beating on Mary Lou. "Why you takin' my clothes off? You gonna rape me too? Hell that ain't no big deal. I been in jail where that happens regular like," he said.

"No Hiram," said Mr. B, "we are not going to rape your sorry ass. We have a proposition for you."

"Proposition? Whatcha' mean? I ain't gonna' make no deals with you guys."

He was terrified, but always the braggart, and always obstinate in the face of a situation that required the utmost delicacy and compromise.

"I'll have the cops on you guys. I'll have ya' put in jail, I will. Just you wait and see if'n I don't," said Hiram, sitting in a chair naked, and totally vulnerable to the whims of one muscular Turk who hated him, and his old boss that he'd screwed over by being too drunk to perform on several occasions.

"You not put anyone in jail," Ivan laughed. "You be too dead."

"Yes, Hiram, you are about to become a high wire walker," said Mr. B.

"Aw, no," Hiram wailed. "Why, I ain't done none of that stuff you say I done. Ya' know I'm scared to death of goin' up high."

"Scare not how you die, sonamubitch! I think last sound you hear when Ol' Sinbad break you neck." Ivan was thoroughly enjoying Hiram's terror, and Hiram was beginning to get the picture of what lay in store for him.

"Sinbad! Oh Lordy, why you guys pickin' on me? I ain't done…"

"Shut up, you nasty bucket of dog vomit. You rotten piece of snot," Mr. B's face was contorted with rage.

Mr. B wanted this over with, and right now.

"I have two incentives for you. One is this .38 revolver. It's going to see that you make the climb. However, if you want to use it to put a bullet in your own brain, and forget the high wire act, you can choose that. But if not, you're getting up on the high wire and you are going to walk across, at least as far as you can get. If you make it, you can walk away Scott free," announced Mr. B.

"Oh, God. You promise, Mr. B? Honest?" asked Hiram.

"Have I ever lied to you?" was all he said.

Hiram figured he had two chances…slim and none. But he was willing to take the gamble.

Mr. B moved the program along by saying, "OK Hiram, old buddy. Upsy daisy. It's show time, time to go up. Oh, by the way, just to make the walk more interesting and help you across, Ivan will be pushing the open top tiger cage underneath the wire with Sinbad and Barbarossa in it. They haven't been fed for two days. Don't you think that's thoughtful of me?"

Hiram groaned and protested that he was innocent, but he thought it was at least worth a gamble. There was a remote possibility he could make it across. He'd seen how it was done enough times. And at least the chance was better than if he just pointed the gun at his temple and fired. Of course, if he didn't make it, there was the prospect of falling and being eaten by two hungry wild animals. Neither choice was too good, but at least with one, he had a chance, and he knew neither of these guys was about to back down. The situation was serious. They truly believed he had killed those children. Hiram figured he'd made the mistake of his life, bragging to Mary Lou about killing children. He fell to the ground and covered his head.

Ivan grasped Hiram by his long shaggy red hair, and jerked him to his feet. Hiram's legs were like rubber. He couldn't even stand up on his own. Mr. B poked him in the backside with the mean looking revolver, but he slumped to the ground.

"Get up. I'd just as soon shoot you myself as play this game. I'm being a good guy to give you a chance to walk free after all you've done to those kids, including my own, you low-life son-of-a-bitch. Stand up. No fucking around anymore. Time's up!" shouted Mr. B. Neither Charlie nor Ivan had ever seen Mr. B so angry, but they understood. His own daughter had been terrorized and murdered by this scum.

Clumsily, the terrified man made several attempts to stand. He finally got on his feet, taking two steps toward the tent where the high wire was constructed. The trio walked him to the foot of the ladder. He planted one foot on the bottom rung, and pleaded for the last time.

"Aw, please you guys. I never kilt' no one," he said with tears streaming down his face.

Mr. B slapped him on the side of his wretched face with the gun and fairly screamed in Hiram's face.

"Do you think my little Becky was this scared when you did your sick deed? Get up that ladder or I'll just shoot you right now and throw you in that tiger cage without further *adieu*," he said.

Hiram began his climb, begging and sobbing the whole way up, while the ladder, unstable as it was, swayed from side to side with each step Hiram took. He finally made it to the platform, presenting a rather comical figure. His skinny knocked knees were clacking together now. From time to time he would grab his long, pendulous balls and tug on them while his limp penis hung there like a rotten banana, urine dribbling out the tip.

Hiram moved slowly out on the wire as Mr. B threatened to shoot him if he didn't start his walk.

Hiram got only three feet out onto the wire, when Mr. B, his anger and grief seeming to overtake him, gave the pole a vigorous push and a pull, and Hiram fell screaming into the tiger's cage beneath him.

Both Sinbad and Barbarossa pounced on him in a fury. Hiram's screams of pain and terror only served to stimulate their hunting instincts more, as he got up momentarily and ran around the cage trying to get out. The tigers stalked him for a few minutes, toying with their bleeding prey.

Finally, hunger and their primitive instinct overtook them, and Barbarossa went straight for Hiram's neck in one graceful leap toward him. His vicious bite came from the back and Hiram was dead before the tiger let go of him.

Blood covered the floor of the cage. It spurted out of Hiram's body at the site of every puncture wound made by the animal's long fangs. It dripped off the sides of the floor and was absorbed in the dirt.

"Holy Mary, mother of God," said Charlie. "I never saw so much blood. I'm gonna' be sick." And he went around the back of the cage and threw up his breakfast.

But Mr. B was practical. He had the hose already hooked up and began hosing the blood out of the cage before the two tigers had finished their meal. As he hosed out the blood, the tigers tore great strips of flesh off of Hiram's corpse, grunting, gulping and slavering in a noisy, sickening chorus.

As soon as there was nothing but bones left, Ivan raked them into a big grain basket.

He put the bones into two gunnysacks and gave Charlie a sledgehammer. He took the other one, and the men pounded the sacks of bones until they were crushed into mush. Ivan loaded them up in the wheelbarrow and pushed it down to the river, where they waded far out into the water and emptied the sacks into the swift current. Then they let the sacks go, too.

"There," said Ivan. "You sleep with the fishes, low life. No, that too good for you. You sleep in hell."

And all traces of the earthly remains, of Hiram Logsdon, "Uncle Toby Toontuck" Lockstep, were forever gone,

Charlie was still bothered by the blood and gore. He had to stop his work and puke now and then before he could go on.

Ivan tried to console him.

"Look here Charlie, my good friend. This very bad man. Not human. He kill little ones to make pleasure for himself. He rape little girls. We no kill man. We kill beast, just like two tigers. Worse. We get rid of beast, make it better for little ones. We give him better chance than a trial give him. So be cheerful. He dead now. So be it. Forget it."

And Ivan forgot it.

Chapter Twenty-Eight:
Star And Billy Part

Star had heard that the circus had been sold. She had not heard it from Billy, but from some of the other performers. When she heard it she knew that she and Billy were probably through. There had been other signs but for him not to have told her first seemed to be something of an insult. She was hurt, but was not about to let Billy know it. She had sensed that there was something not quite right with their relationship for several weeks. He was spending more and more time alone and treating her with a coldness that was unusual. There had been no sex and not even any affection from him for some time, so she had been spending her nights in her own place, sleeping there and preparing meals for herself alone.

She spent many hours at the Crystal Skull. It was an entity in its own right. Not human and yet not just an inanimate object. This Crystal Skull had a life of it's own and "talked" to Star. No, not in an audible voice, but in a silent subtle transfer of knowledge like mental telepathy. Star did not question this phenomenon, she was in awe of it and respected, even feared the thing. Of late it had been giving her messages she could not quite grasp. Mysterious thoughts that seemed to have no meaning. "Visions," if they could be called that, of water and drowning bodies and huge teeth tearing at strange things. Much blood. Rivers of blood. Star became afraid of the Skull. Sometimes it would glow an eerie, iridescent green and at other times it would give off a red flickering light. Finally star quit communing with it so often. It always left her shaken and apprehensive, especially the night it showed her the dead body of little Becky Bailey. That is when she knew it was trying to tell her something but Star could not receive the message. She was frustrated and even angry that her "sight" was not strong enough to take her into the place she knew the Skull was trying to lead her.

This remarkable Skull was an artifact that Tico had found at a jewelry auction in Chicago. He bid on it especially with Star in mind. He was not sure of its origin nor that it had any special power. When he gave it to Star he told her that he believed it had been carved in Egypt, but added that this was only an educated guess. It could have also come from India. He knew that it was from the Middle East, but could not pinpoint the exact origin with any accuracy. It had been crafted from a single piece of flawless and very high quality crystal. Tico's experience in the gem trade allowed him to assess its quality and value as well as the origin of the material, but the origin of the carving remained a mystery. The only thing he knew was that the craftsmanship was way above average. It was indeed a thing of beauty. Tico had only bought it as a gift for Star because she was a "Fortune Teller" and every one of them used a crystal ball. Little did he know what that gift would mean to this fortuneteller.

After the last performance of the night she went to Mr. B's trailer. When she entered, Mr. B said, "Well Star, where you been keeping yourself? I have been wanting to talk to you. I am sure that by now you are aware that I have sold the outfit to Ringling Brothers."

"Yes, of course, Beelee. Do you think I would have not? Do you not think that you should have told me before you told the others?" replied Star.

"I don't know why. I am not married to you, you know. You have no interest in my business. I am going back to Florida after the circus is sold. I will retire in my little house in Sarasota and live happily ever after. My plans do not include you. I do not wish to be encumbered with a woman I do not love. It's been nice while it has lasted but it is over."

"Is OK, my Beelee. Star not to be cut out to be housewife to old retired guy, anyway. Star born to be free and…"

"To fuck other guys. Yeh, I know what you like. Go for it Star. Just to show you I am not a complete bounder, I will give you some money to get you started in your new life if you do not stay with the new owners."

Star laughed a bitter laugh. "You not to think Star want your money. No, I not take anything from you. Hey, Beelee, hope for you to find whatever you looking for. I do not think so. Skull tell me you going into…"

"I don't want to hear any of that 'Hocus Pocus' shit, Star. It's crap. It's a big joke and is something to sell to the suckers. That is not me. So goodnight Star. See you around."

"Good, Beelee. It over for us. I have no regret. It OK while it last. Time for Star to move on to something bigger and better, anyway. Maybe I stay here in California. Yeh, San Francisco. Sure, I like that city. Maybe go home to New York. Well, as Mae West say, 'Thanks for the buggy ride!'"

Star kissed the tips of her fingers and touched them to Mr. B's face but he pulled away coldly. "OK, baby. You the boss. See you in the funny papers." Star then left as Mr. B turned back to his desk and to his work.

But Star was thinking, "Huh, what he look for he no find. I see some bad shit for him." Yet, she figured it was only wishful thinking. She wanted bad shit for him.

As she was walking back to her own place after leaving Mr. B's office trailer, up strolled 'Handsome Harry' Freels. "Hey, Star baby! I been lookin' for you. I need my fortune told, if ya' catch my drift," 'Handsome Harry' was looking for a bit of action from Star, or any woman for that matter.

"OK. Big boy. You got one hundred dollars? My price just go up for guy like you."

"One hundred dollars? Why hell, ain't no piece a' ass worth that much money!"

"Oh, yeh? Well this one be, you stupid, worthless, white trash cracker sonuma bitch. In fact, my price just go up to more. If Star be whore, be expensive one. Fact be, I not do you for two hundred dollars. Star worth a lot more than you fuckers think. Star don't need no asshole like you. Scram! Scat! Beat it! Get lost!"

"Sheesh, Star. What the hell got into you? It's only business," Harry said.

"Only business, huh? You not think woman like you just because she fuck you for money? You stink like old outside toilet! Star just change mind. Star just quit the whore business. Try you left hand if you dummass know you right hand from left one!"

But then with a sweet smile that belied her mood, she placed both her hands on 'Handsome Harry's' shoulders. He relaxed a bit. With a swift, powerful, maneuver, born of a female rage, she brought her knee up between 'Handsome Harry's' handsome legs.

He raised about two inches off the ground and doubled over in the classic position of a man just kicked in the nuts. Bent over like that he looked for all the world like a broke down shotgun.

He let out a scream, "Holy Shit!"

By now the ruckus had been heard by Ivan and Charlie who both came over to see what it was all about. As soon as they saw 'Handsome Harry' and Star standing by, they knew.

Charlie looked down at ol' 'Handsome Harry' and said, "Whatsa' matter Harry? Been a'talkin' when you shoulda' been a'listenin' again?"

Harry looked up into Charlie's face. He had had it. He sputtered through clenched teeth. "Why you big nosed, ugly, fat assed son of a bitch!"

He was crazy with pain, fury and humiliation. He rose slowly to his feet and then he swung a powerhouse right and caught Charlie with a five knuckle tattoo square on the point of poor ol' Charlie's chin, just below the slobber line.

Harry looked down into Charlie's face and said, "Whatsa' matter, Charlie? Talkin' when ya' shoulda' been a'listenin' again?"

Star turned away from the group and to her everlasting bewilderment, began to cry.

Chapter Twenty-Nine:
The Last Hurrah

Frantic preparations were now underway for the last performance of the Billy Bailey "World's Biggest Little Circus."

Each performer was most anxious to make sure that this last show would be a spectacular Grande Finale of momentous proportions and a memorable moment, not only for the crowd, but for the troops themselves.

Tico was gone to Argentina with his *Angelica* and was surely missed, but he was not a performer. Hiram had disappeared into the night and few knew where he had gone and nobody really cared. No matter, the Big Top would have a full complement of talent to entertain the crowds.

Mary Lou would sing the plaintiff "Red Sails In the Sunset" and an old Island song of farewell, "Now Is the Hour." No costume she had ever had would surpass the one she would have for this night. It was of red and silver sequins, laboriously and meticulously sewn on by hand by not only Mary Lou, but by Sylvia, Star, and the Caesar girls. It seemed that everyone understood the importance of this event for Mary Lou. Not only would it be a fashion statement, it would be a celebration of success, an expression of her talent and a glorious show of her new life and freedom; freedom from the fat, from Hiram and from her slavery to it all. The whole group was happy for her and wished to help her in any way they could. The girls also sewed red and silver sequins on her satin high-heeled pumps, the first pair of heels she had ever had. The gown itself had a large stand up collar, not unlike that of "Snow White." It was a princess cut that form fitted her bosom, but was cut dangerously low, showing a very daring amount of cleavage. It fell from the fitted waist to the floor in front, but was caught up in a drape in the front that ended in a large bow of fabric in the back. She wore a lovely diamond pendant loaned to her by Sylvia, who would also do Mary Lou's long blonde hair into a "Lillian Russell" type of hairdo. Long, dangly rhinestone earrings and a huge brimmed red satin hat with a profusion of satin flowers on it that would complete her out fit. Except of course the emerald ring, Tico's final gift to his dear friend.

Sylvia, who would assist her husband "Jack The Cat Man" just outside the tiger cage, would wear a set of sexy pink tights, also decorated with red sequins and fitting her so tightly it looked for all the world like her skin. She would wear a wide snakeskin belt and high snakeskin boots. Her earrings would be sparkly diamonds and she would steal the show from her husband, Jack. He didn't mind one bit, as he was more than proud of his beautiful wife.

Charlie "One Shoe," the Ring Master, had had a new scarlet coat and white tight fitting pants hand tailored especially for this event. He knew he may never have occasion to wear this outfit again, but this was a matter of great pride that he look like the King Of The Ring, and he surely did. The abundance of gold braid was scintillating. When he stepped into the center ring in this outfit, complete with a pair of highly polished English riding boots, and sang out in his glorious voice "Ladies And Gentlemen…." all eyes were on him. Then when the horses and trick dogs and high wire walkers and the wonderful Sun Bear "Peter The Great" riding his bike, elephants, and the clowns on stilts and all the other wonders entered he continued his hype of calling out each act as the crowd became more excited. Then Mary Lou would step out and sing her "God Bless America," When she finished he would seat himself at the calliope and play some lively tunes while the folks watched the warm up performance.

Even Star, who normally was not a part of the performing crew, was in the ring. Her dress was one she had made herself. She had found a piece of watermark taffeta in a blue jewel tone. She had made a circle skirt with a high waistband from it and a peasant type blouse of snow white satin. She wore a black velvet cloak lined in the blue taffeta. Her ears were adorned with the golden and diamond earrings that had been a gift from Tico. She would weave in and out of the acts dancing and shaking her tambourine, winking at the men who ogled her as she danced. She was a hit, to be sure.

The Caesars also had new costumes. Papa had been adamant that they all look their very best at this last performance. It would be a last performance not only for the circus, but for many of the Caesars as well. Although he did not perform, even Papa Primo was in the ring. He wore a gorgeous gold cloth cloak that hid his crooked limbs, and was dressed in his matching golden tights and slippers. The girls were all dressed in their new sky-blue costumes and the boys in their dark blue and white garments.

What a sight it was on this night!

As Mr. B gazed at that sight he was almost sorry he had sold the circus. His heart swelled with pride and he fought the tears of regret, and joy and pride. But mostly because of all of the friendships he would have to abandon. He was sad, yet he was happy. Actually, he did not even know what he was. He watched Star doing her sensuous act and remembered her lush body in his arms. No regrets, he had said. But, maybe a little. It had been fine while it lasted, but he had no place in his new life for her. He needed his solitude.

He would miss them all. Mostly Ivan and Mary Lou. Ivan. Yes there was Ivan, out there in the arena. His magnificent physique was clothed in new black form fitting tights with a skull and crossbones painted on the front. Little Angel had painted it before she left and he had saved it for just such a night as tonight. He wore high black riding boots and looked downright menacing. He lifted his weights, appeared as mean as he could and tried to look the part of "Ivan The Terrible" but tonight it was hard to do. He was so filled with happiness at his stroke of good luck in finding the love of Mary Lou before some other guy beat him to her, that he was constantly shooting her glances of tenderness. Like Phillipe always said, "All's well that ends well, eh', *mon cherie*?"

The show was a great success. It far exceeded anyone's expectation, even Star's who 'Knows all, and sees all.'

The extravaganza ended with a standing ovation for the whole complement of performers, with Mary Lou singing "Now Is The Hour, For Us To Say Goodbye…" followed by Charlie "One Shoe" playing the Souza march "Under The Double Eagle" as the audience left the Big Top.

Most of the crew were tired but still psyched from the exhilaration of the glory of the show. They talked excitedly among themselves about the performances of each and every one. Compliments flew back and forth as one would marvel at the talent of another. As the whole thing wound down, many of them felt the bittersweet nostalgia of an end to this way of life and the anticipation of the next step, wherever it may lead.

Chapter Thirty:
Mary Lou Comes Home

Ivan had been left to dispose of Tico's little trailer. He gave it to a very grateful young couple who owned the cotton candy and soda pop concession. He sold his trailer to one of the new Ringling Brothers people and he and his Mary Lou decided to take her trailer to Florida. Mr. B offered to pull it with his car, which he thought was fully capable of the load. Mary Lou and Ivan reasoned that with that arrangement, they would have a place to sleep during the long grinding trip all the way across the southern half of the country from California to Florida. Once they arrived, the new couple would also have a place to live. Mr. B calculated that it would take about seven or eight days to get to Sarasota.

The night before the departure of Mr. B, Ivan and Mary Lou, there was a great gathering of all the circus performers, those who were leaving and those who were staying. They talked about old times, about how Hiram has sneaked off in the middle of the night, no doubt with the lady they'd seen him with in town, and about their future hopes and dreams. Hiram was not missed. Most of the performers felt it was "good riddance to bad rubbish," and they said so.

There were several announcements and disclosures as to what the future held for each of them. Doc announced that he'd been hired by the Veterans Administration to work at the Fort Miley Hospital in San Francisco. The Caesar family was anxious to get to their new home, and they described all of its extras over and over to anyone who would listen.

Papa Primo unearthed several bottles of good wine, and the singing got louder and louder as many friends said their last good-byes. Parker, "Toot" Sweet and Star were staying on, along with Charlie "One Shoe," Madame Fatima, and her daughter Shaharazade, Rudolpho De Mello and his wonderful white Spanish horses, Skinny and Lenny the two clowns that had carried the show after Hiram no longer showed up, and "Fido" Smith, with his trained dogs were all staying on. So were Jack and Sylvia with the cats. They also took over the management of Peter The Great, the camels, Arnold the elephant and "Sweetie" the seal.

The group knew they might never see one another again and the partings were bittersweet. But there were many promises of keeping in touch through visits and correspondence.

There was a special tribute to Tico. They had all been amazed that Tico had found such a beautiful wife. Mr. B had received an exquisite wedding announcement and a letter from the pair. Tico had been well liked and everyone genuinely missed him, so the toast to his happiness was heart felt by all.

Mary Lou showed off her ring, and Ivan and Papa Primo both proudly displayed the diamond studs planted in their ears. Star wore her new golden earrings and Mr. B flashed his majestic diamond ring. Charlie also had a diamond tie tack. Star thought the notion was pretty funny.

"Tie tack?" she asked. "When you wear tie? When we bury you, maybe. Hey, yeah, you look good with big diamond on tie all dead. The undertaker gonna' get himself nice tie tack, eh?"

The wine eventually made them sleepy and the hour of final good-byes came and the group, at last, went to bed with happy memories and a bit of sadness. But they all dreamed hopeful dreams that tomorrow would be a better day.

Early the following morning, Ivan, Mary Lou and Mr. B set out on their journey to Florida. The California heat was almost overwhelming. It was 105 degrees when they reached "The Nut Tree" near Vacaville where they stopped in for a cold soda. Ivan bought some olives and figs, and Mary Lou got peaches. Mr. B purchased three bottles of ice water and some ice. By the time they reached Sacramento, the thermometer had climbed to 108. All three of them were exhausted, but decided to go on down to Oliveville, the town where Mary Lou had grown up. They discussed getting a hotel room just to get out of the heat, and thought they'd check out the situation first.

The motorists bombed through Lincoln, Wheatland and Yuba City, and Mary Lou felt herself getting nervous as they got closer to her original home. The questions darted through her mind quickly. *What if old Simon Franks was still alive? What would she do? How would she feel? Was she still afraid of the man? Would he still be a drunk?*

She knew one thing. She would have to keep Ivan away from him if he was still alive, and if she wanted him to stay that way. Ivan knew what she had endured as a child and he hated child molesters as only a Turk or Sicilian can hate.

Mary Lou felt nauseated as Mr. B drove into Oliveville. There on Main Street, where it had always been, was the butcher shop her father owned and still open for business! She started to backpedal.

"No, Mr. B, I seen enough," she said in a panicked voice. "Let's go on back to the highway and get to a café. You guys is probably hungry and I need something cold to drink, but no need to stop here."

"Why, honey, there is nothing for you to be afraid of," said Mr. B. "Me and Ivan are right here and we won't let anything happen to you."

She knew neither of them understood her fear, but she did feel a little safer with her duo along for support. But the fear belonged only to her and she had no power to share it.

Mr. B drove back out to the highway where they stopped at a little restaurant called "The Dew Drop Inn," just to give her some time to get used to the idea that Oliveville, and perhaps her father, were close by. They were seated at the counter. The owner kept staring at Mary Lou.

The men ordered fried chicken, the specialty of the house, cooked while they waited, which was at least twenty minutes. As they sipped on ice cold Coca-Cola they waited, when finally the owner came over to the table.

"How are you folks doing in this heat?" she asked. Pleasantries about the weather were exchanged as she went on. "I own this establishment and will see to it that your dinner is just as you ordered it."

She was still looking mostly at Mary Lou with a hint of recognition on her face when it dawned on her.

Startled, she said, "Why I do declare! Little Mary Lou Franks! Where in the world have you been? Why your daddy looked for you high and low until the day he died."

Mary Lou felt a sense of both shock and relief that the old man was dead, but she also remembered the proprietor, now the married Mrs. Elliot, who continued to reminisce.

"I guess you know Mr. Millington the lawyer is looking for you too. I s'pose that's why you came back, to settle your daddy's estate. You know Andy Sousa has been doing a real fine job of running the butcher shop 'til it all gets settled. You gonna' stay here or go back to...uh, I don't know where you live now. Where did you say you come from?" she asked.

Mary Lou had not said a word. In fact she had tried to escape from the woman's gaze. And now she was unable to speak as tears welled up in her eyes. The woman gave her a napkin and said, "S'cuse me for my big mouth. I sure didn't mean to make you cry, losing your daddy so sudden like that. You must be grief stricken. Be thankful he never suffered. His heart just gave out. Right there in Mr. Bramwell's drug store. He sure left you a nice bit of real estate though. You know he bought the Mathews farm here two years ago. A stroke of luck really."

Mrs. Elliot rambled on, and no one stopped her. She was spewing valuable information.

Mary Lou composed herself. She didn't quite understand feeling grief at the passing of her cruel father, but her tears were short lived. She was glad she didn't have to face him.

Timidly, Mary Lou asked, "Which Millington is the lawyer?"

She thought for a moment and said, "Ted. Yes, I believe it's Ted. That's right, you wouldn't know he went to law school over in Sacramento. He was about your age, wasn't he?"

Mary Lou remembered Ted Millington well. He had indeed been her age, and her main tormenter in elementary school, screaming, "Fatty, fatty, two-by-four, can't get through the school house door."

Ted had been the one to slap her on the ass just to hear the smack and then laughing pointed his finger at her. When she cried the teacher would say "Oh, Mary Lou, he's only teasing you. Don't be so sensitive. Now go wash your face and take your seat."

Ted Millington had been the leader of the cruel pack, but there were others.

"Oh," thought Mary Lou, *"this is gonna' be fun. I reckon I got to see the little fucker tomorrow. Me and Ivan and Mr. B."*

The trio finished their supper and rented two small cabins in the trailer park across the street from The Dew Drop Inn. Once inside the cool cabin, Mary Lou began to sort out the state of her affairs.

"Well, Ivan. This sure puts a different light on our trip to Florida, don't it!" she said.

"Yes, Little Blossom, it does. What you want to do? If he leave everything to you then I think we better stay here and see what happen. You know this guy the lawyer?"

"Betcher' ass I know him. At least I used to. He's a nasty little son of a bitch. Made my life hell when I was a kid. They was all pretty mean, but Ted Millington was the worst. I guess we go see the fucker in the morning. Mr. B can come along. He knows about legal stuff and he can maybe see if Millington will try to cheat me. I think I got here just at the right time.

"I didn't know the old man was dead. Course, I never knew anything about him all these years. I never went back after I left. And if he did leave everything to me, there's a real nice house over on Hazel Street he owns, I mean he owned it, and also the butcher shop. And didn't Mrs. Elliot say he bought the Mathews Ranch? Now that there's a mansion. Big farm. I think it was a rice farm. Wonder who's farming it? Oh, God, Ivan! This is just about too much for me.

"I guess you guys is wondering if I'm sad about my old man being dead. The answer to that is 'no.' I don't care if he left me a million dollars, it don't make up for what he did to me when I was just a little girl."

"OK," said Ivan. "We go sleep now. I can't hardly wait to see that lawyer fella.' Come on Little Blossom. We go sleep now. Maybe not sleep all time, eh? Maybe Ivan make you feel good. I rub you, maybe kiss you all over," he promised.

"Well, sweetie, I ain't never too tired for that. I'm sure glad Mr. B got a separate cabin!" As she settled into Ivan's arms, she added, "I gotta' ask you something. How come you like fat girls so much? Most guys don't. They want their girls to be skinny and look like them movie stars in the magazines."

"Well, Little Blossom, I tell you. The first woman I have…ah, she was big fat whore. Pretty too. Biggest titties I am ever to see. So big I put one in each ear and hear me come!" he said.

Mary Lou slapped him playfully on the chest and said, "You do have a way with words."

"Well, OK. Fat ladies look so, so, rich, so…there is much to love," he explained.

"Have you ever had a skinny girl?" Mary Lou continued to quiz him.

"Sure, Little Blossom. I have plenty skinny ones. Fat is best. Worst piece of ass I ever have is skinny, but it be wonderful. But of all, you is best. I fuck maybe a million women all over the world. You my Little Blossom, you are best!"

"Huh, I betcha' tell all the girls that!"

by Loma A. Phegley

"Yeh, sure, all guys lie to woman he is with. Tell 'em big lies. Is fair. She lie, too, I betcha.' Only this time, with you, is true. You betcha' baby." They kissed passionately, which invariably led to love making.

The next morning at ten found Mary Lou, Ivan and Mr. B in the front office of attorney Theodore P. Millington, esq. His secretary, who looked vaguely familiar to Mary Lou said, "Yes?" in a snotty kind of way. So Mary Lou, just as snotty, said, "Yes. We came to see Mr. Millington."

The secretary, as Mary Lou realized, was little Patty Pride, all grown up and so sure of herself.

"Do you have an appointment?" she asked.

Mary Lou was ready to deal with her attitude, so she said, "Well, if you keep his appointment book you know we don't. But I know he wants to see me. Tell him Mary Lou Franks is here."

Patty's demeanor changed.

"Why, hello Mary Lou. Long time no see. How are you?"

But Patty proceeded to Millington's inner office, not interested enough to wait for an answer.

"Just a moment and I'll see if he's busy," she said on her way into his office.

"If he is, we'll find another lawyer who ain't," said Mary Lou.

Patty disappeared into the inner office and it was only a moment before Ted Millington appeared in front of the trio. He hadn't changed much. Still the handsome, spoiled rotten little Millington kid, and still his mamma's pride and joy no doubt.

He pretended great enthusiasm at seeing Mary Lou and extended his hand to her in a gesture she took as insincere. Mary Lou wasn't fooled, and certainly hadn't forgotten nor forgiven their shared past. She was seething with hatred for the man who had tormented her during her tender years. She ignored his outstretched hand.

"OK, Teddy. Cut the crap," she said, "Let's get down to what we came here for. My old man's estate."

· 229 ·

Ted looked a bit miffed, and so unused to rejection he was taken aback.

"I don't know what you are so hostile about, Mary Lou. I have been doing all in my power to see that the corpus of the estate was preserved for you until you arrived."

"It ain't that, Teddy. I just don't feel very comfortable around the people whose cruelty caused me to run away from this here town. Maybe you expect me to forgive and forget how you folks ruined my life. Well I don't. You ain't my friend. Ain't none of you my friend. I just want to get this over with and get out of here. Now let's get on with it."

Ted would not let it rest. He looked surprised.

"Why Mary Lou! I never did anything to make you run away. Maybe a little good-natured teasing, but all kids do that. It didn't mean I didn't like you. We were just children, after all," he said.

"Now ain't that typical of folks who hurts other folks beyond repair. It meant nothin' to you and everything to me. Folks like you just don't care about the pain they cause others. You go on with your lives and forget about all the poor people you treated like crap. Get them papers now and get on with this, or I'll get another lawyer and he'll get to overcharge for his services like you no doubt been doing to me."

"I'm sorry you feel that way, but I can't change the past," he said, rifling through papers.

Mary Lou stopped him.

"In the first place, you could have said you're sorry you done me that way instead of sayin' 'I'm sorry you feel that way.' It might have helped, probably not much though."

Ivan was starting to get itchy. He hated arrogance, felt protective of Mary Lou, and was beginning to make fists with his hands at his sides. He stepped up to Millington, way too close for comfort, and said, "Get on with it," in a low tone.

Ted was about to lay some insulting high-brow talk on Mary Lou when he thought better of it, being that close to Ivan and his fists. Ivan presented a formidable figure with his long, black, drooping mustache and his head shaved as slick as a crystal ball. His chest was massive and blown out in a confrontational stance like a rooster at a cockfight. His arms were the size of tree trunks and he stood several inches above the lawyer.

Ted reconsidered. This guy looked more like King Kong than King Kong did.

"Right," he said. "Let's get started." And he proceeded into his office with Mary Lou, Ivan and Mr. B following behind. Patty Pride was already on the phone spreading the word that Mary Lou Franks was back in town to claim her estate while she filed her fingernails. She spoke quietly into the phone, but was too obvious for her own good.

Ted busied himself retrieving papers and files. He called in to Patty to get him the other part of the Franks' file in the conference room that he'd been working on the night before.

Sure, thought Mary Lou. *Mrs. Elliot called and said I was in town. You knew I was here. Well, it's a small town. News travels fast in a small town.*

She kept her thoughts to herself.

"How long do you think probate will take?" asked Mr. B.

"And you are?" Ted asked, a bit uppity like.

"He's a friend of mine. I brought him along because he's been through all this before. So whatever you have to say, say it in front of my fiancé here, and Mr. Bill Bailey."

"Yes, my name is William S. Bailey. I have been asked by Mary Lou to assist her in this matter. I have considerable experience in this sort of thing," said Mr. B.

"Oh fine, Mr. Bailey. This is Simon Franks' will. He has left all his worldly possessions to his daughter, except for a small pittance. He left five hundred dollars to the Presbyterian Church."

Ted's expression indicated he thought that was a pretty chintzy amount, but Mary Lou ignored him and he went on.

"Here's the list: The house and all it's contents at 230 Hazel Street; the butcher shop property and business, seven hundred acres of farm land; now planted and leased to the Yamamoto family; three city lots; some Pacific Gas and Electric stock; quite a nice block of stock there; some Bank of America stock; the vehicles used for the business; a 1935 Ford pickup and a 1934 Chevy flatbed; his personal automobile; a 1936 Lincoln; and a coin collection worth perhaps two thousand dollars. We've not had it appraised yet. There is some jewelry, a rather extensive gun collection, some farm machinery, and $122,000 in cash that rests in the First Bank of California in Sacramento. Then, of course, there are all of your father's personal possessions. His gold watch and a nice ring. The furniture and household accoutrements. The safe deposit box was sealed by the state upon his death, so we don't know what's in there. If you decide to stay here Mary Lou, you can move into either the vacant Hazel Street house or the Matthews' place, which is also vacant. I do not know if you are aware that your Father Purchased the Matthews' Ranch some time before he passed. The Yamamoto family leases it to grow rice. It's got fourteen bedrooms and twelve bathrooms. A bit large for only one person, I'd say," said the lawyer.

"You ain't got no idea how many people will be living in my house no matter where I choose to live, so you got no say." she snapped. Millington held up his hands in surrender and she continued.

"Have you got the keys? I want to go take a look at the Mathews' place. I ain't never been in the house before."

"Sure. We can finish all this up this afternoon. Of course, there's the matter of my small fee. And to answer your question about probate, Mr. Bailey, it should not take long. There are no other heirs and I doubt that anyone plans to contest this will."

He looked over at Ivan, opened his top desk drawer and pulled out a set of keys.

"No, I truly doubt it. Here are the keys. You know how to get there?" he asked.

"Yep. Out to the highway then go east 'til ya get to the old Brewster Road. Turn right there and it's about a mile."

"You have a good memory, Mary Lou. See you about 3 o'clock then?"

She shook her head yes.

"Holy shit!" declared Ivan once they were out in the street. "You gonna' be rich! Maybe you never look at this old Turk again!"

She smiled. "No, Ivan. We gonna' be rich. This don't make no difference. If you love me, nothing makes a bit of difference. I don't even want none of it if you don't come along with it. Hokay?"

Ivan laughed and said, "Hokay, Little Blossom, hokay."

Mary Lou felt exhilarated when they pulled up the driveway to the Matthews' place. The Matthews had been one of the richest families in town, and when she was a kid she fantasized about that house. She wondered what it would be like to be safe and warm in there, with all those toys. Those kids got new bikes every Christmas. Once, the gardener had fixed up one of their older bikes and had given it to Mary Lou.

There was an elaborate tree swing, and a tree house you could practically live in. It all seemed a lot smaller now, but it was still magnificent. The architecture was different for the area too. There was a Mediterranean influence in it, as beautiful white pillars held up a magnificent front porch that extended around the whole house. White wicker furniture was still scattered around the deck but the house was empty of furniture.

The grounds were huge and still well kept. A grassy lawn was superbly landscaped with different kinds of flower gardens and cement walkways all around the house. Immense hydrangeas were strategically located between mature camellia bushes dotting the well-trimmed hedges that bordered the yard. It was surrounded by huge Oriental Plane trees. Behind the house was a great barn and a shop with several other nice out buildings.

The driveway was paved and not a leaf from any of the giant trees was on the ground. The hedges were well manicured and the walkways swept clean.

"My, my. Attorney Millington sure does keep this up well. I wonder if he has been planning to move in here himself if he couldn't find the one and only heir, I mean heiress," said Mr. B.

There was a small guest cottage in the back and a man of about 55 years emerged from it just as the three were admiring the well-kept grounds. They stood still and waited for the man to approach.

"Helloooo," he hollered from a hundred feet, and he approached with his hand extended.

"How do you do?" he asked, first shaking the man's hand, then Mary Lou's.

"I'm Ira Goodman. Been the gardener and caretaker here for the last twenty years. I been keeping the place up waiting for the folks who inherited this place. That lawyer fellow told me it was Mary Lou Franks. Now, you look a little like her young lady, but you sure are grown up. Would that be you Mary Lou?" he asked.

"Mr. Goodman! Yes it's me," she replied. "I remember you. You used to give me apples from the tree in your yard over on Hazel Street on my way to school. You and your wife was two of the only kind people to me in this whole town," she said as she shook his hand with both of hers.

"It was my privilege. I earned a decent wage and kept this place up. I would like to talk to you, though. If you have no one else in mind, I could stay on. For awhile, at least. Kind of help out some until you decide where you are going to live."

Mary Lou thought for a minute, "Well," she replied, "I am sure we gonna' be needing some help. You don't have no idea what we plan to do. If you want to stay, you are sure enough welcome to. We…I mean I, have some plans that just could include you if you're game to help out." Mary Lou laughed. "Ivan don't know yet just what I got planned for him."

"You can stay right where you are. Let me introduce you to my fiancé and my friend," said Mary Lou. She called Ivan and Mr. B over and introduced them to Mr. Goodman. He addressed her again

"Congratulations on your inheritance. I know Simon Franks wasn't much of a father, sending his little girl to school crying many a day, but now you get your well-deserved reward. Let me take you in and show you the inside," he offered.

The place was immaculate. Carpets were clean and looked like new. The drapes were still there and so were the light bulbs. Ivan looked around in wonder. He had never been in such an elegant house. Neither had Mary Lou for that matter, and now she owned it.

She'd already decided. She and Ivan would live here. There was no way she would live in the Hazel Street house full of ugly memories of her father. Those walls were haunted as far as she was concerned. She didn't really even want to go over there, but she needed some closure on the whole situation, and knew she had to see it one last time. Maybe she'd just have the thing torn down.

"Ivan, me and you is gonna' move in here," she said, returning her thoughts to the Mathews' place, soon to be renamed.

"You expect me to make enough kids to fill up this place! Boy! I better get started to work," he said with a wink.

"Ivan, be serious. You don't have to make all the kids to fill this house," she said. He chortled.

"Ah, Ivan have some help he not know about?"

"Course not. But I got me an idea. I'll tell you all about it when I finish makin' these plans in my head. You gonna' like my idea," she promised.

There were compliments to Mr. Goodman for keeping the place up so well, and promises to negotiate with him for his continued service in the next few days, and the trio drove off the estate and back to town.

After lunch at Panatoni's Bar and Grill, they headed back to Millington's office and finalized most of the paperwork. Then they drove to the trailer park where they had left the little trailer, hitched it up and went back out to the Mathews' place.

"Ya know Ivan, this ain't the Mathews' place no more. It's mine. I mean ours. We gotta find some other name to call it. Not 'the Franks' place,'" she thought out loud.

"My name? Our new name when you be my wife? I do not think anyone can say my name. 'Zianastapelomanisti Place' too long for a name," he said.

Mary Lou laughed. She had never heard his real last name. He was called Ivan the Strong Man at the circus, and she'd heard his last name was Ziana.

"No, I don't think so. That your real name? Then I ain't changin' my name when we get hitched," she teased.

"Well," Mr. B spoke up, "there was once a Turk in history called Osman, I believe. Very famous ruler of Turkey. In fact, it was he who founded the Ottoman Empire. Now that is a short easy name to remember. You could call yourself Ivan Osman. What do you think?"

Ivan, always affable, laughed and said "Sound OK, what you think, Little Blossom?"

Mary Lou laughed too. "Hokay, Ivan, I will be Mrs. Ivan Osman. That's just fine with me. But the farm. I'm thinkin', 'The Haven.' You like that?" she asked him.

"Sure. You like, Ivan like too," he said as he hugged her.

"Ivan, are you and me really gonna get married? 'Cause if we are, I have to ask you if you are gonna agree with what I'm thinkin.' I mean what to do with this place."

"Look, Ivan love you. Long time love you. I marry you now if you ready. I want to marry. I no care what you do here. You want keep, we stay. You not, we go to Florida. This is all for you to say," he said.

"OK, I got me an idea. Me and you had a bad time as kids. I do like the little ones though, and the more the better. I know you do too. I seen you working with the kids at the circus when they was feelin' your muscles, and you rode 'em around on your shoulders. Well, I could go over to the county seat and the county will let us take care of some of the kids that are having a bad time. Little girls like I was. Boys like you was. We could make thing a lot better for them. Help 'em grow up to be strong like you. This is a big house. We could…"

"Listen to me, Little Blossom. You have big heart. That why I love you. You want take care little ones, Ivan help. Is OK. Maybe too much work in house for you. Ivan help. I no good with cooking, but I fix anything inside or outside house. Mr. Goodman, he say he stay. We make out OK. I also help with gardening. There is orange trees, apple trees, plums and peaches. I even see grapevines. This paradise like Eden's garden. We get goats and have milk and cheese too. I tend goats and other animals. We live good," he said.

"OK Ivan. Then that's what we'll do. Take care of kids. Boy, have we got a lot of work to do!"

"Yeah, and Ivan got more work. Got to make kids that belong to you and me too. Hooboy! Poor Ivan!" He kissed her and spun her around like a dancer. Everyone was in a good mood.

"Say, Mary Lou, I was perusing the out-buildings and I found something interesting. Do you know there's a whole house full of furniture in that big room in the barn? Looks like some good stuff too," said Mr. B.

"Good. We're gonna need it," she said.

Mary Lou sat down in the porch swing as Ivan gazed out toward the land they now owned, looks of contentment on their faces.

"Ivan, I'm home," she said. "I'm finally home."

Chapter Thirty-One:

The Evil That Men Do Is Oft Interred With Their Bones

Mr. B stayed with Ivan and Mary Lou for a whole month, helping them get the place furnished and ready for the foster children while Ivan complained good-naturedly every day about the extra work he had to do trying to make kids of his own. But Bill Bailey still had his sights set on living in Florida, and he still owned a little house in Sarasota, so he was getting more and more anxious to head south to a place he called home. In fact, he seemed more visibly agitated and nervous each day.

It was October and still hot in the central valleys of California, so Mr. B decided to take the coastal route, at least as far as San Diego, where he would have to cut across the desert when he finally turned east.

Ivan and Mary Lou were newlyweds by the time Mr. B left, and he had been Ivan's best man in the absence of Tico. Both former performers were sorry to see him go. He'd been a great help to them, and a good friend. They insisted the he was welcome to stay there, or come back at anytime, since he had been like a father to Mary Lou and more than an employer to Ivan. Mr. B had been like a father to many of the circus performers, and was considered fondly in their memories.

But he loved Florida and wanted to go home, so reluctantly, after tears and hugs, Ivan and Mary Lou said good bye to Mr. B.

Traveling alone was a bit lonesome, but he knew how necessary it was. He thought about Star. Some lady, that one. But he had to get away from her, since she was starting to see things in him. Private things that he knew were only his to know.

Bill Bailey traveled from Sacramento Valley due west to the coast, and once there, enjoying the magnificent scenery of the trip, over to the town of Ukiah, then the giant cliffs over the ocean and further south, the spectacular Big Sur coastline. The winding coastal highway was longer, but a lot cooler, and he passed near San Simeon where newspaper magnate Randolph Hearst had built a mansion on top of a hill. He drove past a bustling Santa Barbara seaport, and turned toward Los Angeles for a couple of days of rest and relaxation.

Late in the evening, he checked in at the Knickerbocker Hotel. Hell, he could afford to play tourist for a few days, and planned to see some of the sights. The D.W. Griffen studio lot was on his list of things to see, and after a tour, he had dinner at the Brown Derby where all the pictures of the stars graced the walls. They had been there too. He could tell because all the pictures were signed. He even thought he spotted the actor Doug Fairbanks in one of the booths with a pretty little blonde, and he recognized Joe E. Brown and Joe Penner eating supper together in a far corner of the restaurant.

But the Brown Derby itself was nothing spectacular. He wondered what all the hoopla was about. It just seemed like another nice dinner house, and a mystery why some places became star hangouts. Maybe it was just close to the studios, and that was the attraction.

After two days in Hollywood and Los Angeles, he was getting restless, and decided it was time to go. Mr. B continued South towards Arizona and joined up with Route 66 South East to El Paso and finally eastward toward San Antonio. He was beginning to get itchy even before he got to Houston, but he held himself back, keeping his hands firmly glued to the wheel, and aimed stubbornly eastward. He managed to get through Houston without stopping and he congratulated himself on his single-mindedness.

Hurrying through each small Texas town he came to, he had the feeling swelling up inside him that he tried to ignore, but he knew what it meant. He had known for several days it was coming. He was determined not to give in, and with all the power he had in his soul and in his mind, he tried to fight the feeling that came up through his stomach and was beginning to block his throat. It was like a car hurtling down a street with a child ahead in the roadway. No way he could stop what he knew was about to happen. After awhile, he began to look forward to it.

He called the feeling "The Beast," and it would leave him alone for months, and sometimes, even years at a time. But inevitably it always came back again, and he had to cope with it, trying with everything he had to keep it at bay until he realized its inevitability and gave in to it.

He began to sweat, with the weather and with the feeling that would not leave him alone for long. He drove faster, and as he did, the claws seemed to dig deeper into his flesh. He turned around to look and see if there was something real behind him and it was there. There! Clinging to his back was the great yellow juggernaut. He feared that others could see it too, so he drove on faster. The faster he drove, the more intense the pain, even exquisite, as the cruel claws dug deeper and deeper into him, and his compulsion to relieve himself of its burden became more and more urgent. He wondered if he could hold it together until he could get the relief he knew would come when "The Beast" was finally appeased. The feeling was ambivalent. It would vacillate between fear and exhilaration. Between horror and anticipation. Sometimes it was a comfort, sometimes a hideous burden.

Pretend that it's not there! Try! Try harder! He said to himself silently, his soul screaming the words in his ear. *Oh God! The son of a bitch is back! It excited him when they struggled. A vestigial shiver of anticipation made his mind into a quiver of jelly. What a rush. It was its own kind of strength. Its own fuel to ignite the power he needed to feel when they cried and whimpered. It fed his soul like no other thing could ever do. He was King. In charge of their destiny. He was a God. He knew all men wanted to*

by Loma A. Phegley

feel such power, as he would soon feel when her childish fear turned to terror and she knew she would die. She would not even know what to die meant, but she would know at that moment. Ah, yes she would know.

And then *Hurry! Hurry! I need! I need.* He looked around as he drove, checking his surroundings, noting that he'd been here before. His eyes were dilated. His mouth was slack and nearly drooling. Yes! He recognized the place, and there it was. The playground. It seemed like it was most always at a playground that the beast finally caught up with him.

Sure, there had been other places. The tent in the middle of the night. The barn the day he was first introduced to the ferocity of that part of himself. He thought of that first time. It was his little sister. She was six years old then. She had been his first one. He was fourteen. There had been so many since then.

He remembered the old sheriff asking him about it. He had told them he had seen a man leaving the place where they had found Susan's body. Raped, strangled. He hadn't planned it that way, but they believed him. Who would suspect her own brother, practically a child himself?

He'd never been caught. He was too clever. Nobody even suspected him. Except maybe Star. She knew something, but she never knew just what it was about him. He was too close to her for her to get the message from her mystical sources.

Bill Bailey sat in his car, watching the children play. He remembered how his mother had disappeared into insanity after Susan was found murdered. His father was carried away by drink. And even his wife, Maude, dead by her own act after the murder of her little girl, Becky, who was also six. Collateral damage, he thought. Too bad, but it was not his fault. It had been "The Beast." He liked them that young. About six. He remembered Star's shaved pubis. Exciting him beyond words. She never knew. Stupid bitch. All women were stupid. Star was less so. But she never saw all, nor even told all. How could she? She never knew all. She had failed to detect the pervasive malevolence so deeply imbedded in his soul. So had everyone else. Ah, yes. William S. Bailey was the epitome of everyone's friend and Mr. Nice Guy. Well, the joke's on you, and you, and you. Bill Bailey chuckled. He found it amusing that the innocent had suffered horrendously because of his evil deeds, but he had escaped undetected, unscathed. To all the world, he was still Mr. Nice Guy.

When he grew this agitated, his emotions were all jumbled up between sadness, regret, and the overwhelming need to have the beast appeased. Soon. It welled up inside him and this is the time it wouldn't be denied. It wasn't in his control. Never had been.

He thought of Hiram. Dead for something he had never done, but by God, so what. Better ol' Hiram than himself. No big loss, Hiram. He couldn't be troubled about Hiram now. Just more collateral damage, but not much, Hiram had been a worthless old drunk just taking up space in the world and contributing nothing to anyone. And he knew what Hell was like. It was like this compulsion he couldn't stop, even though he wanted to. And then didn't want to. Heaven-Hell. Same thing? Same place?

He watched the swings and the sandbox and the children. He watched them come down the slides, the little girls' dresses flying up. Their laughter and innocence, fueling the beast's desire to devour them. Then he saw her. Providence was smiling on him this day. She was alone. Playing off by herself. It would be easy.

The little blonde girl was six or seven with golden hair that shined in the sunlight. He loved that color, and wanted to put his hands in it. Feeling the soft silk of it really brought the beast out. It reminded him of his beloved Becky, and like his little sister. He felt affection toward the little girl and thought about how his approach would start out tenderly.

His car was parked strategically, on the other side of the trees and brush, where it would not be seen by those passing by. He got out, checking his surroundings again. He approached her from the back as she played with her dolls on a secluded bench. He feigned worry.

by Loma A. Phegley

"Have you seen my puppy?" he asked. "I lost my puppy. Can you help me find him? His name is Spot. Will you help me find him?"

The little girl was hesitant. Bill Bailey put his face in his hands and acted like he was crying.

"He's my little puppy and he's lost. Won't you help me? What's your name?" he asked.

The little girl was visibly moved by his fake tears. These children were so easily fooled.

"Jackie," she said, with a look of concern on her face. "I'll help you. Where should we look?'

"Come over here, look behind those bushes," he directed.

She looked and called the puppy's name.

"I guess we better drive over there and look behind those trees," said Mr. B.

"OK, but I have to come right back. My mommy's picking me up in 10 minutes," she said.

"We'll be right back. No need to worry," he said, as he opened the car door for her and she got in. His tension was palpable, he practically exuded evil, but the child was intent on the lost puppy, and did not see or feel it.

He drove to a place in the canyon, past where the road ended. It was a place where few people ever ventured. There, he let the child out of the car, and as she called for the puppy, he came up behind her and put his hand over her face. He pulled a handkerchief from his pocket and stuffed it to her mouth. Her eyes were wide with stark terror as he tied her hands and feet with rope. The beast liked that, and it made him more excited.

And the freight train struck!

There in the woods, he raped and strangled the little blond angel and left her dead, alone and abandoned to the elements. When he finished, he stuffed his limp penis back into his pants, buttoned them up, smoothed his hair back, and went to his car. Before the warmth of life had left the child, he was out of town, heading away from what he had done.

"The Beast" had been appeased and he tried to put the whole episode out of his mind, giving it little more thought. It was just something he had to do. It's not as if he was in control of it. He had to do it. He had no more control over the feeling than if he'd been hungry or thirsty and had to quench those bodily needs. He did not know why "The Beast" had chosen him, but it had, and he didn't want to think more about it. Until next time.

The restlessness left him as he traveled on to his Florida destination. He was in the Deep South now where he belonged. He drove faster. When he reached Tampa he looked up at the sky.

Holy shit, he said to himself, *those clouds. The whole fucking sky. Looks like a hurricane coming. And damn, I think I'm right in the middle of it. Wind's getting stronger and stronger. I can hardly keep the car on the road. Looks like water coming up pretty high. Man, I could be in some trouble.*

There were no people on the streets of Tampa. That was a bad sign. And the waves were coming up the street he was driving on. Scary. He stopped the car, then thought he'd better move on fast, but the car was flooded out. He got out and started to run for the shelter of a big building he saw off in the distance. The wind picked him up and drove him through the plate glass window into the inside of the place. His head was bloodied, his arm was broken and his ears and mouth filled with water. He choked and sputtered, trying to catch a breath of air. He snorted water through his nose before another wave washed over him. The wild water carried him where it would. He had no control.

A sign on the wall read "Tampa City Morgue." He could see it through the water.

Oh, God! I'm in the morgue, he thought. *Get me out of here. Oh, God, save me!*

by Loma A. Phegley

But God did nothing. No one was there to hear his frantic screams. The water was so deep he could no longer touch the floor. It kept sloshing him from wall to wall.

He went under, coming up only half conscious from being under so long. And then he saw the bodies. Three of them. Floating in the water, alongside him. He went under again. When he came up he was face to face with the little girl he had just killed. No, it was Becky. No, Susan. No. It was the one in Bakersfield or Redding. The flesh was sloughing off of her little face and her hair had fallen out in patches. The eye sockets were empty. He screamed in terror at the gruesome image of the dead child before his eyes.

The horror of the scene overtook him and he made one last effort to find his feet on the floor. He floundered and gulped great mouthfuls of water. But the flooding was too much. He couldn't hold on. He gulped in more water that filled his lungs. He struggled for a minute and then his body went limp.

And Bill Bailey drowned in the Tampa City Morgue in a hurricane from Hell.

Epilogue

Ivan and Mary Lou got their county foster kids. They also had two boys of their own, Ivan Jr, and Teddy, who they called Tico.

Mary Lou sang every Sunday in the local Presbyterian Church, but never in the Catholic Church. True to his word, Ivan helped Mary Lou with the kids, grew vegetables, milked goats, and made cheese. When Papa Primo came to visit, he taught Mary Lou how to make pasta with his famous clam sauce. He also gave Ivan the recipe for his sour mash sipping whiskey. Ivan, in turn, taught Papa Primo how to make a good Turkish *Cous Cous* and to smoke a bowl of an even finer blend of Turkish hashish in his old Hookah.

Two of Mary Lou and Ivan's foster kids joined the army and went to Korea. One boy became Sheriff of Solano County and the girls all went on to college.

When Ivan died in 1980, Mary Lou sold the ranch and bought a nice neighborhood apartment house in Sacramento so she could be near her children and grandchildren. She seldom thought of Hiram, and Ivan never had either in the years after the circus.

Tico and his Angel lived many years in Buenos Aires. Tico took over his father's business and Angel designed jewelry for the many wealthy patrons from all over the world.

They had four sons, all perfectly normal. One is a very well known Endocrinologist in Buenos Aires, another son conducts the Symphony in Brasilia. Yet another boy is a Gemologist and works in the company founded by his grandfather and the fourth son is an Attorney.

When Tico passed on in 1960, Angel interred him in a full-size coffin, open only at the top so that he looked like a full size man in death. Before she closed the lid, Angel slipped a note in beside Tico. It read *Tico, my beloved…*

He died much as he had lived. Well loved by all who knew him and sadly missed. His sons were much like him, too. He had taught them many of his ways, the least of all not being: "Life is like a river, it will surround you. But you gotta' keep swimming."

"Doc" Brady went to work for the Veterans' Hospital at Fort Miley in San Francisco. He was never again a medical doctor, but he was part of the research team that developed skin grafting techniques for burn victims, servicemen returning from the war.

He reconnected with his children. It was never a close relationship, but it was a pleasant one.

Charlie "One Shoe" came to live with Mary Lou and Ivan. He took a job with Manuel Souza at the butcher shop. He helped with the children and each evening he would play the wonderful Souza Marches on the old Steinway Grand Piano in Mary Lou's living room. He taught the kids to play and even played the organ at church where Mary Lou sang. He died in 1973 a happy and fulfilled man. Of them all, he was the only one who remembered Hiram.

The Caesar family fared well in San Francisco. The boys became iron workers and helped build many of the high-rise edifices in the growing city. Angelo worked on both the Golden Gate Bridge and The Frisco-Oakland Bay Bridge.

by Loma A. Phegley

Carmine became a cab driver and Papa Primo lived in his apartment building with all of his children and grandchildren around him. The apartment was in the North Beach district on Greenwich Street in sight of the Coit Tower and near Fisherman's Wharf. Papa Primo spent his days playing bocce ball with all the other old Wops. He watched his friend, Michael Buonserio, paint murals and pictures for the tourists. He died in 1949, old but happy, with a belly full of his best red wine and a hand in that of his newest Grandson.

Phillipe? Ah, yes, Phillipe. Well, his dear long suffering wife, the lovely Appalonia, met a young Italian fisherman who swept her off her feet so that she swept Phillipe out the door, divorcing him while he was away at war with The Royal Canadian Air Command. He never got over it. He tried and he had much help but life was never quite the same, eh, *Mon Cherie*?

None of the circus people ever knew of Mr. B's fate and only a very few knew of Hiram's.

Starshine Moonstone saw all and knew all. She knew that her Beellee must be dead if not one of the troupe even heard from him. She went to Sarasota to Mr. B's little house and found that no one had seen him there for a long time.

She went to the hall of records and found that the taxes were past due. She called upon one of her old acquaintances in the forgery business, who produced a very credible looking marriage certificate that had her name and that of William S. Bailey as being legally married in San Francisco four years earlier. She paid the past due taxes and took possession of the little house as the grieving widow of the Late Great William S. Bailey. With a few more forgeries and some shrewd manipulation, she also latched onto the money Bill had received from the sale of the circus. Hey, she reasoned, a gal's gotta' do what a gal's gotta' do. She opened a fortune telling business in the little house and also sold colorful chenille bedspreads that she hung on a clothes line in front of the house. A true gypsy to the end, she died in 1990 at the age of eighty.

Way to go, Star.

Skookum and Mirriam. Well, Skookum ended up dead alright, but not by Mirriam's hand. He was shot as an innocent bystander in a bank robbery in Saint Louis.

Mirriam, Star claimed, went back to Turkey, ended up in North Africa at El Alemain, became a spy for the British and had a veritable harvest of German soldiers.

Delaney? Well, he went on to become an agent for the O.S.S. during the war and then an F.B.I. agent when the war was over. He and Honey never did become a permanent item. In fact, their thing had nothing to do with love.

Captain Bumpo, however, fell madly for Honey. When his wife found out, as wives always do, she dumped his cheatin' ass and he has had a long and volatile affair with Honey.

Bumpo got fired. His Father-In-Law saw to that. When he asked Honey to marry him, she said a sweet "No," and Bumpo went to Tuscan and opened a bar for cops.

Ah, yes. Honey. She went to Nevada and got a job at a ranch named after wild horses. She became known for her stamina and dedication to her chosen profession.

by Loma A. Phegley

Mr. B! Oh, he died alright. Deadern' a beaver hat. But someone found his remains after the flood and before the cleanup crews got to his corpse. A young woman dressed in a shabby black dress was looking for the body of her baby girl. The cops had told her she had been found raped and murdered alongside the road and they had taken her body to the Tampa City Morgue. She never found her child but she did find the body of a man drowned in the flood.

She slipped the huge diamond ring off of his dead finger and put it into her pocket. It had been so hard since her husband had been sent to jail. At least it would feed the other children. This man would never know for he was dead. She said a Hail Mary over the cadaver and went on her way.

Poetic justice. It may well be the only kind of justice there really is.

The End.

About the Author

Loma Phegley is a seventy-six-year-old great-grandmother who lives with her daughter, Aloma, and her husband of fifty-eight years on the Olympic Peninsula in Washington State.

Her Grandson, John, and his wife, Cary, live next door along with their two sons, Caylen and Braden.

She has three more books in the grinder.

0-595-24854-3